Prai

Berried Secrets

"A fun whodunnit with quirky characters and a satisfying mystery. This new series is as sweet and sharp as the heroine's cranberry salsa."

—Sofie Kelly, *New York Times* bestselling author of
the Magical Cats Mysteries

"Cozy fans and foodies rejoice—there's a place just for you and it's called Cranberry Cove."

—Ellery Adams, *New York Times* bestselling author of
the Books by the Bay Mysteries,
the Charmed Pie Shoppe Mysteries,
and the Book Retreat Mysteries

"I can't wait for Monica's next tasty adventure—and I'm not just saying that because I covet her cranberry relish recipe."

—Victoria Abbott, national bestselling author of
the Book Collector Mysteries

Berry
the Hatchet

Peg Cochran

BERKLEY PRIME CRIME, NEW YORK

BERKLEY
PRIME
CRIME

An imprint of Penguin Random House LLC
375 Hudson Street, New York, New York 10014

BERRY THE HATCHET

A Berkley Prime Crime Book / published by arrangement with the author

ISBN: 978-0-425-27451-4

PUBLISHING HISTORY
Berkley Prime Crime mass-market edition / May 2016

PRINTED IN THE UNITED STATES OF AMERICA

10 9 8 7 6 5 4 3 2 1

Cover illustration by Dave Seeley.
Cover art: *Vintage label with a cranberry fruit* © amorfati.art/Shutterstock;
Tablecloth square red color © urfin/Shutterstock.
Cover design by George Long.
Interior art: *Cranberries ornaments* © by KateVogel/Shutterstock.
Interior text design by Laura K. Corless.

This is a work of fiction. Names, characters, places, and incidents either are the product of
the author's imagination or are used fictitiously, and any resemblance to actual persons,
living or dead, business establishments, events, or locales is entirely coincidental.

PUBLISHER'S NOTE: The recipes contained in this book are to be followed exactly
as written. The publisher is not responsible for your specific health or allergy needs
that may require medical supervision. The publisher is not responsible for any
adverse reactions to the recipes contained in this book.

Penguin
Random
House

*To all the wonderful cozy readers out there
who support the genre and especially to the cozy reviewers
who help spread the word about our books.*

Acknowledgments

Thanks to my plotting buddies who can always come up with a solution even when I can't—Janet Bolin, Janet Cantrell, Laurie Cass, Krista Davis, Daryl Wood Gerber, and Marilyn Levinson. And thanks to my cozy Facebook group who help spread the word about my books.

Chapter 1

Cranberry Cove was in an uproar.

It was less than six hours until the opening of the town's first Winter Walk, an event designed to bring tourists—and their wallets—to Cranberry Cove during some of the darker days of the year. The festive Christmas season was over, the spring tulips were a long way yet from blooming, and the hope was that the Winter Walk would provide an infusion of much needed capital into the local economy between the two more popular seasons.

The shops along Beach Hollow Road bustled with business all spring and summer and into the early fall months, when tourists arrived in droves for autumn color tours. Then things trailed off until the weeks before Christmas, when Cranberry Cove's quaint shops and traditional holiday decorations drew shoppers from all over the state of Michigan and beyond.

January was one of the worst months as far as business

was concerned. An icy wind blew off the waters of Lake Michigan and the sky was gray and leaden more often than not. The vacancy sign swung from the pole in front of the Cranberry Cove Inn all month long, and the only busy shops were the drugstore, the hardware store and the Cranberry Cove Diner, where locals gathered for farmer-style breakfasts and strong coffee in thick white mugs.

So while other towns were taking down their Christmas decorations two weeks after the holidays, Cranberry Cove was stringing up extra garlands of small white lights, adding festive blue and silver bows to anything they could tie a ribbon around and generally gussying up the place as much as possible. Merchants would be throwing open their doors for the next several evenings and offering hot chocolate (made from the finest Dutch cocoa, of course—early settlers of the area had come from the Netherlands and a good portion of the current residents were of Dutch descent), cups of tea and even bowls of wassail for the shoppers who would hopefully soon crowd their establishments.

Sassamanash Farm had erected an outdoor stall in front of Gumdrops, the local candy shop run by the identical twin VanVelsen sisters. Monica Albertson had been baking and cooking for several weeks to ensure a healthy stock of cranberry muffins, bread, salsa and other goodies made from the farm's fall cranberry harvest. Her half brother, Jeff, had crafted a comfortable shelter to protect her from the winds blowing off Lake Michigan barely a block away, and Monica had installed a couple of electric heaters for extra comfort. The VanVelsen sisters had been more than happy to let her run the power cords into their shop outlets.

The wind was picking up, and Monica wrestled with a cloth imprinted with bright red cranberries that she planned to use to cover the rough wooden table Jeff had made for the occasion. Her fingers were stiff with the cold, making them awkward, and the wind kept flipping the fabric up over her face as if this were some sort of playful children's game. Finally, she gave up. She needed to get warm and needed to do it fast.

"You must be freezing, dear," Hennie VanVelsen said when Monica pushed open the door to Gumdrops.

Gumdrops specialized in Dutch treats like hexagonal boxes of Droste pastilles, Wilhelmina peppermints, and De Heer chocolate, along with a counter full of what used to be called penny candy—like Mary Janes, root beer barrels and nonpareils, which the sisters scooped into white paper bags for their customers.

"We have a pot of nice strong tea going in the back room. I'll get you a cup." Hennie headed toward a beaded curtain that separated the shop from the room behind. "Gerda got us an electric teakettle for Christmas, and I must say, the thing is a marvel," she called over her shoulder as she pushed her way through the curtain.

Moments later she reappeared with a steaming mug, which she handed to Monica. Gerda was right on her heels, wearing an identical pale blue sweater set and blue and gray pleated skirt and sporting the exact same tight gray curls as her twin.

"Hello, dear." Gerda rubbed her hands together briskly. "You look positively frozen."

Monica wrapped one hand around her mug of tea and brushed a tangle of auburn curls out of her eyes with the other. "I am. The wind certainly has a sharp edge to it, although the thermometer claims it's almost thirty-five degrees."

Gerda nodded sagely. "It's the wind that does it, that's for certain. A few miles inland and it probably feels positively balmy."

Hennie quirked a smile at Gerda. "Maybe not quite balmy, love."

Gerda made a sound deep in her throat. "You're right, of course. Certainly not balmy." She gave a tight smile. "But more comfortable than here on the very shore of the lake."

Monica hid the grin that rose to her lips. The VanVelsen sisters might be inseparable, but they had their squabbles, just like any other pair of siblings. But instead of driving them apart, their genteel disagreements seemed to bring them closer together.

While Monica had resented her stepmother Gina for stealing her father away, she had adored the baby brother who had arrived barely a year later. Monica and Jeff were as close as any siblings, although there were times, of course, when they had to agree to disagree.

Hennie glanced out the window with a furrow between her eyebrows. "We really need it to snow." She worked her gnarled fingers into the pleats of her plaid skirt. "Miss Winter Walk is supposed to arrive on a horse-drawn sleigh. It's the highlight of the whole event. That's how Mayor Crowley planned it. I read all about it in the newspaper."

Gerda frowned at the large windowpane that looked out onto Beach Hollow Road. "I don't think we're going to get any snow by this evening. Mayor Crowley had a wonderful idea, and of course we normally have piles of the stuff by now, but this year . . ."

Preston Crowley, owner of the Cranberry Cove Inn, had taken over as mayor of Cranberry Cove upon the death of the former mayor, Sam Culbert.

"I'm sure it has something to do with Tempest Storm." Hennie shuddered.

"The lack of snow?" Monica blew on her tea and took a cautious sip. "How could that be?"

Hennie fiddled with a box of Droste chocolate pastilles, turning it over and over again in her hands. "She's planning on performing some sort of spell on the village green." She shook the pastilles at Monica and the candies rattled inside their box. "No good is going to come of it, mark my words."

"It isn't a spell," Monica explained patiently. "It's called Imbolc, and it's a ritual designed to hurry spring when people are fed up with the cold and ice of winter." She glanced out the window at the gray skies. "Which most of us are, I think." She always wished that winter would end on New Year's Day and that spring would arrive in full force the next morning.

"I'm sure that's why we don't have any snow," Hennie said.

"Sounds pagan to me." Gerda sniffed.

"It's Wiccan." Monica looked at the sisters over the rim of her mug. Their faces were settled into identical creases of disapproval.

"No matter what you call it, I don't like it," Hennie said. "Besides, what kind of a name is that? Tempest Storm indeed."

"She is something of a whirlwind." Gerda laughed and Hennie shot her a quelling look.

"Still, who names their child Tempest?"

"It's hard to imagine her being called something plain like Jane or Martha with all those crazy clothes she wears," Gerda pointed out.

Monica put down her now-empty mug. "I'd better get back outside if I hope to have the stall ready for tonight."

"I hate to think of you out there in the cold. You must come in to get warm from time to time," Hennie said firmly.

Monica promised she would.

The wind had died down slightly, so Monica decided to tackle the tablecloth again. This time she was successful in getting it on the table with all the sides even. She pulled a packet of thumbtacks from one of the boxes she'd lugged with her, and tacked each of the four corners to keep the cloth from blowing away.

She glanced up to see Bart Dykema bustling across the street, headed toward his butcher shop on the other side of Book 'Em, a mystery bookstore and one of Monica's favorite shops in town. He had a number of strands of lights looped over his arm. He waved when he saw Monica, and she waved back. She'd only been in Cranberry Cove since the summer, but she was already beginning to feel like a native. Certainly she felt more at home here than she had in Chicago, where she'd run a tiny café and coffee shop that had been put out of business by one of the big-name chains with whom she couldn't hope to compete. When Jeff had asked for her help on his cranberry farm, it had seemed the perfect time to start over.

The smell of frying food drifted down the street from the Cranberry Cove Diner. Monica's stomach rumbled in response. She'd just get a few more things set up, she promised herself, and then she'd treat herself to a nice hot bowl of the diner's famous chili.

The tablecloth having been nailed down, so to speak, Monica began stringing small white lights around the perimeter of the table. Mayor Crowley wanted the town to sparkle as much as possible. Monica looked at some of the other establishments. She hoped the lights wouldn't prove to be too blinding to the customers.

"Need some help with that?"

Monica looked up to see Greg Harper, owner of Book 'Em, standing in front of her cranberry-bedecked table. He had a knitted hat pulled down almost to his eyebrows and thick gloves on his hands.

"I'm just about done."

Monica and Greg had fallen into an easy friendship soon after meeting in September. They shared a love of books in general and mysteries in particular, especially the grand dames of the Golden Age like Christie, Marsh and Sayers. The relationship was slowly taking a romantic turn. They'd both lost someone—Greg his wife and Monica her fiancé—and it took time and a certain amount of courage to move on.

"I've got Book 'Em done up in so many lights, people are going to need sunscreen just to go near the place."

Monica laughed. "It does seem like overkill, doesn't it? But if the mayor is right, and the Winter Walk does bring tourists to town, I guess we should all be grateful."

"That's true." Greg looked up at the sky. "Now all we need is a dusting of snow to complete the picture." He squinted and pointed toward the clouds. "Those look like snow clouds to me."

Monica followed his gaze. "I think you're right. Now if they would just release their contents at the right moment, we'll be in business."

Greg squeezed Monica's shoulder. "I'll see you later. Maybe after all this madness is over we can grab a bite to eat or something."

"I'd like that."

Monica was giving a final tweak to Sassamanash's stall when her cell phone rang. She tried to dig it out of her pocket, but her bulky gloves made it nearly impossible. She pulled one off with her teeth, retrieved her cell and said, somewhat breathlessly, "Hello?"

"Monica, darling, is that you?"

"Mom. Is everything okay?"

"Yes, of course, why wouldn't it be?"

Monica tried to keep her sigh from being audible. "It's just that you rarely call except for Sunday nights."

"That's because I have some news. I'm coming to Cranberry Cove."

"What?"

Monica took her phone away from her ear and stared at it as if it wasn't working correctly. Because surely her mother hadn't just said she was coming to Cranberry Cove?

"I'll be there in about an hour. I assume you can find me someplace to stay?" Nancy Albertson continued. "I doubt you're overrun with tourists at this time of year."

Monica could hear the sound of tires swooshing and horns beeping in the background of the call.

"But why . . . what . . . ?"

The thought of her mother in the same county, let alone the same town, as Monica's stepmother, Gina, made Monica feel slightly sick.

"I've been dating this wonderful man," Nancy continued. "He comes to Chicago on business somewhat regularly. We met when he helped me hail a taxi outside of Neiman Marcus in the pouring rain. Poor man got completely soaked on my behalf."

Monica realized she had a death grip on her cell phone and tried to loosen her stiff fingers.

"And small world and all that, it turns out he's from Cranberry Cove."

"Really?" Monica managed to say despite the fact that all the moisture in her mouth and throat seemed to have dried up.

"The traffic's picking up, dear, so I'd better get off the phone. See you soon. Try to book me a room somewhere. Somewhere decent."

There was a click and the line went dead. Monica stared at her phone in disbelief. Her mother was coming to Cranberry Cove. Now.

What was she going to do?

Chapter 2

Monica clicked off the call with her mother, punched in the number for the Cranberry Cove Inn and waited, her back to the wind, while the call connected. But instead of getting the cheery voice of the receptionist, she got a busy signal. The Inn wasn't that far—she'd walk over and make the reservation in person.

The wind grew even stronger as Monica approached the Cranberry Cove Inn. Its position on a bluff overlooking the lake gave it little protection from the weather. She felt something stinging her face and looked up to see lazy snowflakes drifting down from the leaden sky. It looked as if Preston Crowley would get his wish after all—there would be snow on the ground in Cranberry Cove for the first Winter Walk. Preston was the sort of person who was used to getting his own way, so Monica wasn't surprised. Even Mother Nature was prepared to oblige him.

Monica walked past the picket fence that would be

covered in dusty pink climbing roses come summer and headed toward the front door. The Inn's white shingles had been painted that spring and the black shutters had been touched up as well. It wouldn't be long, however, before the wind and snow of a harsh Michigan winter stripped them of their luster.

Monica was taken aback to discover that the lobby of the Cranberry Cove Inn was crammed with people sitting on the plump sofas, lounging in the deep armchairs and chatting in front of the massive stone fireplace. If her hands and feet weren't still numb from the cold she would have thought it was the height of the summer tourist season and not the dark, bleak middle of January.

The receptionist was behind the counter with the telephone pressed to her ear and a harried look on her face. She was a plump woman with graying blond hair that was pulled into a puffy twist at the back of her head. A long strand of hair had broken loose from the knot and was hanging over her forehead and along her nose. She exhaled a huge puff of air and blew the errant strand out of the way.

Monica smiled as she approached the desk, but despite her friendly demeanor, the woman looked as alarmed as if Monica were a knife-wielding lunatic. She put her hand over the telephone receiver and glared at Monica.

"If you're hoping to make a reservation, we're completely booked," she hissed. "But if you're looking to arrange a wedding or some such affair, the banquet manager is in an office down the hall." She pointed vaguely to the right.

Monica shook her head. "I was hoping to get a room. It doesn't matter where it is or what the view is—"

The woman was already shaking her head, causing the pesky strand of hair to flop forward onto her forehead again. "No room at the Inn. No room at all." She gave a desperate laugh.

"It doesn't matter how small—"

"Even the old maid's rooms are booked." The woman stared at the telephone receiver for a moment before replacing it in its cradle. "Everyone is here for the Winter Walk."

Monica had hoped the Winter Walk would be popular, but it looked as if it was succeeding beyond her wildest dreams. Her mother couldn't have picked a worse time to come to town unless it was the height of the summer season, when Cranberry Cove was even more swamped.

Reluctantly, Monica left the warmth of the Inn's lobby. Perhaps Primrose Cottage, a bed-and-breakfast nearby, had opened for the Winter Walk? Charlie Decker, the owner, usually shut down at the end of October, reopened on the weekends during the Christmas season, and then shut down again until the spring flowers were blooming.

Monica crossed her fingers as she headed down the street. She was buoyed by the fact that Primrose Cottage was lit up like a Christmas tree, with the parking lot full for the first time since the last leaf had fallen off the trees in early November.

Monica pulled open the front door and approached the reception desk with a feeling of optimism. Charlie Decker was chatting amiably with a couple in matching ski parkas. She looked relaxed and happy—better than Monica had seen her since her mother's death at the end of September. Charlie smiled as Monica approached.

"I was hoping I could book a room," Monica said as she pulled off her gloves and stuffed them into her pockets.

Charlie looked startled. "Has something gone wrong at your cottage?"

Monica had renovated the small cottage that stood on the grounds of Sassamanash Farm. It boasted a living room and kitchen on the first floor and two bedrooms on the second with a bathroom between them. The water heater produced barely ten minutes of hot water at a time and there was a leak in the downstairs hallway, but there was a fireplace in the living room and a large bay window, and Monica adored the place.

"Oh, no." Monica hastened to reassure Charlie. "Everything is fine. I need a room for my mother—she's on her way to town."

"Coming for the Winter Walk, huh?" Charlie stuck the pencil she was holding behind her ear.

Monica didn't think that was the case. She didn't know exactly why her mother was coming, but she'd find out soon enough.

"I hate to disappoint you, but we're booked solid . . . with a waiting list if you can believe it. I couldn't be happier."

"That's great," Monica said, although the words practically stuck in her mouth.

What was she going to do? There were no other accommodations in town. There were houses for rent during the summer but not at this time of year. Besides, that would not be suitable for her mother. Her mother would just have to stay with her.

She'd better warn Gina.

Gina was standing on a ladder inside her aromatherapy shop when Monica arrived. After much discussion, and an entire bottle of champagne over dinner at the Cranberry Cove Inn,

Gina had settled on the name Making Scents for her new venture.

She was wearing leopard-print leggings, a long black sweater and suede booties. It was going to take longer than three months to get Gina to conform to Cranberry Cove's unwritten dress code of clothing chosen for its comfort and function rather than its style.

Gina climbed down the steps of the ladder. "What do you think? Enough sparkle for the mayor?"

Monica looked around the shop. "Preston will love it—it's stunning. I don't see how you could add more pizazz if you tried." She smiled at her stepmother.

"Good." Gina stepped off the ladder. "I started the shop at the wrong time, that's for sure. I didn't realize business would dry up as soon as I hung out my *Open* sign."

"Cranberry Cove definitely has its seasons," Monica said, leaning against the counter where a half dozen glass bottles with medicine droppers were on display. The scents of mint, lavender and citrus filled her nose. "But you did quite well over Christmas, didn't you?"

"I did." Gina straightened a bow on the shelf behind her. "And I'm sure things will pick up when summer comes. If nothing else, aromatherapy will be something novel for the tourists to talk about when they get back home."

Monica traced a circle on the floor with her toe. How was she going to break it to Gina that the two ex–Mrs. Albertsons were going to be occupying the same town at the same time?

But before she could say anything, Gina spoke. "I'm meeting Preston tonight—after the Winter Walk."

Monica looked up, surprised. "I didn't realize you were dating."

Gina shrugged. "We're keeping it rather quiet." She shrugged. "It's what Preston wants. He asked me to share a bottle of champagne with him tonight to celebrate the success of the first Cranberry Cove Winter Walk."

Monica had always been told that it wasn't good to count your chickens before they hatched, but she didn't say anything. She didn't want to burst Gina's bubble—it might make the news about Monica's mother arriving in town go down easier if she didn't.

"By the way," Monica said with studied casualness, "my mother is coming for a visit." Gina, who had been wiping fingerprints off the counter, stopped abruptly and spun around toward Monica. "Your mother! What does she want to come here for?"

"To see me, I guess," Monica said, somewhat dryly. "Actually she said she's been dating a man from Cranberry Cove who she met in Chicago when he was on business."

Gina went back to vigorously scrubbing a spot on the glass countertop, which already looked perfectly clean to Monica. "Just so she doesn't come near me. After the things she said to me . . ."

Monica knew the relationship had been quite heated, almost ugly, between her mother and Gina, but she didn't know the details and didn't want to.

Gina's mouth was open and she was about to continue when the door opened, letting in a blast of cold air and a swirl of snowflakes.

It was Tempest Storm. Her cheeks were bright red, and Monica didn't think it was because of the frigid temperatures. Tempest looked absolutely furious.

"What a bunch of narrow-minded nincompoops these people are."

Gina looked sympathetic. She and Tempest had bonded in their roles as Cranberry Cove's most gossiped about citizens.

"What have they done now?" Gina asked.

Tempest's face became even redder, if possible. She drew the long purple cape she was wearing around her. It made her look like the high priestess of some ancient religion.

"That idiot mayor of ours, Preston Crowley, has started a petition to bar me from holding my Imbolc rite on the village green tonight."

Gina bristled at hearing Preston called an idiot. She glanced at Monica and rolled her eyes but held her tongue.

"What is this rite you're planning anyway?" Gina reached behind her for an emery board that was stuck in a pencil holder on the counter and began to file one of her nails.

"It's not like it's going to hurt anyone," Tempest said.

"It might even amuse the tourists." Gina stuck the emery board back in the cup.

"It's not meant to be amusing," Tempest said rather huffily. "The rite is believed to date back to the Babylonians. It marks the halfway point between the winter solstice and the spring equinox." She frowned. "We're doing it a bit early, but I thought it might be something to draw the tourists in and show them that there is some culture in Cranberry Cove."

"Greg Harper holds a book club at Book 'Em once a month," Gina said.

"That's not what I meant. We need to show them that we're tolerant of different peoples and different practices."

"Good luck with that." Gina laughed.

"We'll have candles and noisemakers," Tempest said. "It will be quite a sight."

"I'm sure it will be." Gina finished wiping down the counter and tossed the paper towels in the trash. "Who is going to be taking part in this ritual?"

"I'm hoping that some of Cranberry Cove's visitors will join in. I've got extra candles for them."

The door to the shop opened again and Gina looked up, a practiced smile on her face.

A woman came in, stamping her feet against the cold. A scattering of snowflakes were melting across her shoulders and leaving wet splotches on her dark coat.

"Can I help you?" Gina glided toward her.

Tempest wandered over to the other side of the shop and began to examine a display of oil diffusers.

The woman seemed like an unlikely customer for Making Scents, although Gina had told Monica she was pleasantly surprised by the number of people interested in exploring essential oils for the treatment of insomnia, anxiety and other conditions.

But this woman didn't look as if she was intent on purchasing anything. She had a clipboard clutched to her rather flat chest, a pen in her gnarled hand and a determined look on her gaunt face.

"I'm here to ask if you will sign this here petition," she said to no one in particular.

Gina, as owner of the shop, obviously felt it her duty to take charge. The woman eyed Gina's leggings and sweater with distrust as she stepped forward, her hand outstretched for the piece of paper the woman was brandishing.

"And what is it you're asking me to sign?" Gina arched a perfectly plucked eyebrow as she accepted the clipboard from the woman.

"It's a petition to stop that . . . woman. . . ." She seemed momentarily overcome by emotion and had to clear her throat several times before continuing. "From holding that pagan ceremony on the village green and ruining our Winter Walk. Mayor Crowley himself asked us to go around and collect signatures." She held out the pen to Gina with a shaking hand. "Mayor Crowley has worked hard to make this event a success and nothing can be allowed to ruin it."

"Oh, balderdash!" Tempest swung around from the display she'd been examining and drew her cloak around her with a flourish. The ends flicked outward and nearly knocked over a shelf of lavender oil. "Our Imbolc ceremony is going to do nothing to tarnish the *mayor's*"—she said the word as if it left a bad taste in her mouth—"precious Winter Walk."

Monica thought she'd better do something to diffuse the tension that was crackling in the air like heat lightning.

"It's very kind of you to bring this around," she said, gently removing the clipboard from Gina's unresisting hands. "But I think we all agree that we'd rather not get involved in something that we know very little about."

Monica handed the woman her petition and reached out a hand to take the pen back from Gina. She handed it over, smiled and opened the door to the shop.

They all watched through the window as the woman crossed the street and entered Bart's Butcher shop.

Tempest clenched her hands into fists and shook them

at the plateglass window. "How dare that man! He's the mayor, not God!"

"I can understand your being angry," Monica said in her most soothing voice. She put a hand on Tempest's arm.

"Angry?" Tempest turned on Monica, her eyes glittering. "I'm going to kill Preston Crowley for this!"

Chapter 3

As Monica hurried to her stall outside of Gumdrops, she was thinking about the scene in Gina's shop and it wasn't until she was halfway back before she remembered about her mother. The thought made her stop in her tracks, and a man, bundled up against the cold with a scarf around his nose and mouth, bumped into her.

"I'm sorry," Monica said, but he hurried past with an irritated look on his face.

Monica shrugged. Some people seemed to walk around with a black cloud over themselves no matter what was going on.

She quickly checked on the stall—the tablecloth was still pinned down against the wind, which was now sending snowflakes into swirls like mini tornadoes. She popped her head into Gumdrops and asked the sisters if they would mind keeping an eye on things for her.

"You go on, dear. We'll keep a lookout," Hennie called from behind the counter.

"I'm sure everything will be fine," Gerda added, waving to Monica.

Monica dashed to her car—she'd gotten to town early enough to snag one of the spaces along Beach Hollow Road. Later, those spaces would be blocked off and the street would turn into an outdoor pedestrian mall. She brushed the accumulating snow off the roof and front and back windows of her Focus and took off.

As she drove up the hill toward Sassamanash Farm, she thought about what lay ahead. Her cottage was always orderly—she'd dusted and run the vacuum only yesterday—but she'd dashed out early this morning without cleaning up the kitchen. Flour still dusted the countertops and baking pans were soaking in the sink. She'd have to get all that taken care of before her mother arrived.

The thought made Monica hit the gas a little harder than she should have, and she crested the hill and flew down the other side, her small car skidding slightly on the increasingly snow-covered road. Mayor Crowley had prayed for enough snow for the sleigh to be able to navigate, but she hoped they didn't get so much snow that tourists weren't able to get there.

Mittens met Monica at the door as soon as she arrived home. Monica had adopted the kitten after the VanVelsen sisters' cat Midnight had given birth to a surprise litter. Monica had chosen the name Mittens because the kitten was all black except for four white paws. And since Michigan was known as the Mitten State, the name seemed particularly appropriate.

Monica had never had a pet before. She hadn't had time when she was in Chicago, and her mother had never wanted to be bothered with a dog or cat—she was afraid they would ruin the furniture and generally be too much of a nuisance. But the fluffy black kitten had already wormed her way into Monica's heart. She slept on Monica's lap when she was reading—occasionally waking up to bat at the pages of Monica's book—and she'd proved her mettle as a mouser, having already proudly presented Monica with several *presents*.

Now Mittens rubbed against Monica's ankles until Monica bent down to pet her and scratch under her chin. She followed Monica out to the kitchen, weaving in and out between her feet, tail held high in the air and swishing back and forth. Monica had learned to be extra careful on the steps. The last thing she needed was to fall and break something.

Monica tossed her jacket toward the coatrack by the back door, where it caught by the edge of the collar, then checked Mittens's bowls. Water—full. Food—full. She glanced toward the clock on the kitchen wall. She'd better hurry.

She filled the sink and began scrubbing the baking dishes she'd left for later. Her arms were still plunged up to her elbows in soapy water when she heard a car pull up. She quickly dried her hands and went to the front door.

By the time she got there, her mother was already standing on the front step. She looked crisp and elegant in a navy double-breasted peacoat, leather gloves, gray slacks, and suede driving moccasins. Her ash blond hair had a few gray strands woven in, but was neat and tidy in a chin-length bob.

"Mom!" Monica exclaimed. She pulled the door wider. "Come in."

Nancy Albertson walked into the small living room. She offered her cold cheek to Monica for a kiss. Monica impulsively gave her mother a quick hug.

"What's this?" Nancy asked as Mittens rubbed up against her legs. "I do hope it doesn't shed," she said, bending down to pat the cat's head.

Nancy straightened and looked around Monica's living room, with its welcoming brick fireplace, comfortable furniture and bay window. Monica held her breath as she waited.

"Well, dear, it certainly is . . . tiny," Nancy finally said. She pulled off her gloves. "I'm positively freezing. A cup of tea would be nice."

"Sure." Monica took her mother's coat and hung it in the closet by the front door.

She hastened down the hallway toward the kitchen, Nancy following, the rubber soles of her shoes silent against the wood floor. Mittens was right behind her, her rigid posture suggesting that she didn't approve of Nancy at all.

Nancy sat at the kitchen table while Monica filled the teakettle. She turned around to see that Nancy had pushed the remains of some flour into a small pile at the edge of the table. Monica quickly went over and swept the grains into her palm and dumped them into the sink.

The kettle finally boiled and Monica filled two mugs with hot water, carefully selecting one without any chips or dings for Nancy. She plopped in two tea bags and carried them to the table. She knew her mother didn't care for any sugar or milk in hers.

Nancy picked up her mug and blew on the tea before taking a small sip. She closed her eyes. "Heaven. My hands have been positively freezing. Leather gloves are not as warm as one would think, but of course it's impossible to drive a car in mittens."

She laughed and Monica smiled politely.

"I assume you've booked me a room somewhere." Nancy put down her mug and wiped a finger along the edge where her lipstick had left a pale pink smudge.

Monica chewed on her lower lip briefly. "I'm afraid everything in town is booked. But I have a guest room that should be perfectly comfortable." She pointed toward the ceiling and the second floor.

Nancy looked doubtful but then gave a quick smile. "I'm sure it will be perfectly adequate. Of course with your Winter Walk going on, it hadn't occurred to me how crowded this poky little town would be."

Cranberry Cove wasn't poky! Monica was about to rise to the town's defense but then thought better of it. No need to antagonize Nancy—they were going to be spending more time together in the next few days than they had in years.

Nancy pursed her lips. "It seemed like the perfect time to come—I could see you, enjoy this Winter Walk I've heard so much about and grab a few moments with Preston. I'm sure he's going to be very busy, but I don't see why we couldn't sneak away for a quick dinner."

Her mother's last words were a blur to Monica. She had stopped listening after the word *Preston* and was trying to convince herself that there could conceivably be more than one person in a small town like Cranberry Cove named Preston. She was having very little success.

"Did you say Preston?" Monica interrupted Nancy's chatter about the new purse she'd bought at Nordstrom.

Nancy looked irritated. "Yes. Preston. Preston Crowley. He's the owner of the Cranberry Cove Inn. I would have asked him to reserve a room for me there, but I wanted to surprise him."

Preston wasn't the only one who was going to be surprised, Monica thought. When Gina found out that both she and Nancy Albertson were seeing the same man, Cranberry Cove was going to have a fireworks display that had nothing to do with the Fourth of July.

Monica got Nancy settled as best she could in the guest room. Nancy wasn't pleased when she found out there was only one bathroom, but Monica assured her she would be up early and finished showering long before Nancy wanted to use the tub.

Monica was about to head back downtown to Sassamanash Farm's little stall when Nancy came breezing down the stairs. She'd obviously powdered her nose and freshened her lipstick, and she had her purse hanging from the crook of her arm.

"Are you going out?"

"Yes." Nancy opened the coat closet and pulled out her jacket. "I called the Inn and Preston is in his office, so I'm going to surprise him."

Monica found her mouth had gone so dry her tongue was sticking to the roof of her mouth. Should she warn her mother about Gina? What if the two ran into each other in town?

In the end, she didn't say anything—just prayed that the two women wouldn't cross each other's paths.

• • •

When she got to town, Monica had to park in the lot at the Central Reformed Church and walk back to Beach Hollow Road. Both hands were full with two baskets brimming with more of her homemade cranberry bread, muffins and salsa. At least two inches of snow blanketed the lawns, sidewalk and street, and it continued to fall in big, fat flakes. The sidewalk was slippery and several times Monica barely kept herself from falling. She should have dropped off her goods at Gumdrops and then gone to park the car. She shrugged. Too late now—she was almost there.

She passed the Pepper Pot and was surprised to find it dark with no signs of activity. Lights had been strung along the roofline in the front, but hadn't been turned on. The Pepper Pot was the newest restaurant in town. Everyone said it was going to give the dining room at the Cranberry Cove Inn a run for its money. According to the newspaper article Monica had read, the owner planned for it to be an eatery somewhere between the extreme casualness of the Cranberry Cove Diner, with its short-order menu and slapdash service, and the Cranberry Cove Inn, with its white linens, extensive wine cellar and waiters in black tie.

The menu had been taped to the window for the past few weeks, and Monica had glanced at it whenever she went by. It looked as if the restaurant was going to feature home cooking—roast chicken and turkey, grilled steaks, beef stew and other old-time favorites served in a nice atmosphere. Upscale, but not so fancy that it would scare off the locals who would be the ones to keep it busy all year long. The tourists would like it, too, for its retro menu and its charm.

Monica knew the owner had planned on a grand opening the first night of the Winter Walk. What had gone wrong? Preston had been vocal in his opposition to the place, claiming it was going to create too much traffic along Beach Hollow Road and make parking nearly impossible. He had tried to rally a group of like-minded people, but had failed.

Everything was in order when Monica got back to the stall. A bell jingled as Hennie opened the door to Gumdrops and put her head around the edge. "We've been keeping an eye."

"Thanks. I appreciate it."

Monica set her two baskets down on the table and began to unpack them. She would have to warn people to warm the muffins and bread before eating them—the cold air was quickly chilling them, and they felt as if they'd been stored in the refrigerator and not in the warmth of her kitchen.

People were beginning to stroll down the street, many arm in arm, their cheeks rosy from the cold. The official start of the Walk was four p.m., when Miss Winter Walk, accompanied by Mayor Preston Crowley, would arrive in the horse-drawn sleigh. Fortunately there was now plenty of snow, so Preston must be pleased. The thought of Preston made Monica's jaw clench, and she quickly turned her mind to something else.

Monica finished arranging her display and looked around. She had to admit, Cranberry Cove had certainly risen to the challenge. Lights twinkled on all the shop fronts, the scent of hot chocolate and mulled cider drifted on the air, and the old-fashioned street lamps gave a ruddy glow to the entire scene. A group of young men and women dressed in period costume stood at the top of the street singing old English ballads. The whole scene was quite magical.

Monica glanced toward Twilight and wondered if Tempest was going to hold her ritual despite Preston's petition. Personally, she thought it would add to the celebration rather than detract. The way Tempest had described it, there would be candles and bells and various other noise-makers. Certainly it would give the tourists something to talk about when they got back home.

The door to Gumdrops opened and Hennie and Gerda came out, bundled to their eyebrows in matching boiled wool coats, knitted hats and mittens.

Hennie pushed back her sleeve and glanced at her watch. "It's almost four o'clock. The sleigh should be arriving any minute now."

"This is so exciting." Gerda clapped her mittened hands together.

"Who is Miss Winter Walk?" Monica asked, suddenly realizing she had no idea who had been chosen for this prime part in the celebration.

Hennie rolled her eyes. "Preston's niece Candy. She's a complete ninny if you ask me. We hired her briefly to help out in the store, and even after a week she couldn't figure out how to make change."

"We had to let her go," Gerda chimed in. "But then I heard she was working at that jewelry store down the street with the unusual name—"

"Bijou," interjected Hennie with an air of superiority. "It's French, I think."

"I heard she's only working because her mother refused to support her anymore." Gerda squared her shoulders. "She didn't want to go to college, so it's time she went out into the world and earned her own keep."

"Yes," Hennie said, lowering her voice confidentially. "Her mother can hardly afford to take care of herself, let alone a twenty-one-year-old girl more than fit enough to hold down a job."

Monica raised her eyebrows.

"Preston has done very well for himself," Hennie explained, "but his sister hasn't been as lucky. She married this complete ne'er-do-well who left her high and dry with a baby to raise."

Monica didn't think she'd ever heard anyone use the word *ne'er-do-well* in conversation before. It was one of the things she liked about the VanVelsen sisters—talking to them was like opening a window into a different era.

There was a noise at the top of the street—it started as a rumble and grew louder until it reached the spot where Monica and the VanVelsens were standing.

"The sleigh is coming," Hennie said, peering into the distance, pressing against the barricade that had been set up to keep people out of the street until after the sleigh had arrived. She checked her watch. "It's early. It's only ten to four."

"Anyone who's late is going to miss it." Gerda pulled a tissue from her pocket and dabbed at her nose. "Mayor Crowley said it was to be at four."

The horse and sleigh came roaring down the center of Beach Hollow Road, scattering the few pedestrians who had ignored the barricades like pinballs.

"It's going awfully fast, don't you think?" Gerda turned to Monica, her face creased with concern.

As the sleigh got closer, they could see the horse's eyes were wide and staring. It looked terrified.

A murmur rose from the crowd, getting louder and louder the closer the sleigh got.

"Something's wrong," Monica said, gripping the edge of the barricade and straining to see.

She saw a man running furiously down the street, his arms pumping. It was Bart Dykema, with his white apron flapping in the wind as he attempted to catch up with the sleigh. His face was bright red, and great clouds of air were coming from his open mouth.

"We've got to stop it," he yelled to the crowd that was now riveted by the spectacle in front of them.

Bart put on what looked to be a last burst of energy, like a marathoner with the finish line in sight, and finally came abreast of the heaving horse. He grabbed the dangling reins and slowly the horse came to a halt, looking relieved that someone had taken charge at last.

Bart stood bent over, his hands on his knees, panting furiously. The horse tossed its head, snorted and pawed the snow-covered road.

"Where is Miss Winter Walk?" Gerda craned her neck. "She must be positively frightened half to death, poor thing."

"I don't see her, either," Hennie said squinting into the distance.

A small crowd had made its way around the barricade and was slowly gathering around the sleigh. There was shouting and finally a collective groan followed by a piercing scream that sent Monica pushing through the barricade and running toward the sleigh.

Chapter 4

The shoppers crowding Cranberry Cove's sidewalks forgot what they were doing or had been about to do and surged toward the sleigh, shopping bags swinging and slapping against their thighs, mouths circled into identical startled *O*'s.

Monica managed to maneuver her way through the crowd, softly murmuring "Excuse me" as she went but occasionally employing a sharp elbow to get through a tight spot. She had no idea what she would do when she reached the sleigh, but she felt a strong need to find out what was going on.

She finally managed to get to the front of the crowd and when she saw the sight in the sleigh, her hand flew to her mouth as if of its own accord, and she stifled the gasp that rose to her lips.

Preston Crowley was the only occupant of the sleigh— Miss Winter Walk was nowhere to be seen. He was dressed in an elegant black coat that looked like cashmere to Monica, although she was hardly an expert in the matter, cashmere being well out of her price range. He had on a skillfully knotted silk and wool scarf in a discrete paisley pattern, with touches of red, at his neck, and he sported buttery soft black leather gloves on his surprisingly small hands.

His head was tilted back against the seat of the sleigh, revealing an expanse of white, carefully shaven throat. Monica could have sworn there was a smile on his face. It was completely at odds with the knife that stuck out of his neck at a jaunty angle.

By now, shopkeepers were coming out of their stores, standing in the chill wind in their shirtsleeves, their arms wrapped around themselves for warmth. Monica saw the VanVelsen twins standing on the edge of the crowd, the round circles of rouge on their cheeks standing out against the white of their faces.

"Someone call nine-one-one!" Monica heard the clerk from Danielle's boutique call out.

Bart Dykema had finally caught his breath. He straightened up and dug around in the pocket of his jeans. "I've got my cell."

The tourists gathered around the sleigh continued to stare in wide-eyed fascination, as if this were a play and the whole thing had been planned for their entertainment. They murmured among themselves, stamping their feet against the cold, but didn't make a move to take shelter in any of the stores.

"Is he alive?" Greg came out of Book 'Em to stand by Monica.

"I don't know. I don't think so."

Someone called out, "Should we take that knife out of his neck?"

"Better not," Greg said, stuffing his hands into his pockets. He'd managed to grab his jacket but had obviously left his gloves and hat behind. "I'd leave everything exactly the way it is."

Moments later they heard sirens in the distance, their wail becoming louder with every passing second. A police car pulled up to the barricade at the end of Beach Hollow Road and two officers jumped out. They were bundled against the cold, with their hats pulled down low on their foreheads, but Monica thought she recognized them. Eventually everyone became familiar in Cranberry Cove.

Greg was standing behind Monica. He put his hands on her shoulders and squeezed. "Are you okay?"

"Yes, I'm fine," Monica said and meant it. She wasn't the delicate flower, fainting type, although she sometimes wondered if she would have gotten more attention from men if she had been. But you can't change who you are, and she really didn't want to anyway.

"I'd better get back to the store," Greg murmured. "In case someone wants to read about a murder mystery rather than take part in the one happening right under their nose. Even though that seems highly unlikely."

Monica spun around toward him. "You think it's murder?" Her breath caught in her throat.

Greg gave a wry smile. "I don't think Preston fell on that knife by accident."

Monica gave a short, humorless laugh. "True." She shook her head. "But another murder in Cranberry Cove? It's hard to believe."

Greg sighed. "I know. But greed and jealousy and all those other turbulent emotions exist in idyllic small towns as well as big cities."

"I guess you can't call them idyllic then?" Monica said with a question in her voice.

"I don't know about that," Greg responded. "I think any place that suits you, personally, is idyllic."

Monica thought about that. Greg was right. Cranberry Cove suited her down to the ground. And Greg was definitely a part of that.

"I'll catch up with you later," Greg said, giving Monica's shoulders a final squeeze.

Monica went back to watching the police, who were now approaching the sled with Preston's body. They carried themselves with an air of self-importance as they pushed their way through the crowd.

"Step back, folks. Nothing to see here."

Nothing to see? There was obviously plenty to see. The tourists had gotten their money's worth and then some. The admonitions of the two officers fell on deaf ears and did little to dissuade the crowd, which pressed even closer to the sled holding Preston's inert body.

Bart Dykema hung on to the horse's reins, whispering softly at it, keeping the animal steady. He wasn't wearing a coat, but he didn't seem aware of the frigid air as he soothed the rattled beast. It continued to snort and prance, pawing the ground with its enormous hooves, but it was clearly calming down after its mad dash down Beach Hollow Road.

The two policemen dispatched to the scene didn't seem to have any idea as to what to do. They stood around with their arms hanging at their sides, their jaws slack, their heads swiveling right and left, lest any of the people in the crowd try to get closer to the scene.

The sound of a car's engine rose above the noise of the crowd, and a black sedan pulled up behind the police car. The front door opened, and a woman emerged. She was dressed warmly in a serviceable navy blue parka, woolen hat and heavy gloves. A fringe of blond hair hung just below the hem of her cap. Monica wasn't positive, but she thought it was Detective Tammy Stevens. They'd met back in September, when a body had been found floating in the bog at Sassamanash Farm. Stevens had been nine-plus months pregnant at the time. The belt tied tightly around her jacket made it obvious that the baby had duly arrived, and she was back on the job.

Her air of authority parted the crowd like the Red Sea, and she came to stand in front of the sleigh and Preston Crowley's body. She spent several long, silent minutes surveying the scene before looking around her at the crowd, which had retreated to a respectful distance. She spotted Monica, and a brief look of relief passed over her face.

"Detective Stevens," Monica said when Stevens approached.

"It's Monica, isn't it? Sassamanash Farm?"

"Yes." Monica nodded. She tipped her head toward Stevens's stomach.

"A boy," Stevens said, reflexively rubbing her now-flat abdomen.

"Congratulations."

"Thanks." Stevens looked back at the body. "Do you have any idea what happened?" She turned toward Monica again.

"I don't know much, I'm afraid." Monica gestured around at the crowd. "Miss Winter Walk was supposed to arrive in the sleigh around four o'clock. At about ten or maybe five minutes to four, the sled came roaring down the street with Bart Dykema in pursuit."

"Is he the fellow holding on to the horse's reins?" Monica nodded.

"He's going to freeze out here in his shirtsleeves." She turned to the two patrolmen who were hovering behind her. "One of you go grab that horse so that poor man can go inside and get warm."

The younger one nodded briskly and headed in Bart's direction. He took hold of the reins and Bart dipped his head in gratitude as he hurried away toward the warmth of his butcher shop.

Stevens turned back to Monica.

Monica shrugged. "That's all I know. The sleigh was supposed to come down Beach Hollow Road at four o'clock, and everyone was startled when it was early. Preston is something of a fanatic about punctuality."

"Our mayor?"

"Yes. From what I understand, the Winter Walk was his idea."

"Was he meant to be riding along with this Miss Winter Weather?"

"Winter Walk," Monica corrected. "Yes. They planned on making a grand entrance together." Monica looked around. "I have no idea where she is."

"Who is she?"

"I don't know her, but according to the VanVelsen sisters . . ." When Stevens looked blank, Monica added, "They own Gumdrops, the shop behind us." She jerked a shoulder toward the pastel pink front of the candy store. "Anyway, Preston's niece Candy was chosen as Miss Winter Walk."

Stevens snorted and rolled her eyes. "Completely unbiased, of course."

Monica had had the same thought. It was unlikely that Candy would have been chosen if she hadn't been Preston's niece. Had anyone else even been considered? But that was always the way.

Monica remembered when she was in fourth grade—every year one lucky girl was chosen to play Mary in the Christmas tableau. Monica had been a donkey, a sheep, and a goat, but never Mary or even one of the angels. But she never gave up hope. One day she told her mother that she was positive that that year she would be chosen to play the part of Mary. Her mother had laughed and said that the girl whose father gave the most money to the school would be chosen as Mary and that definitely wasn't going to be Monica.

Stevens pulled a camera from the pocket of her navy parka and began snapping pictures of the scene from various angles.

"Excuse me." A woman slithered through the crowd and confronted Stevens.

Monica recognized her as Jacy Belair, the owner of Bijou. The jewelry store was relatively new in town, and wealthy tourists shopped there when they were bored of sunning themselves by the lake. She looked to be in her thirties, with frosted blond hair teased high in front, and a bright coral pashmina shawl thrown around her shoulders.

Stevens lowered her camera and spun around. "Yes?" she said, her tone as frosty as the air blowing off the lake.

"We've put a lot of effort into the Winter Walk," the woman said, sweeping an arm toward the crowd, the pile of bracelets on her wrist tinkling melodically. "Can we get this . . . this obstruction out of the way as soon as possible?"

Stevens's face hardened and her eyes narrowed. "I'm sorry, ma'am, but this is a murder scene."

"Murder!" The woman gasped.

The word spread through the crowd like wildfire until a chant went up—*Murder! Murder! Murder!*

Chapter 5

Monica turned to look at the VanVelsen sisters, who were still standing on the sidewalk where she'd left them. Gerda's face was white, and Hennie's was pinched with concern.

"Is everything okay?" Monica asked when she reached the pair.

"Gerda is having one of her attacks," Hennie said. "She gets palpitations."

"Should we go inside? Do you need to sit down?"

Gerda shook her head. "I'm sure they will pass in a minute," she said, although Monica didn't think she looked well at all.

"It's the shock, of course." Hennie put her arm around her sister's shoulders, and Gerda swayed slightly.

"Do you think we should call for an ambulance?" A note of alarm crept into Monica's voice, in spite of her determination to stay calm.

"Oh, no, dear," Gerda said, some color coming back to her face. "I don't want to miss anything. I think they're passing now. Yes, I'm feeling almost myself again."

Monica had to hide a smile. Even a potential heart attack wasn't going to keep the VanVelsens from the scene of all this action.

"This is certainly more excitement than even Preston bargained for." Greg came up behind Monica.

She looked at him quizzically. "Did you close up for the night?"

Greg shook his head. "That teenager I hired as part-time help finally showed up. I thought I'd make sure you're okay."

Monica smiled as they stood surveying the scene. The tourists who had come to town for the festivities and shopping were scattering as quickly as they could, their excited chatter filling the air.

"The tourists are certainly going to have a story to tell when they get home," Greg said.

The two policemen were busy stringing black-and-yellow crime scene tape around the sleigh. A young man in jeans, work boots and a heavy jacket had come and led the poor, frightened horse off.

"Oh, no," Greg said, pointing toward the end of Beach Hollow Road.

"What is it?" Monica craned her neck to see.

A young woman wearing a fake fur coat and a rhinestone tiara balanced precariously on top of her head came running down the street. Her blond hair was curled and piled high in a hairdo that would rival Medusa's, and her cheeks were rough and red from the cold.

"What happened?" she asked of no one in particular.

"I think Miss Winter Walk has arrived," Greg said dryly. "She's a little late to the party, I'm afraid."

Monica watched as Stevens immediately grabbed Candy by the arm. Candy's face looked as if it was about to crumble, and Stevens pulled a tissue from the pocket of her jacket and handed it to her.

"You must be frozen." Greg put an arm around Monica's shoulder. "I don't think anyone is going to be doing much shopping. How about coming back to Book 'Em, and I'll make us a cup of tea?"

Monica realized she *was* frozen—she'd just been too engrossed in watching the drama unfold to notice it. She followed Greg as he made a path for them through the crowd to the sidewalk.

A blast of warm air shot out when Greg opened the door to Book 'Em. Monica closed her eyes in pleasure. The heat felt luxurious after standing in the cold for so long.

Book 'Em was its usual jumble of books tumbling off the shelves and piled willy-nilly in every nook and cranny. The store specialized in mysteries, and Monica had found Greg to be quite an authority on the topic.

She took off her gloves and rubbed her numb hands together while Greg filled mugs with water and put them in the microwave.

A minute later, the microwave pinged and Greg removed the two mugs, plopped in tea bags and handed one to Monica. "If I remember correctly, you take your tea neat."

"That's right." Monica felt absurdly pleased that he'd remembered. She held the cup of tea close. The warm mug in her hands felt heavenly.

"I wonder what poor Preston Crowley did to get himself

killed like that?" Greg turned to Monica. "I only met him a few times, but I found him inoffensive enough." Greg added another spoonful of sugar to his tea and stirred it. "I know he was very generous with his money—he wrote a check to any charity that knocked on his door, and I've heard that he paid for the addition to the library and the repair to the roof out of his own pocket. The library committee wanted to name the new wing after him, but he preferred to remain anonymous." Greg gave a small smile. "As anonymous as anyone can be in a small town."

Monica pulled out the old desk chair that was shoved under a small table in the corner of Book 'Em's back room and collapsed into it. She felt as if she'd been on her feet for decades. She put her mug of tea down on the table, which wobbled slightly.

"I only met him very briefly, at a spaghetti supper fundraiser for Charlie Decker's mother, and we barely spoke." Monica took a sip of her tea and winced as the hot liquid scalded her tongue. "My stepmother is . . . was . . . dating Preston."

Greg raised his dark eyebrows. "I'm sorry. I'm sure this is going to be difficult for her."

More difficult than Greg could even imagine, Monica thought, if Gina found out about Nancy.

Monica thought she had better check on Gina. Gina hadn't been dating Preston all that long, but she'd obviously be upset by what had happened. *Who wouldn't be*, Monica thought. Death was always a shock, and murder . . . She shuddered.

Monica finished her tea, said good-bye to Greg and,

with her scarf tucked securely into the neck of her coat, made her way down the street to Making Scents. The crowd along Beach Hollow Road was thinning. Some tourists, undaunted by what had happened, were going in and out of the brightly lit shops. The twinkling lights, colorful bows and decorations seemed almost bizarre in light of what had happened.

Monica wondered if she ought to go back to her stall. She was about to turn around when she decided against it. She wanted to make sure Gina was okay—she was worried about her.

Monica passed Bart's Butcher shop, where she could see Bart through the window, tidying up and getting ready to close for the night. As she walked by, the tiny white lights affixed to the front of the shop went out. Moments later, the light inside the store was extinguished as well. She could just make out the shadowy figure of Bart shrugging into his coat and pulling his hat down over his ears.

Making Scents was still ablaze with lights. Gina had persuaded the young man who worked at the hardware store after school and on weekends to string them up for her. Monica pushed open the door to the shop and froze.

Gina was behind the counter, and Monica's mother was standing in front of it. Her coat was open, and she'd taken off her gloves, so it looked as if she'd been there awhile.

Monica's first instinct was to shut the door, turn tail and flee, but she stifled the urge.

"Why didn't you tell me Gina had settled in Cranberry Cove?" Nancy said in the tone of voice you would use with a child who was trying to hide the fact that they had just broken your heirloom vase.

"It . . . it never came up." Monica unzipped her jacket.

She was suddenly feeling very warm, although whether it was from the heat in the small shop or from being put on the spot, she didn't know.

"We've been having a lovely conversation, haven't we, Gina? Catching up."

Monica looked at Gina but she didn't seem particularly perturbed—her face was smooth and placid. Of course that could be because of the Botox and not because Gina had superhuman control over her emotions.

The last time the two women had encountered each other—at Monica's college graduation—their hostility toward one another had been buried under a frosty coating of politeness. Nancy had refused to talk directly to Gina and had raised a fit at her ex-husband's suggestion that Gina be included in some of the family photographs.

And now they were chatting like two polite acquaintances. The only things missing were the tea and cookies. Monica felt the way she used to when she played pin-the-tail-on-the-donkey, when they spun you around in a circle, leaving you dizzy and confused about which way to go. She supposed that having been dumped by the same man, each for a considerably younger model, had given them something in common.

Since neither Gina nor Nancy appeared to be upset, Monica suspected they didn't know about Preston.

"Something is going on out there," Gina said, pointing toward the window that looked out onto Beach Hollow Road.

"Yes." Nancy fingered the silk scarf at her neck. "There was a great deal of commotion and people running." She laughed. "It reminded me of those photographs in the newspaper of the running of the bulls in Pamplona."

"I imagine it's Tempest and her spring rite, or whatever she's calling it." Gina wiped at a smudged fingerprint on the glass countertop with the edge of her top. "She probably thought limiting it to the village green wouldn't provide enough shock value. She seems determined to shake up the citizens of Cranberry Cove."

"No, it wasn't Tempest," Monica said wishing that was all it had been. How was she going to break the news to them?

"Something was going on, that's for sure." Nancy looked at her watch. "I imagine the whole thing will be over soon. I have an appointment tonight, and I don't look forward to braving that crowd."

"I didn't know you knew anyone in Cranberry Cove. Other than Monica, of course." Gina was rearranging some spray bottles of lavender essential oil on the counter.

Monica caught a whiff of their delicious scent. Lavender was supposed to be soothing and restful. Had the herb lulled both Gina and Nancy into this eerie state of calm?

Nancy gave a coy smile. "Actually I do," she said preening like a peacock. "We met in Chicago when he was in the city on business, and we just . . . hit it off, I guess you could say."

"That's quite the coincidence that he happens to live in Cranberry Cove."

"I know," Nancy said, her voice sounding throaty. "But coincidences do happen. Lucky ones, too."

"Cranberry Cove is a small town." Gina stopped fiddling with the glass bottles and gave an *It's just us girls* sort of smile. "We probably know him. What's his name?"

Monica felt herself tensing from head to toe. Maybe if she created a distraction she could stop this conversation in its tracks. But what to do? Douse them both in calming lavender essential oil? Sweep all the glass bottles off the counter? Set off the smoke alarm? Panic was making her think like a crazy person.

"You probably *do* know him." Nancy gave that coy smile again. "I'm sure everyone does."

"Don't keep us in suspense." Gina leaned her arms on the counter, her eyes on Nancy.

Nooooo, Monica was screaming inside her head, *don't say it.* For a moment she was afraid she might have actually spoken out loud.

"If you must know," Nancy said, giving a slight giggle, "it's Preston Crowley, mayor of Cranberry Cove and owner of the Cranberry Cove Inn."

Gina became so still that for a moment she reminded Monica of an ice sculpture. Gina's only movement was a slight trembling of her hands that slowly increased until they jerked wildly, scattering the glass bottles of essential oils all over the display counter.

"Preston Crowley?" Gina said, the words coming out in a croak.

Nancy looked half amused and half annoyed by Gina's reaction. "Yes. Do you know him?"

"As a matter of fact, I do," Gina said in a quiet voice with a menacing edge that made the hairs on the back of Monica's neck stand on edge.

Oh no, here it comes. Monica was tempted to duck for cover.

"Is something the matter?" Nancy bristled and arched an eyebrow.

Gina began righting the toppled bottles. "You could say

that," she said. She looked up at Nancy. "I've been seeing Preston Crowley as well."

"Preston?" Nancy looked confused. "Do you mean seeing as in . . . ?"

Gina nodded curtly.

Nancy's face went white and her lips tightened. She gave a mirthless laugh. "I don't suppose there could be two Preston Crowleys . . . cousins or something?"

"No."

"The dog!" Nancy spat out.

"I'm afraid none of that really matters now," Monica said.

"What do you mean?" Nancy turned toward her daughter.

"Preston's dead."

"What?" Gina and Nancy said at the same time.

Chapter 6

Monica hurried down Beach Hollow Road toward Gum-drops and her abandoned farm stall. By the time she'd left Gina's shop, Gina had retrieved a bottle of wine from the refrigerator in her back room, and she and Nancy were drowning their sorrows in large glasses of sauvignon blanc.

Monica found people still milling idly along the side-walks, as if they didn't know what to do with themselves. Some of the shops, like Bart's, had already closed up. Others, like Danielle's and the Purple Grape, were still doing business as if nothing had happened. Monica glanced across the street—the lights were even on at Bijou. The shop had taken over the space vacated by a camera store that had been made obsolete now that everyone took pictures with their smartphones and looked at them on their computers.

The sleigh was still in the center of the road, with two policemen standing guard, although Preston's body had mercifully been removed. The yellow-and-black police tape snapped in the brisk wind.

Monica found everything at the farm stand to be in order. She'd pack up the unsold baked goods and take them to the farm store tomorrow morning. The Winter Walk—with all the shops open until eight o'clock in the evening for the event—was meant to run for another four nights. Monica had no idea whether they would have to cancel the rest of the event or not, but she supposed Jeff could always come and collect their stall in the morning if need be.

Monica didn't relish the idea of being back there in the morning. A sense of sadness enveloped her—the peace, comfort and security she'd found in Cranberry Cove had been shaken by the day's events. She was more than happy to buckle herself into her little Ford Focus and leave Beach Hollow Road behind her.

Monica crested the hill outside of town. Sassamanash Farm was a shadow in the distance, with a few pinpricks of light here and there. She could make out the white smudge that was her cottage and another that was the farm store and cranberry processing building. From this vantage point during the day, you would be able to see the farm quite clearly. And if it was autumn, the ground would be blanketed with a red carpet of ripe cranberries. Right now, with the fruit harvested, there was nothing to see but a dark shadow. Monica sailed down the other side of the hill toward home.

As she pulled into the driveway of her cottage, she realized she hadn't yet taken down the Christmas wreath that hung from her front door, the greenery now lightly dusted with snow. She supposed leaving it up for a few more days wouldn't hurt.

Mittens was at the back door to greet her, and Monica scooped the kitten up and cuddled her close. She purred loudly and butted her head against Monica's chin as Monica carried her out to the kitchen.

Later, as Monica was heating up a pot of leftover vegetable soup, there was a knock on her back door. Before Monica could answer, it opened and her half brother Jeff walked in, bringing a rush of cold air with him.

"How did it go? Did we sell out?" he asked as he struggled to take off his coat.

His left arm had been injured during his time in Afghanistan, leaving it paralyzed. He was slowly coming to terms with the disability and had learned to work around it. Monica itched to help him with his coat, but she knew he wanted to do it himself.

"Didn't you hear?" Monica asked as Jeff slumped into one of her kitchen chairs, his long legs nearly sticking out from under the other side of the table.

"Hear what?" Jeff scrubbed a hand over his face.

"Preston Crowley is dead. Murdered."

Jeff stopped with his hand halfway to the handle of Monica's refrigerator. He'd been tilting the chair on its two hind legs but now dropped it back to the floor with a *thunk*.

"You're joking, right?" He started to smile, but the attempt faded when he saw the expression on Monica's face. "You're not kidding, are you? You're as white as a sheet. Tell me about it."

Monica gestured toward the pot simmering on the stove. "You want some soup first?"

"Sure. I haven't had a chance to eat yet—not that I was exactly looking forward to that frozen potpie I have waiting for me back at my apartment."

"You need to learn to cook a few things for yourself."

Jeff gave her a cheeky grin. "Why? I can always stop by here and get my big sis to feed me."

Monica shook her head but ladled out two steaming bowls of soup and placed them on the table. She rummaged in the pantry and brought out a sleeve of salted crackers.

"Can you grab the butter dish from the fridge?"

"Sure." Jeff swiveled around and, using his good arm, retrieved the butter along with a can of the beer Monica kept on hand for him.

Jeff ate half his soup and a dozen crackers before finally looking up. "So tell me what happened." He swiped his napkin across his chin, which was covered in a day's stubble.

Monica explained about the sleigh arriving with Preston's body.

"There was a knife sticking out of his neck?" Jeff asked in disbelief.

Monica swallowed the bite of cracker she was chewing. "Yes. And it was odd looking. Not that I know all that much about knives."

Jeff shuddered. "That's crazy. First Sam Culbert and now . . ." He looked down at his nearly empty soup bowl. "I feel bad about bringing you out here. If there's any danger . . ."

Monica smiled reassuringly. "I'm sure there isn't any danger. This murder is undoubtedly personal. Although what grief someone would have with Preston, I can't imagine."

"You never know."

Jeff leaned back in his chair. Monica noticed the dusky shadows underneath his closed eyes.

"You look tired," she said as she got up to clear the table.

Jeff's eyes flew open. He rubbed his hand across his face again, then smiled. "I am tired. Farming is hard work." He shook his head. "I didn't realize how hard."

Monica turned to face him with the two soup bowls in her hands. "But the cranberries are all harvested."

Jeff laughed. "Cranberry growing is a four-season business. We're getting ready to sand the bogs."

Monica put the dishes in the sink. "Sand?" she said over her shoulder.

The chair squeaked as Jeff changed position. "Sanding stimulates the development of new roots and helps to keep weeds and insects down." Jeff yawned. "Stop by the bog tomorrow and I'll show you. We're starting over by the pump station." He yawned again. "As a matter of fact, Lauren is organizing a couple of tours. She thought some of the tourists who are in town for the Winter Walk might be interested in seeing the operation."

"She's a smart girl." Monica liked Jeff's girlfriend very much.

"I know." Jeff grinned. "And speaking of Lauren, I want to get her something special for Valentine's Day. I thought I'd go to that new jewelry store in town and pick something out, but what?"

"Frankly, you can't go wrong with jewelry so I'm sure anything you choose will be fine."

"They had a necklace in the window that I liked—a heart on a thin gold chain. Too corny?"

Monica hid her smile by bending over the dishwasher to put in their dirty soup bowls. "Not at all. I think that would be perfect."

"I went inside the store to get the price and got to

talking with the woman behind the counter—Jacy. She said she's the owner. Asked me all about cranberry farming and how it's done. I told her about how we've flooded the bogs and now that ice has formed, we'll lay down sand. She seemed quite fascinated by it."

"It sounds like she was flirting with you." Monica leaned against the counter.

The tips of Jeff's ears suddenly turned red, but then his expression became grim—his mouth set in a hard, thin line. "Maybe. But she doesn't know about this." He motioned to his injured arm.

Monica was about to reassure him, but then realized that he would have to get to that point by himself—she couldn't do it for him.

"I told her about the tours Lauren is organizing, and she said she'd like to go on one." Jeff's entire face was now suffused with red. "She even said she'd give me a discount on the necklace."

As Monica finished cleaning up the kitchen, she thought about what Jeff had told her about Jacy, and she smiled. She certainly didn't want anything to come between Jeff and Lauren, but it was good for Jeff to have another woman flirt with him. It would boost his confidence. And despite his protests, she gathered he'd rather enjoyed the exchange.

Monica checked Mittens's water bowl then peeled aside the curtain to look out. There was no sign of her mother's car.

She was beginning to worry when she finally heard a car pull up outside. Mittens scampered ahead of her as she ran to the front door and yanked it open. Gina's Mercedes was parked in the driveway, slightly askew as always. Jeff always said his mother didn't park her car—she abandoned it. Gina was standing by the passenger side door and appeared to be helping someone out. Monica peered into the darkness.

She blinked her eyes in disbelief. It was her mother!

Nancy was clearly quite tipsy, and leaned heavily on Gina's arm as they approached Monica's door. At one point she stumbled, and Monica started toward her, but Gina caught her and pulled her upright.

"Hello, darling," Nancy said when they finally reached the entrance to Monica's cottage.

"Mother! What have you been doing?"

"Just enjoying a nice glass of wine with Gina, dear. An excellent sauvi . . . sauvi . . . white wine." She hiccoughed and smiled brightly at Monica.

"What . . . what happened?" Monica asked Gina as they got her mother settled in an armchair in the living room.

"I guess you'd call it drowning our sorrows. I had one glass of wine—your mother finished the bottle." Gina jerked her head toward Nancy. "She's not used to drinking, is she?"

"Not really. I don't know."

Monica realized she didn't actually know her mother all that well. Nancy was always so buttoned up—so guarded—that it was hard to tell what she was feeling or thinking.

"I guess she's taking Preston's death rather hard," Monica said.

Monica glanced at Gina. How was Gina taking it? Her expression didn't give anything away.

"I think it's his duplicity that's really bothering her. She thought she was the only woman in his life," Gina said rather dryly. "She hadn't been going out with him all that long, and frankly, neither had I. We both might have ended up disliking him in the end. But finding out that he was a lying, cheating dog is rather hard to take." Gina laughed. "And now that he's dead there's no chance to tell him what we think of him."

Monica could understand that—they'd been robbed of the chance for closure.

Nancy, meanwhile, had slipped down in the armchair, her head dropped back, her mouth slightly open. She was fast asleep and didn't even notice that Mittens had curled up in her lap.

"Maybe I should help you get her up to bed," Gina said. "Or we can transfer her to the sofa if you think that's better."

Monica thought of the steep stairs leading to the second floor. "I think the sofa would be easier."

"Or maybe we should leave her? She *is* sleeping."

They both looked at Nancy, whose head had lolled to one side.

"I'll cover her with the throw."

Monica was reaching for the blanket when the doorbell rang. Monica and Gina jumped, and Nancy's eyes flew open.

"Who could it be at this time of night?" Monica glanced at her watch.

"I suppose we'll find out when you open the door," Gina said rather dryly.

"Right."

Neither Monica nor Gina expected to find Detective Stevens standing on Monica's doorstep.

"I'm sorry it's so late," she said as she stepped into the foyer. "I understand your mother is staying with you? Nancy Albertson?"

Monica wondered how Stevens knew that. The village tom-toms must have been beating overtime. This was a record, even for Cranberry Cove.

"You remember my stepmother, Gina Albertson," Monica said as she led Stevens into the living room.

"Wonderful," Stevens said, pointing at Gina. "I want to talk to you, too. Kill two birds as they say." She laughed. "Probably not the best saying to quote under the circumstances."

Stevens turned to Nancy, who was now awake, although her eyelids had drooped to half-mast and she looked as if she was having trouble focusing. Monica couldn't imagine what had gotten into her mother.

Mittens had jumped down from Nancy's chair and was amusing herself by making her way along the back edge of the sofa, as if she was practicing tightrope walking.

"Mrs. Albertson? Mrs. Nancy Albertson?" Stevens said.

Nancy nodded, then winced and put a hand to her head.

"Won't you sit down?" Monica gestured toward the sofa.

Stevens sat down on the couch with a tired sigh. Gina chose the other end of the sofa while Monica opted for perching on the arm of the chair Nancy was sitting in. She slipped an arm around her mother protectively.

"We're investigating a murder that occurred this afternoon." Stevens rubbed her eyes. "Preston Crowley. You may have heard?" She looked at Gina then nodded toward Monica. "You were there, I know."

Monica nodded.

Stevens continued. "There isn't much to go on at the

moment, but we did find his cell phone in his pocket. We've gone through the log, and it seems he received calls from both you, Mrs. Albertson," she nodded at Nancy then turned to Gina, "and you, Mrs. Albertson."

Monica put a protective hand on her mother's shoulder. "What does that have to do with anything?" she said, trying to keep the defensive tone out of her voice.

Stevens shrugged. "Probably nothing, but we're following up on everything we can. We're trying to piece together Mr. Crowley's movements throughout the day, and I thought one of you might be able to help."

"I never did see—" Nancy began, but Stevens waved her quiet.

"First, let me ask what your relationship was to the deceased. Friends?"

Gina snorted.

Nancy lifted her head, which had begun to droop, and perked up slightly. "We were dating," she said with a smug tone to her voice.

Stevens tilted her head, and her blond hair brushed against her chin. She turned to Gina. "And you? You were a friend?"

Gina fiddled with the scarf around her neck. "Not exactly. We were dating as well."

Stevens looked back and forth between the two women. "So you were both dating Preston Crowley?"

Nancy and Gina nodded in unison.

"Did you know he was dating both of you?"

"No!" Gina said, rather more loudly than necessary.

Stevens looked in Nancy's direction.

"I didn't know either. The miserable dog . . ." she said, her last words trailing off.

"So it was a surprise to both of you." It was more of a statement than a question. Stevens shifted in her seat. "When did you find out—that you weren't the only woman Crowley was involved with?"

Monica's palms became clammy. She didn't like the direction that Stevens's questions were taking.

Nancy pursed her lips and put a finger to her chin as if she was thinking hard. "It was this afternoon," she said, although it sounded more like a question than an answer. She suddenly sat up straighter. "Yes! It was this afternoon."

"She's right," Gina said, her foot jiggling wildly. "It was only this afternoon."

Stevens raised her eyebrows and looked solemnly from one woman to the other. She pulled a notepad from her pocket and sat poised with her pen above the blank sheet.

Monica felt a drop of sweat make its way down her back.

"Do you two ladies mind telling me where you were between three fifteen and four o'clock this afternoon?"

Chapter 7

Nancy was considerably less tipsy by the time Stevens left, and Monica was considerably more worried.

"It sounds like Stevens thinks one or the other of you had something to do with the murder." Monica turned from Nancy to Gina and back again. "And neither of you seems to have an alibi."

"It's not as if we knew we'd need one," Gina said somewhat petulantly, stroking Mittens's soft fur.

"Are you sure you didn't see anyone?" Monica turned to her mother. She realized she was gripping the arm of the chair so hard her knuckles were turning white and tried to loosen her hand. "Did you stop for gas? Or a cup of coffee?"

"I'm afraid not." Nancy sat up straighter in her seat. "I just drove around. I popped in on Preston at the Inn, but didn't stay long—he was busy." She waved a hand in the air. "Then I thought I'd see some of the sights so I just . . . drove around."

"What about you?" Monica turned to Gina.

"I was at the shop getting ready for the Winter Walk."

"Surely someone came in and can vouch that—"

"I'm afraid not. There were no customers all afternoon. I was hoping things would pick up when the Walk started."

"Maybe someone saw you through the window?"

"I was in and out of the stockroom—besides, how would we ever find the person? Put an ad in the paper and advertise the fact that I'm a suspect in a murder case?" Gina's hand jerked, and Mittens darted away.

Monica held up a hand. "I don't exactly think you're a suspect—"

"Of course I am. You heard the questions Detective Stevens asked. Who's to say that Nancy and I didn't know about Preston's two-timing ways before this afternoon? Maybe I confronted him, we had an argument and . . ." She made a slashing motion across her throat.

Nancy shuddered.

Gina turned and pointed a finger at her. "And who's to say Nancy didn't come here on purpose to have it out with Preston, and her anger got the best of her and . . ." Again, she drew her finger across her throat.

"The whole idea that either of us would . . . it's just ridiculous." Nancy crossed her arms over her chest and glared at Gina.

"I'm playing devil's advocate and trying to look at it from Detective Stevens's perspective," Gina said. "We need to be prepared, that's all."

• • •

Monica was up early after a restless night. Even though she knew it was ridiculous that anyone would think her mother capable of murder, it had unsettled her. Mittens watched her from the warmth of the bed while she dressed in some jeans and a cable-knit sweater. The kitten followed her downstairs, weaving in and out between Monica's legs as she headed to the kitchen. Her first order of business was to make coffee—she yawned as she filled the pot with water and poured it into the machine.

Within minutes, coffee began trickling into the carafe, filling the kitchen with its enticing scent. While she waited, Monica got out the ingredients she would need to make Sassamanash Farm's signature cranberry streusel bread—sugar, butter, flour, spices and the cranberries that she'd stocked in the freezer at the end of the harvest season.

Monica had just finished measuring the flour when the last drops of coffee trickled out of the machine. She filled a large mug and set it on the table next to her bowl.

Within half an hour, Monica had her first batch of bread in the oven. She took a moment to sit down while she finished the last sips of her coffee. Next she would start on some muffins and then some cranberry salsa.

Her baking finished, Monica got out the straw baskets she used to carry the goodies down to the farm store. She had no sooner put them on the table than Mittens jumped into one. The kitten peeked over the side, her tail swishing back and forth and the look on her face plainly saying that she, not Monica, was the rightful owner of the basket and Monica should just try to evict her.

Monica laughed. "You think that's yours, do you?"

Mittens's meow was the answer.

"Come on, you little minx. I've got to get going."

Monica went to scoop the kitten out of the basket, but Mittens nimbly jumped out of it and into the other basket. Monica laughed and took the opportunity to line the vacant one with a piece of blue-and-white checked cloth.

She was about to scoop Mittens out of the second basket when her mother walked into the kitchen. Mittens jumped out and scampered over to Nancy.

"How did you sleep?" Monica asked, hoping the mattress in the spare room hadn't been too soft for her mother's taste.

"Not very well, I'm afraid."

"I hope you weren't too uncomfortable?"

Nancy waved a hand. "No, it wasn't that. It's the idea that this policewoman seems to have gotten it into her head that either Gina or I have some responsibility for Preston's death. What a ludicrous notion."

"I'm sure they'll find the real culprit soon."

"I certainly hope so."

Monica finished packing the straw baskets and slipped into her jacket. She wound her scarf around her neck, and Mittens leapt onto the table and began batting at the fringe on the ends. Monica shooed her off the table, where she was pretty sure Mittens knew she wasn't allowed. She was only a kitten, but so far she had proven to be very smart.

Nancy had her head half in the refrigerator as Monica opened the back door.

"Do you have any eggs?"

Monica turned around, her hand still on the door handle.

"Middle shelf, left side." Monica prided herself on keeping a neat refrigerator, which meant everything had a specific place on the shelves. "Do you need anything else? Can you manage—"

"I'll be fine," Nancy said. "You go on about your business. I know you have things to do."

Monica said good-bye and went out the back door. The wind immediately tugged at her scarf, tossing it around in the brisk air. Monica pulled her collar closer around her neck, and headed toward the farm store.

The rush of warmth when she opened the door to the store was very welcome. Her hands were chilled right through her gloves, and her face felt stiff from the cold.

She wondered if anyone would show up for Lauren's tour in this weather.

Nora Taylor was behind the counter wearing one of the Sassamanash Farm aprons. She had short, curly dark hair and round glasses that made her look perpetually surprised. She worked in the store in the mornings and left in time to get her two children off the school bus in the early afternoon.

She looked up and smiled when she saw Monica. "I can smell those delicious goodies all the way over here."

She came out from behind the counter and took one of the baskets from Monica. "I'll just start arranging these, shall I?"

When Monica had arrived at Sassamanash Farm, she'd been dismayed to see that none of the baked goods in the store were homemade. She'd soon changed that, whipping up cranberry bread, muffins, and scones every morning so they would be fresh for their customers. Their business had grown as a result, and even during the winter people made a special trip to pick up some of Monica's baked goods.

Monica had also spruced up the store with decorative trays and platters she'd collected at garage sales and from secondhand shops. Combined with the delicious smells coming from all their products, it gave the store a comforting, homey feel.

Monica was stashing her special cranberry salsa in the cooler case when she heard her name being called.

She turned around to find Jeff leaning against the doorway. He had on a heavy jacket and work boots and had removed his wool cap and gloves and tucked them under his arm. His face was ruddy from the cold.

"We're about to start the sanding. Want to see how it's done?"

"Sure. Let me grab my jacket." Monica pulled on her jacket, hat, gloves and scarf and followed Jeff out the door.

"We're starting with the bog over by the pump house." He pointed to a spot in the distance. "The bogs have been flooded, and we now have a good three to four inches of ice. That's the minimum thickness to hold the weight of the machinery without cracking."

"You said that sanding keeps down insects," Monica said, the wind snatching her words away as she said them.

"Yes. Way back in 1816, when the cranberry growing industry was in its infancy, a Captain Henry Hall of Dennis, Massachusetts discovered that the sand that regularly blew onto his cranberry vines seemed to stimulate their growth. Sanding is now a best practice in cranberry farming."

By now they had passed the pump house, where the

controls for the sprinklers were housed, and had reached the bog in question. It looked so different in winter, Monica thought, without the brilliant ruby red of the cranberries dotting the vines. The bog was frozen over and the vast expanse of ice was a bluish gray that blended with the overcast sky so that the line of the horizon nearly disappeared and you could barely tell where the ground ended and the sky began.

Two of Jeff's men stood around with their hands shoved into their pockets. They were dressed for the frigid weather in thick jackets and heavy work gloves. Monica recognized the one with the green cap pulled down low over his curly blond hair. He'd helped Jeff with the fall harvesting. They were standing next to a machine that looked like a cross between a Bobcat and a dump truck.

"That's our sand buggy," Jeff said, pointing at the contraption. "I adapted it from a crawler. Cranberry growing is all about making do with what you have. There are only around one thousand cranberry farmers in the country, so manufacturers aren't rushing to create equipment for us—we have to do it ourselves." He grinned. "At least it's something to keep us busy during the winter."

At a signal from Jeff, one of the men jumped into the sand buggy and started the engine with a roar. Carefully he guided the strange-looking machine down a ramp and onto the frozen bog. A spreader, hooked to the back of the sand buggy, slowly released a layer of sand onto the ice.

"When the ice melts, the sand will automatically sift onto the vines," Jeff said. "It will choke out any weed seeds or insect eggs and act as a fertilizer, as crazy as that sounds."

As they were talking, a small group of people approached, led by a pretty blonde in a dark blue parka.

Monica caught the glance that she and Jeff exchanged, and she smiled. Jeff had been hesitant to pursue Lauren at first, feeling he had nothing to offer with a farm on the brink of bankruptcy and an injury that was never going to heal. But Lauren had waited for him to come around, and he had.

Together, Jeff and Monica had managed to turn Sassamanash Farm around as well, and they were now making a small profit. A chain gourmet grocery store had taken an interest in stocking Monica's cranberry salsa, and they had their fingers crossed that the deal would soon go through and bring an infusion of cash to the farming operation.

Lauren's brave little tour group huddled together as Jeff explained about the sanding process. One gentleman, who looked like a retired professor with his tweed overcoat and plaid scarf, asked numerous questions, which Jeff patiently answered while the others looked around, stamping their feet to keep warm.

Lauren was about to shepherd them toward the farm store when Monica noticed a woman in the distance headed their way. She was waving at them. Monica watched as she ran down the dirt path toward them.

The woman finally reached them, breathless and red-faced, with her fancy heeled boots coated in mud.

"Jacy!" Jeff said. He looked from Jacy to Lauren. "Lauren, this is Jacy Belair. She owns Bijou, that new jewelry store in town."

Monica could tell Jeff felt awkward. He kept looking back and forth between Lauren and Jacy.

Jacy put her arm through Jeff's, apparently not noticing

his scowl, and looked up at him. "You sound surprised to see me. You did invite me to come tour the farm."

Lauren raised her eyebrows at Jeff, and he smiled sheepishly.

"I'm sorry I missed cranberry picking season," Jacy continued, seemingly oblivious to the tension in the air. "But I'll make up for it next fall, I promise."

Lauren sidled up to Monica and whispered, "Sounds more like a threat than a promise, doesn't it?"

Monica checked in at the farm store and even though they were doing a brisk business, Nora said she was managing just fine. She enjoyed working in the shop while her husband spent time with the kids—he was taking them sledding, yesterday's snow having accumulated just enough to make that possible.

Today was the monthly mystery book club at Book 'Em, and Monica always looked forward to it. They were reading Margaret Yorke's *Dangerous to Know*. She was a new author to Monica and to most of the others, and Monica was very glad that Greg had introduced them to her books. Most were stand-alone novels with fascinating characters and edge-of-the-seat suspense that the author managed to achieve despite most of the stories being set among seemingly ordinary people in small villages much like Cranberry Cove. Monica looked forward to discovering more of her work.

Downtown was crowded when Monica got there. Preston Crowley's Winter Walk might not have gone off as he'd planned, but his death had still lured plenty of people to the small town. They'd obviously come out of some form of morbid curiosity, and the sidewalks along the cordoned off Beach Hollow Road were teeming, as was the street itself.

People darted in and out of the various shops, emerging with shopping bags swinging from their hands. She noticed several people poke their heads into the Cranberry Cove Diner—where it was fairly obvious that the locals hung out—but the tourists had retreated as quickly as a turtle pulling its head in when it sensed danger. The locals kept to themselves and certainly weren't going to swap theories about the murder with perfect strangers who'd come from miles and miles away just to gawk.

Book 'Em was filled with the smell of freshly brewed coffee when Monica arrived. Greg had opened up a small gateleg table and set out hot water for tea, a thermos of coffee and a pot of hot chocolate.

He had pulled every chair he could find into a circle in the middle of the store—folding chairs, slipcovered armchairs that had seen better days and a couple of desk chairs. The VanVelsen sisters were already seated in two of the more comfortable chairs. Every once in a while they left Gumdrops in the hands of the granddaughter of one of their cousins who lived nearby, although Gerda always fretted the entire time they were away from the store.

Grace Singleton was there, too. Monica hadn't been sure she would come. She'd been Preston Crowley's secretary for years and was very devoted to him. She was thin and angular and her clothes—a nearly ankle-length skirt and white cotton turtleneck—had no more shape on her than they would have suspended from a hanger. Her gray hair was pulled back in a ponytail that hung halfway down her back. Her eyes were red-rimmed, Monica noticed, and her hands were trembling slightly in her lap.

Greg came out of the back room. "That looks delicious," he said, taking the cranberry coffee cake Monica had brought as her contribution.

There was already a glass bowl filled with VanMelle fruit toffees from the VanVelsens and a batch of oatmeal cookies from Grace. Greg cleared a space and set down Monica's coffee cake.

Monica helped herself to a cup of hot chocolate and chose one of the folding chairs—not the most comfortable, but she preferred to leave the better chairs for the older women in the group.

They heard voices approaching, and the door opened and two more women came in. One was Eleanor Mason, a retired schoolteacher who always made Monica think of Miss Marple. Today she had on a quilted sweatshirt with a snowman applique on the front. With her was Phyllis Bouma, the local librarian. She was almost as much of an authority on mysteries as Greg.

The two women poured themselves coffee and slid two pieces of Monica's coffee cake onto the paper plates Greg had put out. Eleanor sank into one of the armchairs with a loud *ouf*, and Phyllis sat next to her on a worn leather office chair.

Phyllis brandished her copy of *Dangerous to Know*. "It's hard to believe there's been another murder in our midst," she said. "Just like out of a book."

Grace gave a loud sniff. "Except we know the victim. Or at least I do." She pulled a tissue from her sleeve and dabbed at her eyes. She tucked it back into her cuff and fingered the thin gold chain around her neck. She gave another loud sniff. "Preston gave me this for my twentieth anniversary with him."

"It's lovely," everyone chorused dutifully.

"He bought it in that new shop here in town—Bijou. Preston always did believe in patronizing the local stores."

"It must be odd for that Jacy Belair woman who runs Bijou to be on the other side of the fence now—or should I say *counter*." Phyllis drummed her fingers on the book in her lap.

"What do you mean?" Grace looked at her quizzically.

"She used to be one of the rich summer tourists buying fancy clothes in Danielle's, and now she's behind the counter at a jewelry store."

"She owns the store, doesn't she?" Eleanor asked. "At least that's what I heard."

"As far as I know." Phyllis raised an eyebrow. "Still, it's a bit of a comedown having to work for a living, don't you think?"

"But if she was one of the rich summer tourists, as you put it . . ." Monica said.

Phyllis snorted. "Easy come, easy go, as they say. I heard that husband of hers left her quite well off but she got caught up in some sort of scheme and lost it all. She even had to sell her house down south or wherever it was they came from."

Eleanor glanced at Grace, who was dabbing her eyes again.

"I'm sorry, dear," she said. "All this must be very upsetting for you."

Grace nodded. "I just hope they find out who did it."

"We should investigate ourselves," Phyllis declared.

"Yes. Just like in the books—like Miss Silver or Jessica Fletcher," Eleanor chimed in.

"Do you really think . . ." Gerda started.

"It may not be wise. It may be . . . dangerous," Hennie added, "to get mixed up in murder."

"Nonsense," Phyllis said briskly. "But we do need some clues."

Greg, Monica noticed, was listening to the conversation with an amused look on his face.

"What kind of clues?" Grace lifted her head, and for a moment her face became almost animated.

"I don't know," Phyllis said in exasperation. "Maybe like who hated him or who stands to benefit—things like that."

"He had a huge argument with someone the day he died," Grace said with the air of someone presenting a gift. "It was right before he left the office to go to the Winter Walk. They were shouting so loudly I could hear them clear out to my desk, even though the door was shut."

The rest of the women leaned forward eagerly in their seats.

"Who was he arguing with?" Eleanor asked.

"I don't exactly know," Grace admitted, her bony shoulders sagging.

"Gerda and I know almost everyone in Cranberry Cove, right, Gerda?" Hennie turned to her sister. "Perhaps if you describe the person, we can figure out who it was."

"I don't know. . . ." Grace slid her feet in and out of the clogs she was wearing.

"Well, was it a male or female?" Hennie asked impatiently.

"It was a woman," Grace answered.

"And?" Hennie raised her eyebrows.

"Nicely dressed."

By now even Eleanor was beginning to get impatient. "If this person had an argument with Preston that was so loud you heard it out at your desk, it's probably significant. You must try to remember. What color hair did she have? What kind of clothes?"

Grace squeezed her eyes shut as if that would jog her memory. "She was wearing a jacket—the kind that buttons over like this." She demonstrated with her hands.

"Double-breasted. Go on," Eleanor said. "Color?"

"Dark. Navy or maybe black, I'm not sure."

"Was she wearing anything else besides a jacket?" Eleanor asked and everyone laughed.

"Pants. Gray pants and suede shoes," Grace said triumphantly. "I remember thinking the shoes looked very comfortable—almost like those slippers they sell that look like moccasins but are lined in fur." Grace closed her eyes again. "Her hair was blond," she finished and looked around almost as if expecting applause.

Monica had felt herself grow cold as Grace's description continued, and by the end she was positive. It was her mother who had had the argument with Preston right before he died.

Could she be the one who had killed him?

Chapter 8

Monica was so distracted by the thought of her mother as a potential suspect in a murder case that she couldn't focus on the book discussion that swirled around her. Several times someone had to repeat her name to get her attention, and she caught the brief look of concern that crossed Greg's face at one point.

Finally the meeting came to an end, and everyone got ready to leave—donning coats, pulling on hats and winding scarves around their necks. Discussion about the book had been lively and continued even as the members of the book club prepared to depart. Monica was about to leave when Greg put a hand on her arm to stop her.

"Have a minute?" he asked with a smile.

Monica hesitated. "Sure," she said at last.

Greg plopped down into one of the armchairs, which sent up a puff of dust while emitting a loud groan. Monica took the seat opposite him—a rickety wooden folding chair. She unbuttoned her coat and took off her gloves.

Greg was silent as he fiddled with his reading glasses, twirling them around and around by the earpiece. Finally he spoke.

"I'm worried about you."

"Me?" Monica said, pointing at herself.

"Yes. Is something wrong? You're normally an active part of our book discussion, but today you seemed . . . you seemed as if you were somewhere else." Greg smiled. "Your mind that is."

Monica laughed, but it didn't sound right, even to her ears. "I guess I was a little preoccupied." She hesitated for a moment. Should she tell Greg? Why not—he'd proven himself to be her friend. "The woman Grace described as having been in Preston's office arguing with him sounded a lot like my mother. Actually I'm quite sure it *was* my mother."

"Your mother?" Greg looked confused. "But isn't she in—"

"She came to Cranberry Cove for a visit. Although not to see me—to see Preston Crowley. Apparently she met him when he was in Chicago on business, and they began dating. She thought she would surprise him."

"But why would that make you think she had anything to do with Preston's murder?"

Monica fiddled with the gloves in her lap—turning them over and over and over. "I'm not the one who thinks she murdered him—Detective Stevens does."

Greg looked even more perplexed. "But why? What reason could she have for jumping to that conclusion? From what you've told me, your mother is a perfectly normal suburban housewife, not a psychopath—hardly the sort to go around killing people."

"Stevens discovered the fact that my mother and my stepmother Gina were both dating Preston—unbeknownst to each other, of course. But she's convinced that one of them actually already knew she was being two-timed." Monica stopped for a second and took a deep breath before going on. "The theory is she then got angry—angry enough to stick a knife in Preston's neck."

Greg jumped up and began pacing the small open space in the center of the bookstore. He had his hands behind his back and his head down.

"Does Stevens have any evidence? Anything that puts either your mother or stepmother on the scene?"

Monica shook her head. "Not that I know of . . . but the police don't always reveal all the information in their possession."

"And neither your mother nor your stepmother has a convenient alibi, I presume?"

Monica shook her head. "Sadly, no. My mother claims to have been driving around, and Gina says she was in her shop but had no customers."

Greg stopped in mid-stride. "Then it's up to us to find out what really happened." He crossed his arms over his chest.

Monica felt the ghost of a smile hover around her lips. "Like Hercule Poirot?"

Greg straightened his shoulders. "I prefer to think of myself as more of an Inspector Lynley type—not very tall but certainly dark and handsome."

Monica laughed. "Fine. Who shall I be then?"

"You're way too young and pretty to be Miss Marple

or Miss Silver." Greg tilted his head to one side, considering Monica. She could feel the blood rising to her face under his scrutiny. She forced a laugh to cover her discomfort.

"Who do you think?" Greg asked.

"I . . . I don't know," Monica admitted.

If Greg's objective was to take her mind off her mother and the murder, it was working admirably.

"Maybe Stephanie Plum? Sort of bumbling and comical," Monica suggested.

"No, you're much too classy to be Stephanie Plum." He snapped his fingers. "I know! Gemma James from Deborah Crombie's books. You've got the same tumble of auburn curls, the same tenacity, honesty and goodness."

Now Monica was blushing in earnest. Of course Greg was just joking, but she was enjoying it nonetheless.

Monica left Book 'Em in a good mood, which vaporized into thin air the moment she got home and saw her mother's car sitting in the driveway. It was fine for her and Greg to joke about investigating, but the reality was that they had nothing at their disposal and the police had everything at theirs.

Monica scooped up Mittens and held her tight as soon as she walked in the back door. The sweet little tabby always soothed her, no matter what her mood. Mittens rubbed against Monica's face as if saying *I understand*.

Nancy was sitting in a chair in the living room, staring at nothing. She didn't move when Monica walked in.

"Is everything okay?" Monica put Mittens down on the floor and sat on the edge of the sofa.

Nancy lifted her shoulders and let them slump. "Nothing has gone right." She wound a handkerchief between her fingers. "I only wanted to surprise Preston—and look what's happened!"

Monica cleared her throat. Now was as good a time as any to ask her mother about the argument Grace had overheard—assuming she could find the words. Every sentence she composed in her head sounded accusatory.

She cleared her throat again. "Preston Crowley's secretary is in my book group. She said she overheard someone arguing with Preston right before the Winter Walk. She didn't know the woman's name but the description fit you." The words came out sounding stilted—rehearsed.

Nancy whirled around to face her. "You can't believe that I—"

"Of course not," Monica said briskly. She let the silence draw out for several minutes. "What were you arguing about?" she finally asked.

"Nothing, really."

"It must have been something if Grace heard you all the way out at her desk, through the closed door."

"The woman probably had her ear to the door," Nancy said, clenching her fists. "And I wasn't the one shouting." Nancy looked affronted. "I told Preston to keep his voice down, but he wouldn't listen." She folded her hands primly in her lap. "It was unseemly the way he was carrying on."

"Yes, but what was it about?" Monica persisted. "When this gets out, the police are going to want to know."

Nancy sat up straighter in her chair. "I should hope you're not going to tell them!"

"Of course not. But if they question Grace about that afternoon, she's bound to mention it."

"But the police won't know I was the woman he was

arguing with, will they?" Nancy ended the sentence on a plaintive note, her voice sounding almost girlish.

"I don't think it would take them long to figure it out. Stevens is a detective, after all."

"Preston was so *rude*."

"About what?" Mittens jumped up on the sofa, and Monica stroked the cat's soft fur. The kitten purred loudly.

"I just wanted to surprise him. I thought he'd be pleased. But he . . . wasn't. He was furious. I don't understand why."

"I think it's obvious. He didn't want you to find out about Gina. While you stayed in Chicago, and she stayed here in Cranberry Cove, the chances of you finding out about each other were slim."

Nancy sagged in her chair again. "True. And here I thought we had the start to a good relationship. We enjoyed many of the same things, always had plenty to talk about. . . ." She balled up the handkerchief in her hand. "And now I find out he was dating another woman. And not just any woman—Gina!"

Monica felt a pang of sympathy. All these events certainly had to have been hard on her mother. She got up, went to Nancy and put her arms around her shoulders.

"I'm sure everything is going to be fine. Detective Stevens is smart—she'll find out who did it soon enough."

"I just want to go home." Nancy sniffed.

"Maybe that would be best." Monica patted her arm. "You'll feel better surrounded by your own things—"

"But I can't," Nancy wailed.

"Why not?"

"The police won't let me. That Detective Stevens called and made it quite clear that I wasn't to leave Cranberry Cove until she said I could."

• • •

Monica was surprised when she looked at the clock—it was already past lunchtime, and she hadn't had a chance to go to the grocery store. What could she feed her mother and herself? She studied the contents of her pantry and fridge. Maybe some potato soup—it would use up the last of her spuds along with the two slices of bacon and the piece of cheddar cheese in the refrigerator. She might not be Dutch, but living in Cranberry Cove, she had picked up some of their thrifty ways.

She was giving the soup a final stir when she heard a car pull into the driveway and around to the back of the cottage, so it was no surprise when the back door flew open.

"What smells so good?" Gina said, wiping her feet on the mat.

"Potato soup. There's plenty if you'd like some."

Monica wasn't sure how well Nancy and Gina would get along sitting across the table from each other, espe- cially without any wine being involved, but she wasn't going to ask Gina to leave. They would have to be civil to each other, even if it killed them.

"Oh," Nancy said when she walked into the kitchen and saw Gina. "Are you staying for lunch?"

"Yes." Gina slid into the place Monica had set for her.

Monica ladled out bowls of soup and then took her place at the table.

"I wonder what Preston was thinking," Nancy blurted out. "Dating both of us at the same time."

"Maybe that he could have his cake and eat it, too?" Gina patted her lips with her napkin.

"He didn't seem like the sort," Nancy said, then laughed. "Of course neither did my ex-husband."

Gina shifted in her seat, keeping her eyes on her bowl.

"I didn't know that much about Preston really—only superficial things." Nancy put down her soup spoon. "I knew he liked opera but preferred *La Boheme* to *Figaro*. He didn't care for fish—especially salmon. He bought his clothes at Brooks Brothers, and he had a sister." She stared into the distance. "It doesn't add up to much in the end, does it?" She sighed. "And it certainly doesn't seem like any of that would have gotten him killed."

"I know his first wife left him," Gina said, stirring her soup around and around in the bowl. "She took off with another man. He never got over it."

Nancy gave Gina a piercing look. "That sounds terribly familiar."

"Are you insinuating—" Gina got halfway out of her chair.

"I'm not insinuating anything." Nancy lifted her chin. "The facts are the facts. You lured my husband away like that man lured away Preston's wife."

"If you had treated him like a man and not a child— always after him to pick up his things, complaining when he came home late even though he was working hard to support his family—he might have stayed."

This time Nancy half rose from her chair. "If some floozy hadn't come along and sunk her claws into him, he never would have left."

The two women stared at each other, nostrils flaring, faces turning red. Monica knew she had to do something.

"Enough!" she said, startling not only Nancy and Gina

but herself as well. "If we're going to solve this case we have to work together." She pointed at the two women.

"Well!" Nancy said, although Monica noticed she looked somewhat chastened.

"You're right." Gina pushed back her chair. "Squabbling isn't going to get us anywhere." She picked up her purse and slipped into her coat. "And on that note, I'll be going. The gal that's minding the store has to leave soon to go pick up her kids."

Nancy didn't say anything but watched as Gina went out the back door, slamming it slightly harder than necessary.

As soon as they heard Gina's car start up, Nancy turned to Monica.

"How can you tolerate that woman? After what she did to us. . . ."

"Believe it or not, I like Gina," Monica said, lifting her chin defensively. "She's been a good mother to Jeff, and she's been kind to me. It's time to move on."

Nancy looked as if someone had thrown a bucket of ice water at her. She fiddled with her napkin, then sighed dramatically. "I suppose you're right. It is time to move on. We've both been hurt by the same man—that should make us allies, not enemies."

"That's right," Monica said with relief. "And we have to work together if we're going to find out who really killed Preston Crowley."

Chapter 9

Since Cranberry Cove was still teeming with tourists, it was decided that the Winter Walk would continue as originally planned. The police had reopened Beach Hollow Road, and it was slowly filling with shoppers. Monica hurried back to the farm stand outside of Gumdrops. She had few baked goods left but plenty of her signature Sassamanash Farm cranberry salsa. She decided she would concentrate on selling that, in hopes of creating enough buzz that some of the chain gourmet stores might consider stocking it. An order like that would mean investing in a professional kitchen, but with a solid plan, she was hopeful the bank would give them a loan. Jeff had already decided where to build—they could create an extension of the farm store and cranberry processing building.

Nancy had gone to lie down for a bit—she still had a slight headache from yesterday's wine binge. Monica made sure she had everything she needed and was comfortable and then went to carry the containers of salsa out to her car. Three trips later, she slammed the trunk lid of the Focus and took off for downtown Cranberry Cove.

Parking was scarce, even on the side streets, so it was obvious that the Winter Walk was still in full swing. Monica parked at the church and walked back toward town. It seemed odd to see the storefronts sparkling with lights and the street and sidewalks bustling with people— and poor Preston wasn't alive to see it. His idea was definitely a success.

Monica passed the window of Making Scents, where she could see three women clustered around the counter. Gina was putting pink tissue into a pink and white Making Scents shopping bag, so at least one of the ladies must be buying.

Bart was in the window of his butcher shop, tying up what looked like a pork loin. It reminded Monica that she needed to plan something for dinner. More often than not, when she was alone she made a sandwich or heated up a can of soup, but that wouldn't do for her mother. She'd pop in to Bart's later and pick something up.

She passed Book 'Em and peeked into the window but didn't see Greg. He must be in the back room.

A couple of Cranberry Cove residents sat on the stools in front of the counter at the diner. Monica recognized one fellow with a Lions baseball cap and the plaid flannel shirt from the garage just outside of town. They were all sipping coffee and keeping a watchful eye on the door lest any of the tourists, lured by the smell of bacon and potatoes frying, attempted to cross the threshold.

Monica was passing Twilight, Tempest's new age shop, when Tempest ran out of the store and grabbed her by the elbow. She was wearing a long jacket embroidered with silver and gold threads that looked as if it came from India, with black pants that were almost as fitted as leggings.

"I need to speak to you," Tempest said, as she pulled Monica through the open doorway of her shop.

"Is something wrong?"

Tempest put a finger to her lips as she closed and locked the door behind her. Her face was as white as a Kabuki performer's.

Twilight was almost as disorderly as Book 'Em, with candles scattered everywhere—tall and short, chunky and tapered. There was also exotic looking jewelry on black velvet stands, stacks of tarot cards and displays of crystals.

Monica's heart began to beat faster. Something had obviously frightened Tempest . . . badly.

"What's wrong?"

"I can hardly believe it," Tempest said, fingering the large, ornate amulet she wore on a ribbon around her neck. "I assumed they just wanted to know if I'd seen anything, but that wasn't the case."

"Who are *they*?" Monica put a hand on Tempest's arm to calm her.

"The police. That woman detective."

"Detective Stevens?"

"Yes." Tempest put a trembling hand to her face. "It's terrible. I don't know what to do."

"Why don't you tell me what's happened. What did Detective Stevens have to say?"

"It was about Preston's murder." Tempest shook her head. "That man is managing to cause me trouble even after his death."

"What . . . how?"

Tempest played with a loose button on her jacket. "There hasn't been a lot about the murder in the papers. I suppose the police don't know very much at this stage, but people are saying that Preston was stabbed in the neck."

Monica shuddered. "Yes, he was. I saw it myself."

"You poor dear," Tempest said, momentarily forgetting her own troubles. "It can't have been a pretty sight."

Monica shook her head as if to dislodge the image that rushed to fill her mind. "But what did the police want with you if you didn't even see anything? Maybe it's routine?"

Tempest shook her head. "It was about the murder weapon—the knife in Preston's neck."

"But what does that have to do with you?"

Tempest touched the amulet hanging from her neck. She held the pewter charm toward Monica. "This is the Sigil of Defense—a magic symbol that is supposed to protect you from harm." She made a wry face. "Maybe it really is all hocus-pocus after all, because it's certainly not working."

"I think you'd better tell me all about it."

Tempest's lower lip trembled, and for a moment Monica thought she would cry.

"The police researched the murder weapon. It wasn't an ordinary kitchen knife or hunting knife or anything like that. It was an athame."

Monica frowned. "What on earth is that?"

"It's a double-edged ceremonial dagger." Tempest paused as if the words were stuck in her throat. "It's a magical tool used in Wiccan rituals."

Monica gasped.

Tempest moved to the glass counter that dominated the center of the store. She went behind it, opened the back and took something out. She placed it on the counter. It was a long dagger with an ornately carved black handle.

She pointed to it. "This is an athame."

"Oh," Monica said, understanding dawning as swiftly as a wave rushing across Lake Michigan to the shore. "But the police couldn't possibly think . . ."

"What else are they going to think? It's not like you'd find one of these in every kitchen drawer or toolbox." Tempest managed a brief smile. "It's not your everyday household item."

"And the police think it belongs to you?"

"Everyone knew that Preston and I had butted heads over the Imbolc ceremony I wanted to hold on the green."

Monica thought back to the previous day in Gina's shop when Tempest had threatened to kill Preston. She hadn't believed her, of course. Tempest certainly hadn't meant it—but the police didn't know that. Monica was quite certain there were any number of people in Cranberry Cove willing to make sure the police knew about the animosity between Tempest and Preston.

Tempest put the dangerous-looking dagger back in the case. "The problem is the athame might have come from my shop. I'm hopeless at keeping inventory. Obviously there isn't any place else in town where you would find one of these."

"The murderer might have bought it somewhere else— another town or city perhaps."

"There aren't all that many new age stores around. Maybe in Chicago. . . ."

"Is it possible someone stole it from you?" Monica asked.

"I suppose so. I don't worry about shoplifting all that much—it's never been a real problem." Tempest waved a hand around the shop. "Besides, I doubt I would even notice if something went missing."

"Someone might have bought the knife from you," Monica said. "And just waited until the right time to use it."

Tempest fiddled with her loose button again. Monica was convinced it was going to come off in her hand.

"That's possible. I don't sell many of these though, and I think I'd remember it."

"It looks to me like the murderer is trying to implicate you, but why?" Monica mused.

"As I said, I make the perfect candidate. It was well known that Preston and I didn't see eye to eye, and the locals obviously distrust me underneath their polite facade—if anyone has to be held responsible for the murder, they'd rather have it be an outsider like me than one of their own."

Monica understood—for her part, she couldn't help wondering if this new evidence would clear both her mother and Gina. Of course it was no better having the police suspect Tempest. She had always been welcoming to Monica, and Monica liked her offbeat personality.

"I don't know what to do. Should I call a lawyer or will that make things look worse?" Tempest smoothed back a strand of hair that had escaped from the white streak that cut through her otherwise black hair. "I feel like I need to be prepared."

Now Tempest was picking at the threads on her exotic jacket, her fingers twitching like chickens pecking at grain.

"Where were you during the opening of the Winter

Walk?" Monica asked as delicately as possible. "Did you have your ceremony on the village green?"

"I had everything planned," Tempest said. "Candles, noisemakers, everything that would be needed. I didn't expect the entire village to join in, but several people had indicated an interest in taking part—even Zoe Farthing, who teaches history over at the high school."

Tempest fiddled with that loose button again and this time it came away in her hand. She looked at it as if she'd never seen it before—as if it were some sort of ancient artifact. She finally put it in her pocket.

"If there were people around, they can vouch for the fact that you couldn't have committed the murder," Monica told her. Even Tempest couldn't be in two places at once.

"That's the problem. No one showed up. They were scared off by Preston and his wretched petition."

"But someone must have seen you. You lit candles and shook noisemakers, didn't you?" It seemed to Monica that Tempest would have been hard to miss out there on the green, chanting and shaking noisemakers.

Tempest looked over Monica's shoulder. "I decided not to go ahead with it in the end. It seemed pointless out there all by myself. . . . I suddenly felt foolish."

"Did you go to the green? Did anyone see you?"

Tempest shook her head. "I don't think so. I don't remember seeing anyone myself, although I seem to recall . . ." Tempest paused.

"Have you remembered something?"

"I don't know. I have a feeling I did see someone, but maybe I'm imagining it."

Monica sighed. It seemed as if Tempest didn't have even a shred of an alibi.

Tempest looked at Monica as if entreating her to do something, but what could she do? She tried to find the words to reassure Tempest, but they didn't come—the evidence was damning. An athame wasn't your common, everyday weapon.

And it pointed straight at Tempest.

Chapter 10

Monica left Twilight with her mind going in every direction—whirling with thoughts that floated away and were quickly replaced by new ones. She knew Tempest didn't kill Preston, no matter how bad it looked, but what was she going to do? It was obvious that Tempest was looking to her for help, and she couldn't let her down.

The sidewalk and the blocked-off street were crowded with people, and Monica felt herself being jostled repeatedly as she made her way toward Gumdrops. Laughter and loud conversation filled the air—it seemed wrong in light of Preston's murder.

Monica glanced across the street. The front of Bijou twinkled with tiny white lights. She could see there were several people standing around the counter inside the shop, while others peered at the display of diamonds and other gems in the window.

Next door was the Purple Grape. The wine store did

most of its business during the summer when tourists were in town, but the locals were becoming more and more interested in learning about grapes and various vintages. It, too, had been decorated with lights, which created a distinct contrast with the storefront next door.

A sign with *Pepper Pot* in paprika-colored script hung outside the darkened space, and Monica could see the menu she'd looked at the other day still taped to the window. She'd have to ask the VanVelsen sisters about it—they knew virtually everything that went on in Cranberry Cove. The restaurant should have been open by now to take advantage of the crowds gathered for the Winter Walk. At least Monica understood that that had been the plan. Grace had told the book club that the dining room of the Cranberry Cove Inn was fully booked with a waiting list as long as her arm, so another restaurant in town would have been a boon. People wanted atmosphere and good service, which the Cranberry Cove Diner couldn't provide, although the merits of its chili were known far and wide.

Monica finally reached the makeshift booth Jeff had created for the Walk. She was relieved to set down her baskets—they'd grown heavier with each step. She carefully arranged the containers of salsa—each glass jar topped with a piece of cloth printed with cranberries and tied around the lid with a red grosgrain ribbon.

She was setting the last few in place when the door to Gumdrops opened and Hennie stepped out. She had a gray cardigan draped around her shoulders, and her arms were crossed over her chest.

"Glad to see you're back, dear." She pulled the sweater around her more tightly. "We've been doing a brisk business. A very brisk business indeed." She pointed at

Monica's tower of cranberry salsa. "Those will be gone in no time. We're fresh out of pastilles and root beer barrels." She shook her head. "That's never happened before—not even on summer holidays like Memorial Day and the Fourth of July."

"Everyone seems to be busy. It's a shame that new restaurant hadn't been able to open." She pointed across the street toward the Pepper Pot.

"They were supposed to." Hennie frowned. "I heard something about a permit being delayed. Apparently the owner was furious. Edith DeHamer—she works over at the town hall—told me about it. The fellow raised quite a ruckus apparently." Hennie shivered. "I'd best be going in. I don't want to catch my death of cold out here."

Monica gazed longingly at the warmly lit front of Gumdrops. Her fingers and toes were already turning numb. She thought of Jeff and his crew working out on the bogs, where there was nothing to block the frigid wind blowing in off the lake.

Soon Monica had sold all the stock she had with her. She picked up her empty baskets and was about to leave when she changed her mind. She'd go into Gumdrops and get something to take home to her mother. Nancy needed cheering up, and who didn't love candy?

"You must be frozen," Gerda said when she spotted Monica standing by the counter. "Can I get you a cup of tea?"

"That would be lovely." Monica took off her gloves, shoved them into her pockets and rubbed her hands together briskly.

The shop momentarily emptied of customers, and Hennie went over to Monica.

"Are you calling it a day?" she asked.

Monica nodded. "Yes. I've sold everything I had. I'm going to have to do some serious baking tomorrow morning."

"It's a shame Preston's not here to see what a success the Winter Walk is. A lot of people balked at the idea in the beginning, but obviously it was brilliant. Normally at this time of year, we'd be lucky to have a handful of customers a day—mostly mothers coming in to buy treats for their child's birthday party—but today, like I mentioned to you, we've actually started to run out of stock."

Monica felt something brush against her leg and looked down to see Midnight weaving in and out between her legs. Midnight was the mother of Monica's kitten Mittens, having presented the VanVelsens with an unexpected litter.

Midnight gave a plaintive meow, and Monica bent down to scratch her head.

"Midnight!" Hennie scolded her in pretend stern tones, but Monica could hear the affection in her voice. "You've had plenty of attention already today. And a bowl of cream, too."

Monica laughed. "Mittens takes after her mother, I think!"

The door opened, and a customer came in. She was wearing a royal blue parka trimmed in fur and a pair of sheepskin boots lined in fleece. Monica glanced at them and was reminded of her half-frozen toes. She was going to have to go shopping for a new pair for herself. Hennie glanced at her customer and raised her eyebrows at Monica. Monica waved her away. She could wait until Hennie had served the woman.

The woman spent several minutes studying the cases

of candy, then nodded at Hennie and left without making a purchase.

Hennie shrugged. "You can't please everyone." She smiled.

A thought had been formulating in Monica's head while she waited. She motioned for Hennie to step closer and with a lowered voice she said, "I've been thinking about the restaurant across the street and how they weren't able to get their permit in time for the Winter Walk."

Hennie tipped her head to the side. She was obviously all ears.

"Everyone has been talking about how the Pepper Pot was going to give the dining room at the Cranberry Cove Inn a run for its money. Preston was mayor of Cranberry Cove. Do you suppose he might have—"

"Had a hand in delaying the permit?" Hennie finished for Monica. "An intriguing thought. I'm afraid I have no idea how these things are done. I wonder . . ." Hennie put a finger on her chin. "I imagine Edith might know. Of course she won't be at work until Monday morning, but she lives quite close. She has an apartment over the hardware store, which her parents used to own. She grew up there. When her folks died and the new owner took over, they let her stay on as part of the arrangement."

"Do you think she'd mind if I stopped by?"

"On the contrary. You'd be lucky to get out of there in less than two hours. Poor Edith. She's quite alone . . . and a little . . . peculiar, if you know what I mean."

Was Hennie trying to warn her, Monica wondered? When Monica ran her café in Chicago, she'd met her share of unusual types—she was pretty sure she could handle it.

Gerda emerged from the stockroom with a mug of tea

for Monica. Monica accepted it gratefully, enjoying the warmth of the cup in her hands and the steam that rose to bathe her face.

"Who *is* the owner of the Pepper Pot?" Monica looked from Hennie to Gerda and back again.

Both the sisters shrugged their shoulders.

"Whoever it is has stayed in the background," Hennie said. "No one knew anything about the restaurant until the work crew showed up that one morning and began tearing out the interior of that notions shop that used to be there. Never could figure out how they'd stayed in business as long as they did. The stock never changed and old Mrs. Veenstra could never be bothered to run a feather duster over things. Not very appealing."

"I heard they got a good price for the shop, though," Gerda said.

"I should imagine so. It's a prime location—right on Beach Hollow Road." Hennie fiddled with the glasses that hung from a chain around her neck. She looked around the shop. "I wonder what this place would be worth?"

Gerda got a panicked look on her face, and Hennie put a hand on her arm.

"Don't worry, I'm not thinking we should sell. I'm only curious."

Gerda looked relieved.

Monica looked at her watch. "If I'm going to visit Edith, I'd better get going so I don't interrupt her dinner." Monica peered into the glass candy case. "I wanted to pick up something for my mother."

"Does she like chocolate?" Hennie asked.

Monica wrinkled her nose. "Not so much."

"I know." Hennie went behind the counter, opened the

case and pulled out a package. "Katjes winegums. I'm sure she will like these."

"I'll take them," Monica said, digging around in her purse for her wallet.

Hennie waved a hand at her. "Never mind. Our treat. To welcome your mother to Cranberry Cove. You must bring her by someday."

Monica promised she would as she took her leave and plunged back into the cold and crowded night.

The hardware store was at the other end of the block from Gumdrops. Monica stepped off the curb and into the street, where it was slightly less crowded. Chatter filled the air around her—it was impossible to believe that someone had been murdered here only the day before.

Monica arrived at the entrance to the hardware store, and then took a few steps back—she'd gone too far. Off to the side was another door, red with a brass doorbell alongside it. Monica pressed the button. She heard the buzzer ringing inside and waited.

Monica was about to turn away—perhaps the VanVelsen sisters were wrong and Edith had decided to go out—when the door opened a crack.

"Yes?" A woman's voice came through the small opening.

"Edith? I'm Monica Albertson. I live out at Sassamanash Farm. The VanVelsen sisters told me you lived here. Could I possibly come in and ask you a few questions?"

"Are you a reporter? Because I don't want my name in the paper. My mother always said the only time a lady should have her name in the paper is when she's born, when she's married and when she dies."

"No, no. I'm not a reporter."

"I suppose it's okay." Edith pulled open the door.

She was wearing an old silk peignoir ensemble, the sort actresses wore in movies made in the thirties and forties, although Edith's set was frayed at the hem and cuffs and sported several tiny holes. Her thin hair was dyed a red that bordered on fuchsia, and her lips were extravagantly colored with bright orange lipstick.

Whatever Monica had been subconsciously expecting, this certainly wasn't it.

Monica followed Edith up a set of bare wooden stairs that ended in a small landing. The door to the landing was propped open with a rolled-up newspaper. Edith kicked it aside as they entered the apartment.

The apartment itself looked as if time had stood still. The sofa and chairs were Victorian era with antimacassars draped over their backs and knickknacks—porcelain ladies in stiff petticoats and gentlemen in knee breeches—were scattered everywhere. A Victrola stood on a tabletop in the corner.

From the living room, Monica could see a small kitchen and the door to what looked like a bedroom. Noise from the street—the rise and fall of voices and far-off horns—drifted in through the closed windows. Edith had a chair pulled up next to one of them—Monica suspected she sat there and watched life go by downstairs.

"It's so nice of you to visit me. I don't get many visitors." Edith sat down opposite Monica and crossed her ankles primly, her hands folded in her lap. Suddenly she struggled to her feet. "I'm forgetting my manners. Would you like some tea?"

"No, thank you. I just had a cup with the VanVelsen sisters."

"Oh, yes. Hennie and Gerda." Edith resumed her seat. "I knew them when we were all in school together. Our families have been in Cranberry Cove for several generations."

And I'm a newcomer, Monica thought.

"I understand from Hennie that you work at the town hall?"

"That's right, dear. I've just had my fiftieth anniversary. They threw me quite a lovely party to celebrate in the private dining room at the Cranberry Cove Inn. Even the mayor was there. Of course, I've worked with numerous mayors, as you can imagine."

Monica smiled. "The Cranberry Cove Inn is lovely. I imagine you had a wonderful time."

Edith clasped her hands to her chest. "Oh, we did. We certainly did. A steak dinner with all the trimmings. Wine, too, but I don't care for liquor."

"It looks as if there'll soon be a new restaurant in town—the Pepper Pot."

Edith nodded, and her bright red curls bobbed with the movement. They looked almost neon in the light cast by the lamp next to the sofa. "There was quite a to-do over the opening. I understand the owner wanted everything to be in order for the Winter Walk, but for some reason the permit was delayed. Something to do with an inspection not taking place on time. Rieka would know. She's a secretary in the health department."

"I imagine the owner must have been very upset?"

"Oh, he was. He definitely was. There was quite a scene."

Two patches of color brightened Edith's cheeks. Monica imagined it must have been the highlight of what were usually rather boring days occupied with filling out forms and photocopying documents.

"I've heard that our mayor, Preston Crowley, was not in favor of the restaurant?"

Edith's posture stiffened. "May he rest in peace." She bowed her head briefly and then looked up at Monica. "The mayor had his reasons, I'm sure."

"Of course," Monica said soothingly. "But I've heard rumors. . . ."

Edith sniffed. "People will always talk, even when they don't have anything useful to say."

"So you don't think it's true that Mayor Crowley somehow had a hand in delaying the necessary permit?"

"Who said that?" Edith bristled.

Monica shrugged. "Just rumors going around. . . ."

"Mayor Crowley would never stoop to something so low." Edith quivered with indignation. "Those are lies. Just lies."

Her entire face was now flushed with color. Monica suspected that Edith may have developed a crush on the mayor.

"Do you have any idea who owns the Pepper Pot?" Monica thought it best to change the subject, however slightly.

"His name is Roger Tripp."

"Is he from out of town?"

Edith plucked at the torn lace on the cuff of her peignoir. "I know I've been seeing him in town here and there for a couple of years now, but I'm sure he's not *from* here, if you know what I mean."

"Did he work in town somewhere?"

Monica knew that while the shops along Beach Hollow

Road offered employment to some, most Cranberry Cove residents commuted to jobs in bigger towns.

Edith brushed her hand back and forth across the worn velvet of the sofa's arm. She pursed her lips and the wrinkles around them folded in on themselves as if pulled by a drawstring. "I don't know. I remember seeing him in town but he might have been doing his shopping. Maybe Rieka will know?"

Monica smiled. "Good idea." She picked up her purse and put it in her lap. "Will Rieka be at work on Monday do you think?"

"I imagine so. We have the same hours—Monday to Thursday from nine in the morning until three in the afternoon. There's enough to keep us busy, but the job doesn't require a full eight hours. Besides, both Rieka and I are getting on in years, you know. We can't work as hard as you young people." She smiled at Monica.

Monica stood up and began to put on her jacket.

"Are you sure you wouldn't like some tea? I've already had my dinner—only a bowl of pea soup, but I don't eat much these days. I have a lovely coffee cake if you'd care for some."

Monica looked out the window where the shadows had deepened and the sky was darkening. She could see the longing and loneliness in Edith's eyes, but she wanted to get to Bart's before he closed.

"That's very kind, but I'm afraid I have to be going."

"But you've only just gotten here."

Monica was beginning to see what the VanVelsen sisters had meant about it being hard to get away from Edith. "Perhaps I can come another time?"

Edith's face brightened. "That would be lovely." She struggled to her feet.

"Please don't get up," Monica said as she pulled on her gloves.

"I'm fine. Don't worry about me. I'll just walk you to the door."

After a few more minutes of conversation standing by the open door, Monica was finally able to get away.

Bart was about to close up when Monica pushed open his door.

He looked up and smiled. "Monica. Nice to see you. What can I get you? I'm almost cleaned out, but I do have some lamb chops and a porterhouse left."

"I'll take the lamb chops then." Monica decided.

Bart pulled a piece of butcher paper from the roll. "I didn't expect my business to increase because of Preston Crowley's Winter Walk, but I'm pleased to say it has. The day-trippers wanted something to take back home for dinner. My homemade sausage has been selling especially well."

"All the stores have been doing well." Monica pulled her wallet from her purse. "And I gather the Cranberry Cove Inn has been booked full—the dining room as well."

"Too bad that new place hadn't been able to open on time. It's time someone gave Crowley a little competition." Bart slipped a paper-wrapped bundle tied with string into a white bag. "Something went wrong with the permit, I gather." Bart handed Monica the parcel. "The owner is a guy named Roger Tripp. I don't know him well, but he seemed nice enough. Shame it didn't work out for him."

"Is he from around here?"

"Roger?" Bart wrinkled his brow. "Not born here, that's for sure. But I think he's been around for a couple of years. He used to work at the Cranberry Cove Inn as a bartender, then obviously decided to go out on his own."

"That's interesting."

"Yeah. I hope he makes a go of it."

Monica thanked Bart and left. As she passed Book 'Em, Greg was in the process of putting some new books in the window. He held up a hand, signaling for Monica to wait. A second later, the door to the shop opened and Greg popped his head out.

"How did your day go?"

"Very well. I sold everything I had. I'm headed back to the stall to pick up my empty baskets."

"That's great. Preston Crowley might have been a bit of a pain at times, but he had a good idea when it came to this Winter Walk."

Monica nodded. "Everyone has been doing well—even the butcher."

"Listen." Greg opened the door a bit wider. "If I can snag a reservation, would you like to go to brunch tomorrow at the Cranberry Cove Inn? If we go early enough perhaps the tourists won't have arrived yet to take up all the tables. Since it's Sunday, most of the shops aren't opening before noon anyway."

"I'd love to. But why don't I meet you there? Afterward I can head straight to our farm stall."

"Okay—say nine o'clock?"

"Perfect. See you then." Monica waved and continued down the street.

By the time Monica got back to her cottage, the light had faded and night had set in. Snow had started falling on her way home—fat, lazy flakes swirling down from above. She peered up at the clouds that were moving swiftly across the sky. It was most likely lake-effect snow, created when cold winds blew across the warmer waters of Lake Michigan.

Monica hoped it wouldn't last. Bad weather would keep visitors from Cranberry Cove. They already had had just the right amount of snow—a light sprinkling that had turned downtown Cranberry Cove into a picture postcard.

Monica opened the back door. The kitchen was dark, and she flicked on the light switch with her elbow. Mittens came running in from the living room to rub against Monica's legs and purr loudly. She put her packages and the empty baskets on the table and picked up Mittens's dish. The kitten seemed put out by the fact that Monica was five minutes late in preparing her dinner—she sat in the corner, with her back to Monica, grooming her paws with great precision.

Monica opened a can of food, emptied it into a bowl and put it down on the floor. Mittens scampered toward it, her irritation obviously forgotten.

Monica went down the hall to the living room. The room was in darkness, and she reached for the nearest lamp. Her mother's car was parked outside—perhaps she was upstairs resting?

Monica was startled when the light flicked on and she saw her mother sitting in the armchair by the fireplace.

"Why are you sitting in the dark?" Monica took a seat on the sofa opposite her mother.

Nancy gave a small smile. "Just thinking."

"What about?" Monica asked, although she could guess.

"Preston. The murder. My life."

"Your life?"

Nancy nodded. "Yes. I thought Preston and I were headed toward something—at least a permanent relationship, if not marriage." Nancy played with the fringe on Monica's throw pillow. "I'm not getting any younger, to use a trite phrase. I've been alone since your father left."

Monica started to open her mouth, but Nancy waved a hand to silence her.

"Oh, there have been dates here and there. But until Preston came along, there wasn't anyone I could see myself staying with for any length of time." She gave a smile that faded almost as quickly as it came. "Maybe I'm still a little in love with your father."

"After what he—"

"Don't wait too long to let someone into your life. I know Ted's death has made you leery of getting involved again."

Monica was surprised to realize it had been several weeks since she'd thought about her late fiancé.

And then she remembered her date with Greg for brunch, and she smiled.

"What's that smile for? Is there something you're not telling me? Is there someone?"

Monica wasn't ready to talk about it. "There could be. I just need to give it some time."

Chapter 11

The snow stopped sometime during the night after leaving about three inches on the ground—nothing that would stop a true Michigander, Monica thought. It took at least two feet of the white stuff plus whiteout conditions to do that.

She woke up early so she could do some baking and still have time to wash her hair and take a stab at doing something with it. Her curls usually had a mind of their own, and today was no exception. Monica concentrated on applying some mascara and lipstick—things she rarely ever bothered with.

She had a bottle of perfume in the bathroom vanity that Ted had given her, but when she opened it, she realized it was too old and had gone bad. She'd have to be content with smelling like soap. She doubted Greg would mind.

She did take more care than usual selecting her clothes, though. Her normal attire generally consisted of jeans and a sweatshirt or old sweater. The ones she'd worn last night were now discarded in a pile, as she'd been up late baking and had gotten up while it was still dark to do some more. The whole cottage was infused with the smell of butter, sugar and cranberries.

Finally, Monica stood in front of the mirror on her dresser. It didn't afford her a full view, but there wasn't anything she could do about that. She kept meaning to pick up a full-length one at the hardware store to attach to the back of her bedroom door, but it kept slipping down her list of priorities.

Monica heard her mother stirring as she left her room, and she had just entered the hallway when the guest bedroom door opened. Nancy's face was shiny with night cream, but her hair was combed, and she was wearing white pajamas piped in navy blue with a matching robe and navy terrycloth slippers.

She looked Monica up and down and smiled. "Something special must be happening today."

For a moment Monica thought of confiding in her mother, but she wasn't quite ready to show her hand yet. Better to wait until the relationship was more established.

"Not really," Monica said as she turned to head down the stairs. "I was tired of living in jeans and sweatshirts and thought I'd make more of an effort today."

"You look lovely."

"Thanks."

Monica started down the stairs.

"I just hope whoever you're meeting appreciates it," Nancy called down the steps.

• • •

Monica could tell Greg appreciated the care she'd taken with her appearance by the look in his eyes when he met her at the Cranberry Cove Inn.

The Inn was bustling. Three people waited at the reception desk, and more milled around the lobby, coffee cups in hand. The Inn did Sunday brunch in the dining room, but also set out a complimentary continental breakfast of coffee, tea, fresh fruit and pastries in the lobby.

"I've managed to snag us a table," Greg said, as he put his hand on Monica's elbow and steered her toward the dining room, "although I can't guarantee it will be by the window."

The maître d' bustled over with a stack of leather-bound menus in his hand. "This way, please."

He led them to a small table for two tucked into the corner. As they passed the large picture window that was a feature of the Inn's dining room, Monica caught a glimpse of the sun glinting off the ice floes on Lake Michigan.

"Why don't you sit there?" Greg said, pointing to the chair against the wall. "You'll at least have a view of the dining room."

Once again, Monica was struck by how thoughtful Greg was.

Greg looked around the packed room. "Preston would love this if he were here."

"I know." Monica closed her menu—she'd decided on eggs Benedict.

They chatted amiably until their order had been taken and the food had arrived.

"Have you heard about Tempest?" Monica asked,

unable to stay away from the subject on everyone's mind any longer.

"No. I hope nothing's happened to her."

"Not exactly."

Greg looked up sharply at Monica's tone.

She put down her knife and fork. "The police have discovered that the weapon found in . . . in Preston's neck was an athame."

Greg raised his eyebrows. "What on earth is that?"

"It's a dagger of some sort. It's used in Wiccan ceremonies."

"I know Tempest has a lot of unusual things in that store of hers—I'm jumping to the conclusion that the police think the dagger came from there?"

Monica fiddled with the salt and pepper shakers on the table. "It's a logical conclusion. It's certainly not something you can pick up in the hardware store or supermarket. Tempest claims it must have been stolen from her store."

"Claims?" Greg's eyebrows shot up again. "You don't think she had anything to do with it, do you?"

Monica shook her head vigorously. "No. No, not at all. But you know Tempest—she can't remember when it went missing or even if she might have sold it to someone."

Greg dabbed at his lips with his napkin. "If I was going to murder someone, I'd certainly steal the weapon, not buy it. It looks like someone is trying to implicate Tempest. Unless there's some reason why she—"

"No," Monica said, cutting him off. "I don't believe for a minute that Tempest had anything to do with it. She was furious with him, of course—because of the petition to stop her ceremony on the village green, but she would never go so far as to . . . murder him."

"I certainly can't imagine it, either."

Greg put his napkin down on the table. "If you'll excuse me for a moment?"

"Certainly."

Monica pushed her empty plate to the side and leaned her elbows on the table. She looked out over the dining room—it was still packed, with the only empty tables being ones that were in the process of being cleared. She heard the rattle of cutlery and clink of plates being stacked behind her. She glanced over her shoulder—two busboys were making short work of preparing the table for the next diners.

They chatted with each other while they worked, and the words flowed over Monica until she heard one of them mention the name Roger Tripp.

For a moment, Monica couldn't remember why the name sounded so familiar and then it came to her—he was the owner of the Pepper Pot, and former employee of the Cranberry Cove Inn.

Monica leaned back against her chair so she could hear better.

The two young men continued to chat, and now Monica was listening intently.

"I thought Roger's place was supposed to open for the Winter Walk," one said.

"Yeah, I think it was. I heard he ran into some trouble getting the right permits."

The other one snorted. "No wonder, with Preston Crowley as mayor. Tripp's probably still holding a grudge."

"Do you think he did it? Roger, I mean."

"What? Killed Crowley?"

There was silence for a moment. "I never thought of that. No, I meant, stealing from the Inn."

"He wasn't stealing exactly."

"Sure he was. He was charging customers for top-shelf booze but giving them the cheap stuff and pocketing the difference. That's why Crowley fired him."

There was a loud clatter as plates tumbled into the bus tubs, and Monica lost some of the busboys' conversation.

"I think Crowley got his own back," one of the young men said.

"Seriously?"

"Yeah. He was the mayor, wasn't he? No reason he couldn't stop the permit from going through so Roger couldn't open on time for the Winter Walk."

"Yeah. But maybe Roger got the last laugh by plunging that knife into Crowley's neck."

"You think?"

The busboys began to head toward the kitchen with their overflowing bus tubs and Monica couldn't hear the answer.

Greg came back to the table moments later and sat down opposite Monica. He gave her a peculiar smile and picked up his spoon, turning it over and over and over again.

Monica had the sense that he wanted to say something or tell her something, but what, she couldn't begin to imagine.

"Can I ask you a question?" Greg said finally.

"Sure."

Greg continued to play with the spoon, his eyes not quite meeting Monica's. He gave a deep sigh.

"Are we officially dating?" he said. He gave a self-conscious laugh but then turned serious, his eyes searching Monica's for an answer.

Monica was startled. Of all the things she expected him to ask her, that question had never crossed her mind.

"I . . . I don't know," Monica said. "Are we?"

"I hope so." Greg put the spoon down and smiled at Monica.

"Yes, me too." Monica felt her heart lift as if it had suddenly been attached to a helium balloon. She felt a grin break out across her face.

Monica put a hand out and Greg grasped it.

"Good," Greg said and smiled again.

Monica didn't so much drive home as float home. The ride was a blur and when she pulled into the driveway of her little cottage, she couldn't imagine how she'd gotten there. Obviously she must have stopped at all the stop signs and red lights and made all the right turns without even realizing what she was doing.

She felt as giddy as a young girl but at the same time, she knew a lot more about relationships now that she was older and realized that they weren't always smooth sailing. There would be ups and downs, but she was confident that she and Greg could weather them together.

Monica went in through the unlocked kitchen door. She peeked into the living room, but her mother wasn't there, although her car was in the driveway. Monica supposed she must be upstairs taking a nap or reading in bed.

Monica's little car's heater didn't always work, and today was one of those days when it had refused to function. She was chilled to the bone so she retrieved the teakettle from the top of the stove and swung it under the tap to fill it with water.

While the kettle boiled, she hung her coat on the coat-rack and then mopped up the drops of dingy water her snow-covered boots had deposited on the floor. Mittens, who had been sleeping in her basket, woke up, gave a huge stretch and ambled over. She thought it was a wonderful game to try to catch the paper towel as Monica swished it back and forth across the floor.

Monica was grateful when the water boiled and she was able to wrap her hands around a warm mug of tea. She'd just taken her first sip when she heard a noise on the stairs. Moments later her mother appeared in the doorway.

She was elegantly dressed in the same gray trousers she'd worn the day before, topped with a pink cashmere sweater and a colorful silk scarf tucked into the neckline.

She paused at the entrance to the room, and Monica had to suppress the uncharitable thought that she wished her mother would go back to Chicago so she'd have the cottage to herself again.

Instead she said, "Good afternoon," with as much good grace as she could muster. "Would you like a cup of tea?"

"That would be lovely."

Nancy took a seat at the table while Monica readied a mug of tea for her. She stirred in a drop of milk and handed her mother the cup.

"You look different," Nancy said, tilting her head to one side as she regarded Monica.

The last thing Monica wanted to talk about was Greg. She made a noncommittal reply.

"So tell me," Nancy said with enthusiasm, "how was your date?"

Monica was about to deny it had been a date when she

remembered her discussion with Greg. She could feel color flooding her face.

Nancy looked smug. "Something tells me you had a good time. When do I get to meet him?"

"Mother, please. I'm way too old to go on dates and have boyfriends. That part of my life is over."

"It most certainly is not!" Nancy pushed her mug of tea aside and leaned her elbows on the table. "That's never over. Certainly you're not going to be going to a prom or out for milkshakes at your age, but you never outgrow the need for companionship."

Nancy looked away, and Monica thought she wiped a tear from her eye.

"Do you miss Dad?" Monica asked gently.

"Yes. No. Sometimes." Nancy gave a loud sniff. "I thought I'd found someone in Preston—someone who would be a friend as well as a . . . lover."

Monica felt uncomfortable with her mother's confidences and looked down into her cup of tea.

Nancy clenched her fist and banged it on the table, making the sugar bowl jump. "It's all Gina's fault. She wasn't content with stealing John away from me, she had to take Preston, too."

"But she had no idea that Preston was seeing both of you," Monica said. It felt strange to be defending her stepmother for a change.

Nancy shook her finger at Monica. "I just can't believe she didn't have something to do with it."

Monica stifled a gasp. "You don't mean . . . you can't think that Gina had anything to do with Preston's . . . murder?"

Nancy lifted her chin. "I wouldn't put it past her."

"That's ridiculous!"

Nancy shrugged.

"Besides," Monica blurted out, "the police found that the weapon used to kill Preston was an athame—"

"What on earth is that?" Nancy sat up straighter at the table and glared at Monica.

"It's a sort of dagger that Wiccans use in their ceremonies. The police think it came from Tempest's shop."

"Isn't that the woman Gina has become friends with? Two peas in a pod, if you ask me." Nancy lifted her chin.

"Yes. But I don't believe for a minute that Tempest had anything to do with the murder."

Nancy snorted. "Of course not. It's obvious what happened. Gina took advantage of her friendship with Tempest to steal that . . . that . . . thing—whatever you said it's called. And then she used it to kill Preston."

Monica couldn't believe that her mother really thought Gina might have been involved in Preston's death. They'd seemed to be getting along quite well—perhaps it had been the bottle of shared wine that had lubricated things and not any real desire to bury the hatchet and let go of the past.

Monica was relieved when her mother announced that she was going out. Nancy insisted that she would take care of dinner so that Monica could put her feet up and rest. Monica had given her directions to Fresh Gourmet just outside of town, where she trusted her mother would find the ingredients she needed for the tarragon chicken in white wine sauce she planned to make.

Monica heard the churn of gravel as Nancy's car backed out of the driveway, and she breathed a sigh of relief. She sat for a moment with her cooling mug of tea and savored the silence broken only by the soft breathing of Mittens, who had jumped onto one of the chairs and fallen asleep curled into a tight ball, her long tail wrapped protectively around her.

Monica's own head was nodding when there was a peremptory knock on the back door, and Jeff stuck his head into the kitchen.

Monica jumped up and banged her knee against the kitchen table. She winced and put a hand over the sore spot.

"Sorry. I didn't mean to scare you."

"I was falling asleep, I'm afraid."

"You've been working hard, sis," Jeff said as he kicked off his mud-caked work boots and tossed them onto the old rug Monica kept by the back door. "I hope you know how much I appreciate your help."

Monica smiled at her younger brother. Despite having different mothers, there was a strong resemblance between them—they had the same curly auburn hair, similar noses and the height they'd both gotten from their father.

"You're working awfully hard yourself." Monica regarded the lines of weariness on Jeff's face that made him look older than his twenty-five years. "Today's Sunday. Do you ever take a day off?"

Jeff laughed. "There's no such thing when you're a farmer." He ran a hand over his face. "But I don't mind. I'm determined to make Sassamanash Farm a success."

Jeff pulled open the refrigerator door. He looked over his shoulder at his sister and grinned. "Is it too early for a beer?"

"Not at all. Did you know that early American settlers drank beer instead of water? Water was often polluted and unsafe for drinking."

"Must not have been too bad back then." Jeff grinned, and Monica playfully cuffed his ear.

He popped the top off his bottle and sat down opposite Monica. Mittens stood up, stretched and jumped into his lap. He put his beer down on the table and stroked the kitten's glossy fur.

"Did you finish your sanding?" Monica drank the bit of tea left in her mug. It had gone cold, and she made a face.

"Just about. There's one spot on that bog closest to the road—do you know which one I mean?"

Monica nodded.

"The sun hits the far end of it when it's at its peak and despite the cold temperatures, there are places where it's still too slushy to chance using the spreaders." Jeff sighed. "We're going to have to do it by hand." He took a pull on his beer and wiped his mouth with his sleeve. "Fortunately you only have to sand every three years or so."

Jeff's cell phone went off, playing the sonorous notes of Beethoven's Fifth. Jeff grinned at Monica and shrugged. "Gina," he said as he put the phone to his ear. "I thought that piece suited her."

Gina seemed to do most of the talking in the conversation, with Jeff mumbling the occasional *yes* or *no* or *not yet*. Several minutes later he punched off the call and scowled at Monica.

"What's the matter?"

"She got me to agree to having dinner with her tonight." He sighed and slumped down in his chair. "I was looking forward to a hot shower, another beer, take-out pizza and television. Now I have to get dressed for the Cranberry Cove Inn." He ran a finger around the collar of his open-necked shirt.

"How is Gina doing? Do you think she's okay? It's hard for me to tell."

Jeff wiped a streak of condensation off the beer bottle with his thumb. "It's ridiculous." Jeff half turned away. "Promise you won't get upset."

Monica was taken aback. "I'll try."

"Gina is convinced that Nancy killed Preston. Her logic," he gave a strained laugh, "is that Nancy is getting back at Gina for stealing Dad away by taking Preston from Gina."

"By killing him? Seriously?"

Jeff took another swallow of beer and rolled the liquid around in his mouth. "Like I said—ridiculous."

"What's funny—or maybe I should say ironic—is that Nancy thinks Gina killed Preston."

Jeff choked on his beer. "Gina? Why on earth would she kill Preston? She was falling in love with him."

"I have no idea. Personally I think they both need their heads examined."

"You can say that again." Jeff tilted his chair back on two legs.

"Instead of knocking heads, they need to put them together and help figure out who *did* murder Preston before Stevens zeroes in on one of them as the killer." Monica frowned.

They were both quiet, listening to the tick of the kitchen clock as the hands moved forward. Jeff opened his mouth and then shut it.

"Out with it," Monica said when he did it a second time.

Jeff looked down at his hands.

"Come on. Tell big sister what's wrong."

Jeff let his chair fall back into place. "It's something Gina said."

Monica tried not to roll her eyes.

"You know Lauren is graduating from college this spring, right?"

"Yes."

"Gina thinks that Lauren isn't going to be content to stay in Cranberry Cove once she graduates. She's been commuting back and forth to Davenport University for her classes and once she has her degree in business, what kind of a job is she going to find here?"

Monica wasn't sure what to say. "If she's commuting now, what's going to stop her from continuing to commute once she has a job? Lots of people do it."

"It's not just that." Jeff chipped away at the label on the beer bottle with his thumbnail, shredding it into long, thin strips of paper. "She hasn't had a chance to see much of the world yet. Would it be fair of me to try to keep her here in Cranberry Cove just because that's what I want?"

"Lots of people are born here, grow up here and then stay here. And are perfectly happy."

"But Lauren's smart. She deserves a chance at a career, at experiences, at . . . I don't know . . . life."

"What about you?" Monica leaned forward in her chair. "Are you going to be content in Cranberry Cove forever? Here on Sassamanash Farm?"

"Me?" Jeff pointed at himself. "I've seen enough of the world to know it can be a horrible place. Even with Preston's murder, and Sam Culbert's before that, Cranberry Cove is freaking idyllic compared to the things I've seen."

Chapter 12

That afternoon was the end of the Winter Walk. Shops were staying open until seven o'clock—even those that never opened on Sundays, like Bart's Butcher Shop and the hardware store. The Cranberry Cove Diner had expanded its hours, too—it normally only served lunch on Sundays but had put up a crudely lettered sign indicating that it would be open for dinner as well. Monica found that amusing, since the diner was hardly known for throwing its doors open to tourists, and they would be the ones strolling Beach Hollow Road tonight.

Tempest was alone in the store when Monica passed Twilight, and on impulse she pushed open the door and went in. The strain of recent events was showing on Tempest's face—the lines between her nose and mouth and across her forehead were deepening and there were bluish shadows under her eyes.

Monica put her baskets down by the door and went up to the counter.

"Something smells delicious," Tempest said, attempting a quick smile.

Monica jerked her head in the direction of the baskets. "Cranberry banana bread with streusel topping, scones and cranberry coffee cake."

"It smells heavenly, although I have to confess I've lost my appetite lately."

"Are the police still bothering you?"

"Detective Stevens has been around a number of times asking the same questions but in different ways. I suspect she's trying to trip me up in a lie or something. Like they do on those police shows on television." Tempest fiddled with the corded silk ties that hung from her patchwork jacket. "I don't have an alibi and can't prove I didn't kill Preston."

She picked a piece of paper up off the counter and began pleating it as if she was doing Origami. "And of course they found my prints on the weapon since I'd handled the athame when I put it in the case—I had to go down to the police station and have my fingerprints taken." Tempest shivered. "Never in my life did I think . . ." She shook her head. "Afterward I scrubbed and scrubbed to get the ink off—the black blobs were like . . . like some sort of stigmata. Unfortunately that rules out the possibility that the killer purchased the athame somewhere else and brought it to Cranberry Cove."

"So it had to be someone local?"

"Tourists were coming into the shop even before the Walk officially started. And I didn't notice whether or not the athame was missing. I was being run off my feet as it was. Unfortunately I can't afford to hire any help. If I need to leave the shop for any reason I lock the door and hang a *closed* sign out front." Tempest tossed the piece of paper she'd been playing with back onto the counter, where it began to unfold like a butterfly emerging from its chrysalis. "Of course my fingerprints being on the weapon only adds to the case against me."

"But that doesn't mean anything. You'd have had to handle it at some point—getting it out of the box, placing it on the counter . . ."

"I probably touched it half a dozen times in all innocence, but try to convince Stevens of that. They're making a big deal out of Preston's petition to stop my Imbolc ceremony, thinking that gave me a motive for murder."

Monica shook her head. "I can't believe that."

Tempest's shoulders stiffened. "There are a lot of narrow-minded people here who don't like me, or at least don't like what they think I stand for. I wouldn't put it past them to be making more of that petition than there was. I had nothing against Preston before that, and even then . . . certainly it infuriated me, but I would hardly kill a man over something like that."

Tempest had her hand in her pocket and was fiddling with some object. She pulled it out and Monica saw that it was a large, ornate cut crystal button in the shape of a flower ringed by dark red stones. Tempest put it on the counter.

"What's that?"

"That?" Tempest pointed at the button. "I found it on the floor when I was cleaning up. It got stuck in the vacuum cleaner and I had the devil of a time getting it out. I only saved it in case someone came looking for it. It's not your ordinary black or tortoise plastic button. I don't imagine it would be easy to replace."

Monica glanced at it again. "It's pretty."

"Yes. It could almost be a piece of jewelry." Tempest held the button up to her ear like an earring.

"Please don't worry too much. I'm sure the police will find the real killer." Monica put a hand on Tempest's arm.

Tempest's shoulders sagged. "I suppose you're right. It's the waiting that's so horrible. It's all I think about . . . and dream about."

After offering a few more comforting words, Monica said good-bye to Tempest, left Twilight and continued down Beach Hollow Road. She glanced in the window of Bijou across the street, where Jacy Belair was waiting on a young couple. Monica wondered if they were looking at engagement rings. The girl kept glancing at the boy and smiling at him. She passed Danielle's and stopped briefly to admire a sweater in the window. It looked hand knit—cream-colored wool in an intricate pattern that Monica had never seen before. She stared at it wistfully for a moment and almost went inside to ask the price when common sense took over. If the garment was in Danielle's window, then she certainly couldn't afford it.

She wondered briefly if she could learn to knit, but then thought better of it. When would she find the time? She spent all her spare hours baking, and in the evenings she generally fell asleep in front of the television before the program was even half over.

Monica was grateful when she reached her makeshift farm booth and could put her baskets down. Before she'd even finished setting out all her freshly baked goods, a couple stopped and bought a dozen cranberry muffins and a container of salsa. They'd driven over to Cranberry Cove from Kalamazoo just for the Winter Walk.

Monica packed their purchase in the new Sassamanash Farm bags she'd ordered and stuffed the cash into her pocket. She was rearranging her stock when she heard a noise coming from down the street. It sounded like chanting. Heads were turning in the direction of the voices.

Monica stepped out of her booth and strained to see what was going on. It sounded like some sort of protest, but what was there to protest about the Cranberry Cove Winter Walk?

With a last backward glance at her stall, Monica made her way past Danielle's, through the people who had gathered there on the sidewalk, toward Twilight. She managed to get to the front of the crowd where she stopped abruptly. Her hand flew to her mouth in dismay. The sidewalk in front of Tempest's store was filled with people shouldering placards that read *Murderer*, *Witch* and *Black Magic*. They marched in a loop in front of Twilight shouting "Arrest the murderer now!"

Monica was horrified. Tempest must be frightened half to death. She scanned the group of protesters. She thought she recognized the stock boy from the hardware store and a couple of ladies who occasionally stopped by the farm store. What had gotten into them?

Monica felt a tap on her shoulder and spun around. It was Greg.

"News must have gotten out about the murder weapon being from Tempest's shop."

"So many people are already distrustful of Tempest. It's ridiculous—she's perfectly harmless and actually quite nice. And normal," Monica added almost as an afterthought. She looked back at the group parading in front of Tempest's shop door. She caught a glimpse of Tempest's horrified face through the window and felt her anger rise. "I wish there was something we could do."

"I think it's being taken care of," Greg said, pointing to two uniformed patrolmen hustling down the sidewalk.

"Break it up, folks. Break it up," they could hear the officers saying to the protesters.

Slowly the group dispersed, their placards hanging down as if they'd been defeated. Some shouted "murderer!" over their shoulder one last time as they were ushered away. Monica found herself trembling with fury.

She gave a glance back toward her stand. "I'd better see if Tempest is okay."

"Go on," Greg said, taking her hand and squeezing it. "I've got someone minding the shop if you want me to stand guard over your booth."

"Thanks. I'd appreciate that."

Monica made her way through the milling crowd to Twilight, where she found Tempest as upset as she had expected.

"I feel like I've fallen down a rabbit hole—it's the sixteen hundreds again in Salem, Massachusetts and I'm on trial for witchcraft," Tempest said, pacing back and forth.

She stood erect with her shoulders braced, but Monica could hear the quaver in her voice and see her hands trembling.

"The police are bound to find the real culprit soon."

"I hope so." Tempest looked around the shop. "I've started thinking that perhaps I should close up. Move somewhere else."

"No!" Monica put out a hand as if to stop Tempest. "I've

had a couple of ideas. "I'm going to be following up on them soon."

"Please hurry," Tempest said. "I don't know how much longer I can take this."

Nancy was in the kitchen when Monica got back to her cottage. Ambrosial scents filled the air, and she inhaled deeply as she opened the back door, her mouth watering immediately. Chicken was sautéing in a pan on the stove, and Nancy was chopping tarragon leaves, releasing their fresh anise-like aroma into the air.

Nancy looked up, her knife poised in the air. "What's wrong? You look dreadful."

Monica told her about the protest outside of Tempest's shop.

Nancy shook her head and went back to chopping. "Small towns, small minds, you know."

Monica felt herself bristle. "That's not entirely true. Most of the people I've met here in Cranberry Cove have been interesting and open-minded."

Nancy raised an eyebrow but didn't say anything.

Monica barely registered the delicious dinner Nancy had made. Her mind was so occupied with trying to fit together the various puzzle pieces of Preston's murder—Tempest's athame as the murder weapon, the killer striking right before the start of the Winter Walk, the various people who had turned out to have grudges against Preston. She wondered about the timing of the attack. How had the killer known that Preston would be alone in the sled and that the young man taking care of the horse would wander off? He had to have done, or else he would have seen the murder. Had the killer gotten lucky or were they so diabolical that they had planned the whole thing out in cold blood?

After dinner, Monica and her mother retreated to the living room, where Monica stretched out on the sofa, snuggled under a knitted mohair throw. Her mother got comfortable in the armchair, her feet propped on the matching ottoman. She, too, had an afghan wrapped around her. The wind had picked up and now it was rattling the loose panes in the windows and knocking at the door.

They turned on the television and watched a game show followed by a police show where the crime was handily wrapped up in an hour—even less if you considered the time taken up by the commercials. Monica watched the closing credits and stifled a yawn. Wouldn't it be nice if the solution to Preston's murder was as tidy?

By the time Monica and her mother started up the stairs to bed, the temperature in the cottage had dropped considerably. Monica had a moment of panic thinking that the furnace might have gone out, but then she heard the ancient piece of equipment rumble on and felt a blast of warm air issuing from the vents.

It had been quite the day. First, brunch with Greg—who she was now *dating*, she reminded herself. She gave a spontaneous smile and saw her mother look at her strangely. And then her talk with Jeff, and finally the incident in front of Tempest's shop. She felt tired down to her bones and couldn't wait to slide beneath the covers, spend a few moments with the book she was reading and then turn out the light as sleep blissfully descended.

But in the end she couldn't fall asleep. Monica crawled out of bed, perched on the bench under the window, pushed aside the lace curtain and looked out. Sleep was as elusive as the thin wisps of clouds passing over the moon in the dark night sky. She dropped the window curtain into place, climbed back into bed and burrowed under the covers, praying that oblivion would eventually descend.

Downtown Cranberry Cove was quiet the following day as Monica drove down Beach Hollow Road toward the village green and the town's city hall. The tourists had obviously pulled up stakes and headed back toward home. There was even a vacancy sign swinging outside the Cranberry Cove Inn—something they hadn't seen in days. It had been nice while it lasted, Monica thought. The next big bump in tourism would come during the tulip festival, when thousands of the bright flowers popped up all over Cranberry Cove.

The town hall was a serviceable brick building whose only imaginative feature was a large, ornate clock above the front door. The locals couldn't remember back far enough to when the clock had actually been functional.

An icy drizzle was falling—the temperatures had reached a few degrees above freezing for the first time in a long time—and Monica was grateful that she was able to get a parking space close by.

She locked the Focus and dashed to the front door of the town hall, her face stinging from the frozen drops of rain that were pelting her cheeks and bouncing off her jacket. Monica pushed open the door gratefully and stepped inside. The warmth of the lobby felt stifling after the frigid outdoor temperatures, and Monica hastily unzipped her jacket, shoved her gloves in her pocket and yanked off her knit hat.

She had no doubt that her hair was standing up around

her head in a halo of frizz thanks to the static electricity created by her wool cap, but she didn't care. She was bound and determined to talk to Edith's friend Rieka to learn more about the owner of the Pepper Pot and his failed quest for a permit to open his restaurant.

She couldn't believe Preston Crowley hadn't had a hand in delaying the permit. He must have been furious with Roger Tripp for stealing from him. Monica had only met Preston a couple of times, but she got the impression that he didn't allow anyone to make a fool of him. At least not gladly.

The lobby floor was wet and slippery and Monica almost fell several times, despite the rubber soles of her boots. She was grateful when she reached the receptionist. Her modern computer appeared incongruous sitting on her old-fashioned wooden desk—a manual typewriter and a stack of carbon paper would have looked much more at home. She gave Monica a distracted smile as she approached.

"Can I help you?" she asked with one eye on the papers she was going through.

"I'd like to speak to Rieka, please. I understand she works here?"

"Rieka?" The woman looked up from what she was doing.

The way she said it made Monica wonder if she'd gotten the name wrong—or the place. Edith had seemed lucid enough, but perhaps she was a bit . . . forgetful?

"Yes, Rieka. I believe she works here," Monica said with slightly less conviction, her voice rising toward the end of the sentence like she was asking a question.

"She does," the woman said with no elaboration as she continued shuffling through her papers.

"Can I see her, please?" Monica attempted to arrange her face into pleasant lines even though she was feeling far from pleasant toward the receptionist who was using her position to be a bully.

The receptionist sighed, picked up her telephone, gave Monica an irritated look and finally spoke briefly.

She listened with one hand over the mouthpiece and said finally, "She'll be right out." She glared at Monica, and returned to her paperwork once more.

Monica sidled away from the reception desk and went to look at a group of framed photographs on the wall. They were black-and-white pictures of Cranberry Cove from two centuries ago, complete with horse-drawn carriages and women in long dresses.

"Are you the person who's looking for me?"

Monica spun around at the sound of the woman's voice. The speaker was short and stocky with broad shoulders and a thick head of short gray hair. Monica recognized her from a spaghetti supper she'd gone to last September. Rieka had been in charge of making the oliebollen—a Dutch version of doughnuts that are fried and then rolled in powdered sugar.

"I'm Monica Albertson." Monica held out her hand.

"From out at Sassamanash Farm." It was a statement, not a question.

Once again Monica marveled at how quickly and how far news traveled in a small, close-knit community.

The woman looked Monica up and down. "Come back to my office. I'm sure you could use a cup of hot tea. You look frozen half to death."

Monica didn't argue. Her fingers were still like ice, despite the heat being pumped into the building.

She followed Rieka down the hall, the older woman's black, lace-up, rubber-soled shoes making no noise on the stained linoleum floor.

The term *office* was too grand to describe the space allotted to Rieka—it was little more than a large cubbyhole with a desk crammed into one end and a chair opposite at the other. The desk was covered in neat stacks of papers precisely aligned with each other.

Rieka retrieved a mug from her desk drawer and filled it from a thermos. She handed it to Monica.

"I hope you don't mind a spoonful or two of sugar. I've got the tea already made up the way I like it."

"That's fine." Monica put both hands around the warm mug and let the steam bathe her face.

Rieka took the battered wooden chair behind the desk and placed her folded hands on top of an ancient, stained green blotter. "So?"

Monica felt her mouth go dry. She hated asking questions and poking her nose where most people would argue it didn't belong. But she'd promised Tempest, so she'd have to buck up and just do it.

"I talked to your friend Edith—"

"Edith from down the hall?" Rieka jerked her head to the left.

"Yes. She told me you'd be the one to ask about restaurant permits."

"Opening a restaurant, are you?" Rieka opened a drawer and pulled out a form.

"No, no," Monica hastened to correct her.

Rieka looked puzzled, her rather doughy face reflecting her confusion. "Then what do you want a permit for?"

"I don't," Monica hastened to assure her. "I want to ask about someone else who applied for a permit."

"Why would you want to do that?" Rieka knitted her rather thick gray brows together.

Things were not going the way Monica had hoped. She wet her lips. What could she say? That she was curious? Looking at Rieka's stern expression, Monica didn't think that would fly—not for a minute. Finally she decided that her best course of action was to pretend that she was letting Rieka in on some secret investigation. Appeal to her love of gossip and desire to be in the center of what was going on. Monica was pretty sure that those two things were on the universal hierarchy of needs. In her experience humans lived for gossip and yearned to be in the thick of things.

"It's for a . . . an investigation."

Monica could hear Rieka's indrawn breath. Rieka leaned forward farther in her seat and lowered her voice.

"Are you a private investigator?"

Monica squirmed in her seat. "Sort of." Her hand almost flew to her face to see if her nose had grown like Pinocchio's.

"So what is it you want to know?"

"It's about the permit for the new restaurant in town— the Pepper Pot. Do you remember it?"

"Sure I do. We're all wondering if it's going to be the sort of place we can afford." She gave a slightly bitter laugh. "Not like the Cranberry Cove Inn. Only rich tourists can afford those prices."

"Do you know the owner of the Pepper Pot?"

"Roger Tripp? I only know him by way of him coming

in here all the time to check on the permit he applied for. Seemed like a nice young man—at least till the last time."

"The last time?"

Rieka leaned even farther forward in her seat and put a finger to her lips as if cautioning Monica not to tell. "He came in and asked if the permit was ready—he wanted to open the restaurant at the beginning of the Winter Walk. He'd already been taking reservations for a month, and from the sound of things, none of the tables were going to go empty."

"Did something happen to the permit? I noticed that he didn't open in the end." Monica felt her stomach tightening. She might be on to something at last.

Rieka leaned back in her chair, and it gave a loud groan. She crossed her arms over her broad chest. "I'm not supposed to tell anyone." She began picking at a spot on her gray wool sweater.

Monica felt as if frustration was grabbing her by the throat and shaking her. She had to convince Rieka to talk.

The printer behind Rieka's desk suddenly sprang to life and after much clicking and groaning, spat out a piece of paper.

Monica heard a noise and glanced at the door to see a young man lingering there.

"Sorry to interrupt. I've sent something to your printer. The one in the workroom needs toner." He rolled his eyes.

"I heard you asking about the permit for the Pepper Pot restaurant," he said to Monica as he leaned across Rieka's desk and retrieved his document. "Roger Tripp did apply for one more than a month ago. The last step was the on-site visit by the health inspector, but someone," he rolled his eyes again, "cancelled the appointment."

Monica looked from him to Rieka. Rieka was stony faced.

The young man seemed oblivious to Rieka's censure as he continued. "I think we all know who's responsible for that."

"Who?" Monica said without thinking.

"Let me put it this way," the young man said, "our mayor doesn't like competition."

"Do you mean Preston Crowley deliberately—"

The young man put a hand over his mouth. "Did I say that?" He gave a high-pitched laugh. "I'm not naming names, but I'm sure you know what I mean."

Before Monica could say another word, he was gone.

Rieka's face had gone even more sour. "Young people!" She blew out a puff of air and her short bangs fluttered as if in a breeze. "They don't understand the word *confidential*. They're always gossiping and putting stuff on the computer that they shouldn't and then acting surprised when everyone knows their business."

Monica thought it prudent to stay quiet and let Rieka vent. Finally Rieka wound to a halt and slumped in her chair, as if the effort had leached the air out of her.

Monica decided it was best not to ask for confirmation that Crowley had been the one to engineer the delay of the permit—that young man had certainly made it clear enough that that was the case. Monica had another question to ask and she sat in silence for a moment, debating how best to phrase it to keep from alarming Rieka.

"I hope the Pepper Pot will open eventually. It looks like a nice place. I saw the menu in the window—"

Rieka snorted. "Yes, for once an ordinary person can not only pronounce everything on the menu, but recognize what it is as well. The husband and I made a trip to Chicago for our anniversary and went out to dinner at one of them fancy French places. Didn't understand a word on the menu. Turns out the dish I'd ordered was just a plain old roast chicken, so why couldn't they just say so?"

"I guess since Roger Tripp is from Cranberry Cove, he understands what we like."

Monica felt a little funny using the word *we* since she knew perfectly well that she would have to live in the town for a couple more decades before being considered anything close to a local.

"There's the thing," Rieka said as she leaned back, causing her old-fashioned wooden swivel chair to groan audibly again. "Roger Tripp isn't from Cranberry Cove. At least not originally. By my account he's only been here a few years."

"I imagine he must still live here somewhere if he's going to be running his restaurant," Monica said, trying to maintain an innocent look on her face.

"I should guess so."

"Maybe he's rooming somewhere like Primrose Cottage." Monica twirled a piece of hair around her finger. Primrose Cottage was only open part of the year so that was unlikely, but she wanted to throw something out to see if Rieka would take the bait.

"I don't think so. I heard he bought a place for himself."

"In that new development going up outside of town? I heard it's quite pricey. He must be expecting the restaurant to do well."

Rieka shook her head. "No, not there. An older place." Rieka laughed. "He said he didn't know why he bothered to buy at all since he was practically sleeping at the restaurant."

Monica's ears perked up. Maybe Roger Tripp would be at the Pepper Pot right now. It would be easy enough to check. If she played her cards right, he might even invite her in for a tour.

And then she could ask him some questions. In all innocence, of course.

Chapter 13

By the time Monica left the Cranberry Cove town hall, the icy drizzle that had been falling earlier had turned to snow. It was a slippery combination—ice hidden under a thin blanket of powder. She nearly fell as she made her way to the car, and breathed a sigh of relief when she was safely inside.

There were only a handful of parking places along Beach Hollow Road. Monica pulled into a space in front of the hardware store and got out. She paused briefly to pull her hat from her jacket pocket and put it on.

The snow was coming down more heavily now as Monica carefully made her way down the sidewalk past the butcher shop. She was approaching Book 'Em when she hit a patch of ice and started to slip. She threw her arms out in an attempt to regain her balance, and her purse went flying.

"Steady there." She felt a hand on her arm, grabbing her just before she went down.

She turned around to see it was Bart from the butcher shop. He had a parka on over his white apron. He made sure Monica was steady on her feet and then went to retrieve her handbag.

"You ought to get yourself a pair of these." Bart lifted up his foot so Monica could see the bottom of his boot. It was covered in coils of metal that reminded Monica of the chains cars used to use on their tires in the winter.

"The hardware store carries them." Bart jerked his head toward the shop front Monica had just passed. "The metal coils grip the ice and keep you from falling. You can slip them on over your boots or even an ordinary pair of shoes."

"Very clever. I'll have to get myself some."

"I'll walk with you. I'm headed toward the diner for something to eat."

"A late breakfast or an early lunch?" Monica asked. It was ten o'clock in the morning.

"It's lunchtime for me," Bart said. "My day starts long before I hang up the open sign at nine o'clock. The daily shipment of meat needs to be prepared, but first I have to sterilize the butcher block and surrounding areas. I don't want any bacteria getting into the fresh meat and making my customers sick.

"When the meat comes in it doesn't look anything like the finished product you see in my display case or in the grocery store. I have to carve it up and make it look attractive first. Then I separate out the prime pieces from the rest and arrange everything on trays. Then it's the little touches I know my customers appreciate—like the paper frills on the ends of the crown roast of pork, and the bits of curly parsley I use to brighten things up."

"I didn't realize there was so much to it," Monica said when they stopped in front of the diner.

Bart chuckled. "I'm at the shop by six o'clock every morning. Of course I'm falling asleep in my chair in front of the television by nine o'clock, much to the dismay of my missus." He laughed again. "By ten o'clock in the morning, I'm more than ready for some lunch."

"I can understand why," Monica said.

Bart pulled open the door to the diner, releasing a cloud of air fragrant with the smell of frying bacon and browning potatoes.

Monica said good-bye and continued down the street, even more carefully this time, toward the Pepper Pot.

The menu was still taped to the window of the restaurant, although the edges were curling a bit now, and the writing had faded slightly. Monica put her hands around her eyes and peered through the glass.

A light was on somewhere in the back of the restaurant, which was a good sign. All the tables were draped in white tablecloths and set with plates, silverware and unlit candles.

Monica tried the door and was surprised when it opened. She stepped inside and quietly shut the door behind her.

"Anyone here?" she called. "Your front door is open."

She heard footsteps coming from the direction of the light she'd noticed, and a man appeared around the corner. He had a stocky build with powerful-looking shoulders and a shock of blond hair. He was wearing jeans and a fleece pullover. It was cold inside the restaurant—the heat must have been turned down or even off.

"Can I help you?" he asked, running a hand through his hair and sweeping his bangs off his forehead.

"Are you Roger Tripp? The owner?"

"One and the same." He smiled at Monica.

He wasn't handsome but he had a pleasant, open face, which surprised Monica. Based on the stories she'd heard about him, she had expected someone more sinister.

"What can I do for you?" He gestured around the empty restaurant. "As you can see, we're closed."

"I didn't mean to bother you, but the door was open." Monica pointed to the entrance.

"I usually come in the back way, but this time I didn't, and I guess I forgot to lock the door behind me. Fortunately most of the citizens of Cranberry Cove are law-abiding."

"Except for one," Monica said.

Tripp tilted his head.

"Someone murdered Preston Crowley."

Tripp looked taken aback. "True," he conceded finally with a sharp exhale.

"When do you plan to open the restaurant? Everyone expected a grand opening for the Winter Walk."

"So did I," Tripp said. "But there was a mix-up about the permit." His smile was bitter. "It's all been taken care of, and the health inspector is making his final round on Thursday."

"Rumor has it that Preston Crowley was behind the delayed permit."

Tripp's eyes narrowed. "The rumors are correct. Preston

never admitted it, but I know he did it." A dusky flush crept up Tripp's neck to his face. "It's not enough that he's gone around town telling tales about me that aren't true and ruining my reputation—he had to destroy my business as well."

Monica noticed that Tripp's hands were clenched into fists and there was a steely glint in his eyes. His friendly, open face had become so cold and calculating that without thinking, she took a step backward.

"I'm sorry," Monica said, at a loss for words.

Suddenly Tripp's shoulders sagged, and the expression on his face eased so that he once again looked like the very approachable man she'd thought him to be.

But it was too late. Monica had seen the other side of Roger Tripp, and she could now easily picture him as a murderer.

As Monica drove back to the farm she thought about her encounter with Roger Tripp. He certainly had a motive for killing Crowley. He must have been furious when Crowley unjustly accused him of stealing . . . and then the trouble with the permit coming on top of that. That would stir up murderous feelings in almost anybody. The question, though, was had Tripp done anything about it?

Was he even around during the Winter Walk? Monica wondered if there was someone who could put him at the scene—but how would she find out?

Monica pulled into the parking lot of the Sassamanash Farm store, pleased to see that a number of the spaces were already taken and three people were waiting in line with baskets full of baked goods when she entered the shop.

Nora ran a hand through her curly dark hair as she punched some numbers into the register. Monica cleared her throat and she looked up and smiled.

"Are you managing okay?" Monica slipped behind the counter and held out her hand for the cranberry-printed towels the next woman in line was buying.

"No problem." Nora pushed her glasses up her nose with her index finger. "There's been a steady stream, but nothing I can't handle."

"There are a few things I need to do . . . if you're sure you can manage?"

"You go ahead. I'll be fine."

Monica finished the transaction, left the store and headed back to her cottage. Nancy was dressed when she got there and looked as if she was going out. She was wearing the same gray wool slacks but with a white cashmere pullover this time, and a silk scarf tied just so around her neck.

"Are you going out?" Monica dropped her purse on the floor by the table and slung her jacket over the back of a kitchen chair.

"I was hoping you'd join me for lunch." Nancy tucked a piece of hair behind her ear. "My treat."

Monica felt her stomach growl and glanced at the clock, surprised to see that it really was already lunchtime.

"The diner makes an excellent chili—"

Nancy wrinkled her nose. "I thought we'd go to the Cranberry Cove Inn and have a nice lunch. Just the two of us."

"Sure."

"Do you want to freshen up?" Nancy asked, looking Monica up and down.

Monica sighed and dutifully headed up the stairs. She changed into a pair of tweed slacks and a green sweater that picked up the color of one of the threads in the pants.

Mittens sat on the bed, her tail swishing back and forth, watching as Monica changed.

Monica scratched the kitten under her chin and Mittens meowed and immediately rolled over onto her back for a tummy rub. Monica obliged for a couple of minutes.

"Now I've got to get ready," she said to Mittens as she dashed into the bathroom.

She splashed some water on her face, powdered her nose and added a touch of lip gloss. *That ought to be good enough for the Cranberry Cove Inn*, she thought.

Nancy was wearing her coat and stood with her leather gloves in her hand as Monica came down the stairs.

"Let's take my car," Nancy said. "There's more room."

Monica had no objection to saving the gas and happily got into Nancy's silver Sonata.

Nancy drove smoothly and competently toward town. Monica enjoyed being a passenger for a change so she could enjoy the scenery. The snow had stopped and the sun was now peeking out from behind a cloud. *If you don't like the weather, wait five minutes*, Monica thought. It was an old Michigan expression that had proven true on numerous occasions.

A handful of cars were in the parking lot next to the Cranberry Cove Inn.

"It doesn't look as if we'll have trouble getting a table," Nancy said as she locked the car doors with a beep.

The roaring fire in the lobby looked exceptionally inviting, but today no one was sitting in front of it when they entered. The receptionist was leaning her elbows on the counter, engrossed in a word search puzzle, and a gaggle of bellhops stood off to one side chatting with each other.

The maître d' glided forward to greet them at the entrance to the dining room.

"Right this way, ladies, please." He grabbed two leather-bound menus from the stack and led them toward a table for two in the corner.

"We'd rather sit by the window, if you don't mind," Nancy said, indicating a vacant table for four that commanded a spectacular view of Lake Michigan.

"Certainly." The maître d' led them to the table Nancy had requested and pulled out a chair. He handed them their menus with a flourish. "The waitress will be right with you to take your order."

They scanned their menus, and Nancy snapped hers shut decisively. Just then the waitress appeared.

"Can I get you ladies something to drink?" she asked with her pencil poised above her pad.

"I'll have a glass of the La Cruz Chardonnay, please."

The waitress turned to Monica.

"A diet cola for me, please."

The waitress glanced at Nancy's closed menu. "Do you ladies know what you want?"

"Yes." Nancy handed back the menu. "I'll have the salad of baby greens with walnuts and raspberry vinaigrette, and a slice of the quiche Lorraine."

"And you?" The waitress turned to Monica.

"I'll have the croque monsieur, please."

The waitress laughed as she made a note on her pad. "Pretty fancy name for a grilled ham and cheese, don't you think?"

As the waitress walked back toward the kitchen, Monica thought about what Rieka had said—how the Pepper Pot was going to serve food they could both pronounce and recognize. She had a feeling the restaurant was going to do well when it opened.

"So," Nancy said when their drinks arrived and she'd taken a sip of her wine, "what are your plans? You haven't said."

"Plans?"

"Yes. For the future. Are you going to stay here in Cranberry Cove?"

Monica was taken aback. She hadn't thought much beyond the next year or two and helping Jeff get Sassamanash Farm out of the red.

"I don't know," Monica answered as an idea crossed her mind—something that had never occurred to her before. Perhaps she could open a small café in downtown Cranberry Cove—like the one she'd had in Chicago—good coffee and baked goods. Nothing fancy. And if people liked her coffee cakes and muffins, she could direct them to the store at Sassamanash Farm so they could take some home.

"Monica!" Nancy said sharply.

Monica jumped. "What?"

"You've been a million miles away. I was asking you about the gentleman who took you to brunch yesterday."

"Greg?"

"Is that his name? You didn't say." Nancy leaned back

as the waitress put her salad and quiche in front of her. "Are you dating?"

Monica couldn't control the smile that came to her lips. "Yes. Yes, we are."

"Good," Nancy said, spearing a lettuce leaf with her fork. "It's about time."

"That's what Gina said."

Nancy stiffened at the sound of Gina's name. "Don't make the same mistake I did."

Monica braced herself for another tirade about Gina. She'd been listening to them for years.

"Take Greg the way he is. Don't try to change him."

Nancy put down her fork and looked at Monica. Monica was surprised to see there were tears in her eyes.

"I tried to change your father, and that wasn't right. When he began making good money, I fussed at him to buy better clothes, move us to a bigger house, drive a more expensive car. That wasn't John. He loved his job—the money was merely a pleasant by-product."

Monica stared at her mother. This was the first she was hearing about this. Her mother rarely ever admitted to making a mistake.

"Then Gina came along. She thought he was fine the way he was. She didn't turn her nose up at some of the things he enjoyed as not being sophisticated enough. It didn't take much to lure him away." Nancy took a sip of wine. "Not that I approve of stealing another woman's husband." She shook her finger at Monica. "And John certainly had some responsibility in the whole thing. Gina wasn't . . . the first." Nancy took a large gulp of wine.

"What?"

"There were other women, and there had been for quite some time."

Monica's mind was whirling, trying to adjust to these new facts about her father. "Then maybe it wasn't you who drove him away after all."

"You're probably right." Nancy put down her fork and dabbed at her lips with her napkin. "But I don't think I made it pleasant enough for him to want to stay."

Chapter 14

It was almost two o'clock by the time Monica and Nancy finished lunch and left the Cranberry Cove Inn. Monica was still reeling from what her mother had confided to her. What had prompted her to tell Monica those things now?

Her mother backed the Sonata out of the parking space and turned onto Beach Hollow Road. They passed Book 'Em, and Monica couldn't help but think of Greg. She certainly didn't want to change him. She liked him exactly the way he was.

A delivery truck was parked outside Danielle's boutique, and there wasn't enough room to get around it. Nancy drummed her fingers on the steering wheel as they waited.

She gestured toward Danielle's. "I might have to pop in there for some more clothes if that Detective Stevens doesn't let me leave town soon."

"I'm sure the police must be nearing a solution. It's been

several days." Monica hoped they had found some clues that pointed to the real culprit and that they weren't still wasting their time trying to pin the murder on Tempest.

The truck still hadn't moved but as Nancy's hand hovered over the horn, the red taillights went out, and the truck began to move forward.

Nancy glanced in her rearview mirror. "Isn't that Gina behind us?"

Monica turned around and looked out the back window. "It looks like her car."

"I don't imagine there are too many Mercedes in Cranberry Cove."

They came to the four-way stop at the intersection of Beach Hollow and Elm. Nancy braked and then proceeded through the intersection.

The squealing of brakes took Monica by surprise as her mother slammed her foot down hard on the pedal. The car coming the other way through the intersection braked as well but it wasn't enough to keep the two cars from bumping fenders. Monica and Nancy sat in silence for a moment. Monica was sure the astonished beating of her heart was audible in the suddenly quiet car.

"What on earth—" Nancy looked over at Monica. "Are you okay?"

"Yes. A little shaken maybe."

"Me too."

Monica could see her mother's hands trembling on the steering wheel.

The driver of the car that had tapped them was getting out of his vehicle—an SUV desperately in need of a wash. He was overweight and balding, and his fleshy face was bright red. He bent down to look at the damage to his car, and when he straightened up, Monica could tell he was cursing. He shook his fist at the Sonata, and Monica sank down in her seat.

"I'd better get out and talk to him," Nancy said. She opened her purse, took out her wallet and retrieved her driver's license. "If you open the glove compartment, you'll find my registration and insurance card."

"Maybe we'd better wait for the police," Monica said as she looked through the glove box where Nancy had stored an extra pair of gloves, a packet of tissues and a small bottle of hand sanitizer.

"I'm sure we can sort this out. There can't be much damage and there's no doubt that he hit me."

Monica sighed and opened her car door. She wasn't letting Nancy go out there alone.

The other driver immediately approached them, his fist raised, his face still mottled red. He began yelling as he got closer.

"What kind of driver are you?"

Nancy bristled. "Excuse me? I could say the same about you. You hit me, after all."

"I did not hit you." The man shook his fist at Nancy.

She held her ground. "You most certainly did!"

By now Monica had taken her phone out and called the police. She could already hear the siren in the distance—they obviously hadn't been too far away.

The driver took another step toward Nancy, and grabbed her by the lapels of her jacket. Nancy's face went white as she put up her hands to try to defend herself.

Gina, who was still behind them in her Mercedes, jumped out of her car and approached the pair.

"You let go of her this instant!"

Startled, the fellow released his grip and took a step backward. Gina got between him and Nancy.

"You hit her, do you understand me? You hit my friend." Gina emphasized each word with a poke of her index finger to the man's chest.

The man made a noise like a growl and went to grab Gina. But before he could, Nancy sprang into action, putting her hands against the man's chest and giving him a sound shove.

By now a patrol car had pulled up. The officer jumped out of his vehicle and quickly approached the trio.

"Steady on," he said, pushing his hat back to reveal a red crease across his forehead. He pulled a pad and pencil from his back pocket. "Want to tell me what happened?"

They all began talking at once, and he held up a hand for them to stop. He turned toward Monica who was standing slightly apart.

"Can you tell me what happened?"

"Yes. We approached the four-way stop and my mother," she indicated Nancy, "stopped the car. Since we were the only car stopped at the intersection, we proceeded to go through. We could see another car—the SUV—was coming toward the stop on the other street, but knowing it was a four-way stop, we obviously had the right of way. But he sailed on through without stopping and hit us."

The policemen took down all their pertinent information and then slowly walked around both cars, squatting down to look at the damage. "Hardly more than a scratch," he said, pulling his hat back down. "And judging by the skid marks you both tried to stop."

He turned to the driver of the other car. "I'm afraid

I'm going to have to issue you a summons. License and registration, please?" He held out his hand.

"Can we go now, officer?" Nancy interrupted.

"In a minute. I'll need to see your papers, too."

The officer took the documents from both drivers and headed back to the patrol car while Nancy and the other driver stood fuming at each other.

Finally the officer returned, handed Nancy's license and registration back to her and said they could go.

Nancy turned to leave but stopped briefly to put her arm around Gina.

"Thanks for sticking up for me. That means a lot."

If Monica didn't know better, she would have sworn there were tears in Nancy's eyes.

Gina dashed a hand at her own eyes. "No problem. I owe you one."

Jeff's pickup was in the driveway when Monica and her mother pulled in. Nancy had met Jeff before, but they hadn't seen each other recently. Nancy could be very critical—Monica hoped they would get along.

"Hope you don't mind. I let myself in," Jeff said as Monica pushed open the kitchen door.

Mittens immediately sprang out of nowhere and began to wind in and out between Monica's legs. Monica bent down and scratched her chin. Mittens arched her back and swished her tail in the air.

"Is something wrong?" Monica asked as she hung her jacket on the coatrack.

"No. Everything's fine."

Nancy tapped Monica on the shoulder. "If you don't mind, dear, I'm going to go upstairs and lie down for a bit. That whole event this afternoon has worn me out, I'm afraid."

"What happened?" Jeff asked as he settled into one of the kitchen chairs, his long legs stretched out under the table.

Monica told him about the car accident and how Gina had come to Nancy's defense.

"My mother's a real spitfire," he said, grabbing a soft drink out of the refrigerator. "I'd have liked to have seen that."

Monica sat down at the table opposite Jeff. "I'm sure the other driver is still wondering what hit him—no pun intended. Gina really gave him what for."

Jeff took a long pull on his pop then set the can down on the table and reached into his back pocket.

"I went by the Bijou today and bought that necklace I'd noticed in the window." He placed a midnight blue velvet box in front of him and lifted the lid. Nestled in a bed of white satin was a small gold heart on a delicate chain. "Do you think Lauren will like it?"

Monica smiled. "It's beautiful. I'm sure she'll love it."

"I just hope I'm doing the right thing." Jeff sighed. "I don't want her to feel . . . obligated."

"Lauren seems like a smart girl. I imagine she knows her own mind, and if she decides that life with you in Cranberry Cove is what she wants, I'm sure she won't regret it."

"I hope not." Jeff ran a hand over his face. "I'd like to ask her to marry me and settle it once and for all, but that wouldn't be fair to her. I don't want to rush her into something without giving her time to think. She needs to finish her classes and get through graduation first."

"A lot of girls graduate with engagement rings on their fingers."

Jeff screwed up his face. "I'm planning on building us a house. Nothing too grand or anything, but something we can add on to as time goes by and we need more space."

Monica thought she noticed a blush coloring his face, and she fought the urge to smile.

"There's a spot that'd be perfect—on a small rise with a view of the cranberry bogs. I'd build one of those big wraparound porches," Jeff gestured with his hands, "where we could sit on summer nights and watch the sun go down."

"It sounds lovely."

"Anyway, you think this necklace will do?"

"Certainly."

Jeff let out a whistle. "Boy, that Jacy Belair sure made a big play for me while I was in the shop. She was wearing a low-cut top, and she kept leaning over so that . . . well, you know what I mean."

Jeff's face colored again. He'd been to hell and back fighting in Afghanistan but the sight of a woman's cleavage could still make him blush. Monica found it terribly touching. She could still remember her excitement when she learned he'd been born—excitement she had tried to hide from her mother, who didn't want to know anything about it. An image of Jeff as a young boy flashed across her mind—with dirt on his face and a cowlick that refused to be tamed. And then it seemed as if all of a sudden he was an endearing but awkward teenage boy—tall with long skinny limbs he didn't seem to know what to do with.

And now Jeff was a young man. The time had gone

by so quickly, like one of those flip-books where you fan the pages and the image changes in front of your eyes.

"Has there been any more news about Crowley's murder?" Jeff put the can of pop to his lips and tilted it back.

Monica shook her head. "I have no idea what leads the police are following, but I'm following one of my own."

Jeff sputtered and coughed. "You?"

"Yes," Monica said a little defensively.

"Listen sis, last time you stuck your nose into a murder investigation, you almost got yourself killed."

"I'm not sticking my nose into anything," Monica said even though she knew that wasn't true. "I've merely had a couple of ideas about the case."

"Which are?"

"You know that new restaurant that's slated to open in town—the Pepper Pot?"

"Sure. I plan to take Lauren there as soon as it opens."

"Apparently Mayor Crowley had a hand in delaying the permit that would have allowed it to open in time for the Winter Walk."

"Seriously?" Jeff crushed the pop can in his good hand. "He must have been trying to eliminate the competition."

"Exactly."

"I imagine the owner was furious."

"He certainly was, and on more than one account. Apparently he used to work for Crowley at the Cranberry Cove Inn. Crowley accused him of stealing and fired him."

"Who is this guy?"

"His name is Roger Tripp. I tracked him down this morning. He claims he hadn't stolen from Crowley, and it was just a rumor that Crowley started."

"I can't say I knew Crowley, but from what I've heard of him, that doesn't sound like something he'd stoop to." Jeff scowled. "Anyway, what's your plan, Dick Tracy?"

Monica laughed. "More like Miss Marple, I'm afraid. I'd like to know if anyone saw Tripp around during the Winter Walk—especially near where the horse and sleigh were waiting for Miss Winter Walk."

"Sounds like a good plan."

"The only problem is, I don't have a picture of Tripp." Monica laughed. "I suppose I could sneak up on him and snap one with my phone."

Jeff frowned. "If he is the murderer, that could put you in a lot of danger."

"I'd be discreet," Monica protested.

"Nope, you're not doing it," Jeff said. "I won't let you. If nothing else, I'll do it myself."

Monica marveled at how the tables had turned—now Jeff was looking out for her.

Suddenly Jeff snapped his fingers. "I think the paper ran an article about the Pepper Pot, and there was a picture of Tripp. It was black and white, but it ought to be enough for someone to recognize him."

"How long ago was that?"

Jeff shrugged. "Couple weeks ago maybe? I do remember it was on the front page."

"You don't happen to still have the paper, do you?"

"I doubt it. As a matter of fact, I think I picked it up at the diner and read it while I was eating breakfast." Jeff tilted his chair back on two legs, and Monica held her breath as she always did, fearing he would tip right over. "But don't you have a subscription?"

"Yes, but I've already recycled last week's papers."

Jeff let his chair fall back into place. "Mine wasn't picked up this week, although I don't know why. Why don't you check?"

Monica felt a tiny jolt of optimism. She grabbed her coat from the coatrack, slipped it on and went out the back door.

Both the garbage can and the recycling can were kept beside the cottage, screened from the street by a small wooden enclosure that was supposed to keep the animals out but didn't. Raccoons weren't put off by a simple latched door, and more than once Monica had gone out to find the cans overturned.

The wind had picked up, and Monica shivered as it sent cold, stealthy fingers creeping down her back. She quickly pulled her jacket closed and buttoned it securely.

Monica lifted the lid on the recycling can. Jeff was right—it hadn't been picked up as it normally would have been. Monica vaguely remembered receiving a postcard in the mail that they were going to an every other week system, but she'd paid little attention at the time—her can was usually only half full anyway by the time they came around to pick up. She had no idea that the change in schedule would turn out to be a blessing.

Monica had to dig through a layer of cans and plastic containers to unearth a stack of newspapers that she'd tied neatly with string before depositing them in the recycling receptacle. She pulled them out and headed back toward the cottage.

Monica shivered as she shed her jacket and let the warmth of the kitchen envelop her.

"Looks like you struck gold," Jeff said when he saw the papers.

"Let's just hope that's not the one issue I used to wrap up the potato peelings or onion skins," Monica said as she teased the knot out of the twine.

A faint smell of decay rose from the newspapers as Monica went through them, fingers mentally crossed that she would find the one she wanted.

"It was on the front page?" She turned to Jeff.

"Yes, I'm pretty sure. Bottom half of the paper if that helps."

"It does." Monica flipped the papers over and went through them again.

She almost missed the story—the headline was about the Winter Walk, but the reporter mentioned the expected opening of the Pepper Pot and along with a photograph of the front of the restaurant was a small picture of Roger Tripp. A small spot—moisture, grease?—made a blotch on the left side of Tripp's face, and Monica hoped that it wouldn't make him too hard to identify.

"Here." She put the paper in front of Jeff, and pointed at the article.

He stared at the photo. "He doesn't look familiar to me, but I spend most of my time out here on the farm." He pushed the paper back toward Monica. "Hopefully someone in town will be more of a help."

Chapter 15

Monica drove back into town. The sun was lower in the sky now, and she had to put her visor down to shield her eyes from the glare. She crested the hill that was between Cranberry Cove and the farm and was tempted to stop for a moment to enjoy the view. No one was behind her so she put on the brake and paused briefly. Lake Michigan was spread out below her. Its crystal water sparkled in the light in the far distance, but closer to shore, the water was frozen into sculptural ice forms, dripping from the jetty and clinging to the sides of the lighthouse.

She could see people moving about on the frozen lake although their parkas and scarves were mere dots of color from this distance. The newspaper had warned the public against trusting the ice, but there were always those who didn't listen. Just the other day a young man had had to be rescued when a patch of ice gave way, plunging him into the frigid waters. Monica shivered just thinking about it.

She took her foot off the brake and continued into town. The view never failed to amaze her, and she didn't think she'd ever become jaded enough to where it didn't cause her to catch her breath in wonder.

She pulled into Cranberry Cove proper and parked her Focus at the end of Beach Hollow Road, in front of the hardware store. The hardware store had been there through several generations and still had wooden floors that creaked when you walked over them. The new owners had brought in an old-fashioned popcorn machine so that the store always smelled of popped corn and melted butter.

Monica pushed open the door and went inside. There was a line at the checkout so she pretended to study a display while she waited. She had the picture of Roger Tripp that she'd cut from the newspaper tucked into her purse.

Finally the woman behind the counter had waited on all the customers in line. She began to flip through a seed catalog and looked up when Monica approached her. She gave a practiced smile but then raised an eyebrow quizzically when she realized Monica didn't have any purchases to be rung up.

"Can I help you?" she said with a puzzled note to her voice.

"I hope so." Monica smiled and reached into her purse for the folded newspaper clipping. She opened it up and pushed it across the counter. "Do you recognize this man?"

The woman ran a hand through her hair, which was blond with dark roots. She pointed a finger, with a knuckle that was red and rough and a nail that was bitten to the quick, at the caption under the picture. "It says right here his name is Roger Tripp." She looked up at Monica with a confused expression on her face.

Monica suppressed a sigh. "Yes, you're absolutely right. What I'm wondering is if you've ever seen him around town. Particularly the first night of the Winter Walk."

The clerk shrugged. "I don't know. Maybe. But there were so many people about that night." She pushed the clipping across the counter toward Monica. "Sorry."

Monica smiled. She was disappointed, but she hadn't really thought it would be that easy.

"Can I help you with anything else?" The woman looked pointedly at the empty counter in front of her.

Monica grabbed a pack of gum from a display by the register and handed it to the woman. She looked at it for a moment without moving then rang it up and handed it to Monica.

"Bag?" she said belatedly.

"No, I'll put it in my purse."

Monica slunk out of the shop feeling slightly defeated but ready to continue her search for someone, anyone, who might be able to put Roger Tripp in the area of the murder the afternoon Crowley was killed.

She stood on the sidewalk for a moment, thinking, but the icy wind soon sent her walking. She peered into the window of the butcher shop, where she could see Bart preparing a roast behind the counter. Several people were waiting, and Monica didn't want to disturb him, nor did she want to wait till everyone left.

She passed Book 'Em, and Greg must have seen her through the window because he came out of the shop and called after her, motioning excitedly.

Monica turned back and smiled.

"Do you have a minute?" Greg brushed back the hair that the wind had blown across his forehead.

"Sure." Monica smiled again. The sight of Greg always seemed to make her smile.

"I want to show you something," Greg said as he held the door open for Monica. "It's a real treasure. I'm not sure I'll be able to part with it, but I know a collector in Detroit who would definitely be interested if I want to sell."

Now Monica's curiosity was truly piqued.

Greg went behind the counter, pulled a book off the shelf and reverently placed it on the glass countertop.

He ran his hand over the dust jacket as if he was caressing it. "Dorothy Sayers's *Gaudy Night*. Signed first edition."

Monica could only guess how special the book was. "Where did you find it?"

"Believe it or not, at a garage sale. Someone obviously didn't know what it was worth. I told them it was very valuable, and that they should consult a dealer about it, but they weren't interested in going to all that bother. I gave them several times their asking price for it to ease my conscience." He grinned. "They seemed more than satisfied with that."

Greg leaned his elbows on the counter. "So where are you off to this afternoon? Have time for a cup of coffee?"

Monica sighed. "I'd love to, but I'm on a mission I'm afraid."

"Uh-oh, you on a mission. Now that's scary." Greg laughed.

"I'm canvassing all the shops to see if anyone can put Roger Tripp, the owner of the Pepper Pot, at the scene of Crowley's murder. It's a long shot, I know." Suddenly Monica realized just what a long shot it was, and her spirits plummeted.

"Oh, I don't know," Greg said. "People around here are quite observant—especially when it comes to an unfamiliar face. And I gather Tripp wasn't all that well known around town even though he's been here for a couple of years."

"I'm off to Twilight next. I don't quite have the nerve to approach the diner."

"I grew up here and Gus scares even me," Greg said, referring to the short-order cook who gave the evil eye to any stranger who dared to darken the diner's door. "It sounds like you have your work cut out for you. I won't keep you then." Greg carefully slid the Sayers book back onto the shelf behind him.

He came out from behind the counter and walked Monica to the door. For a moment she thought he was going to kiss her, but he merely squeezed her arm and wished her luck.

The air felt extra frigid after the warmth of the bookstore. Greg always kept the heat blaring in Book 'Em so his customers were motivated to take off their coats and spend time browsing or reading in the comfy armchairs that dotted the shop.

The enticing smells from the diner reminded Monica that her mother had offered to cook dinner again that night. Nancy was an excellent cook, and Monica was looking forward to another delicious meal.

A bell tinkled when she pushed open the door to Twilight. Tempest was behind the counter with her back facing Monica. Monica was shocked when she turned around. More of her black hair seemed to have become consumed by the white streak at her temple almost overnight, and her face had lines that hadn't been there before.

"Oh, Monica," she said when she turned around. The words came out sounding like a sob.

"Is everything okay?" Monica asked in concern.

"Okay? Of course not. The police still suspect me of murder, and it's all I can think about." She gestured toward the tarot cards spread out on the counter. "Even the cards think I did it." She tried to smile, but her lips trembled and turned down at the corners.

She was wearing a flowing purple satin top with a jeweled neckline. She began to pleat the fabric between her fingers. "I don't know what to do." She looked at Monica beseechingly. "Have you discovered something new?" A spark of hope lit her eyes briefly.

"Yes and no. I've learned that Roger Tripp, the owner of the Pepper Pot, had more than one reason to hate Crowley. Not only did Crowley manage to delay the opening of Tripp's restaurant, but he apparently accused him of stealing when Tripp worked at the Cranberry Cove Inn."

"Do you think this Roger Tripp is the one who killed Crowley?" Tempest looked down at her blouse, which was now wrinkled where she'd been clutching it. She pulled a strand of worry beads from her pocket and began fingering them.

"I don't know. But it's the best lead we've had so far."

"I won't keep you then." She put a hand to her chest. "Unless you'd like something to warm you up? Tea? I've a lovely herbal brew. . . ."

"Thanks, but I'd rather get going while the shops are still open. I know it sounds lame, but keep your chin up."

Tempest lifted her chin. "I will. And Monica," she put a hand on Monica's arm, "I appreciate what you're doing for me."

• • •

Once again Monica found herself on the sidewalk. There
weren't very many people about. Two men came out of
the diner carrying the scent of fried food with them. A
woman left Bart's Butcher with a large white bag in her
arms, and a young man with close-cropped hair was entering Book 'Em.

Monica looked around. She could try Danielle's boutique or the Purple Grape across the street, where they
sold expensive wines and specialized in bottles from the
Michigan vineyards on the Leelanau Peninsula.

Bijou was next to the Purple Grape. Monica made a
quick decision—she would go in there next. It would be
interesting to talk to the woman who seemed to have taken
such a shine to Jeff.

Jacy Belair was cleaning the top of one of her glass
display cases when Monica entered. Her ample curves
were wrapped in a pink cashmere scoop-neck sweater that
revealed the very top of her lacy push-up bra as she bent
over to wipe the sides of the case.

Her manicure—pink polish that matched her sweater,
with a rhinestone glued to each pinky nail—accentuated
the diamond chunk in the ring on her right hand. The
strand of pearls around her neck swung forward as she
sprayed the other side of the display case with cleaner.

"Can I help you?" she asked Monica, lifting her head
without straightening up.

"Yes. I hope so."

Jacy put down her cleaning tools and put on her best
smile. Her lipstick matched her sweater and manicure and
accentuated her white teeth and the dimple in her cheek.

Monica couldn't help wondering if she changed her nail and lip color along with her outfits.

Jacy's skirt was short and tight and her shoes high-heeled with a peek-a-boo toe. She slid behind the counter. "Are you looking for a gift perhaps? Or something for yourself?"

She gave Monica a look that suggested she doubted Monica was after a piece of jewelry for herself. Monica realized the only jewelry she was currently wearing was a pair of gold stud earrings.

Monica glanced at the glittering array of gems underneath the glass countertop—diamond rings, heavy gold bracelets, necklaces of every length and style.

Jacy cocked her blond head to one side as Monica pulled the newspaper clipping from her purse. "Don't you live out at Sassamanash Farm?"

"Yes, I do."

"The young man that runs the farm—is that your brother?"

Monica was tempted to say he was her boyfriend but then thought better of it. She wanted to get information from Jacy, not antagonize her.

"Yes. Jeff."

"Handsome young man. Is he seeing anyone?"

Monica stared at the heavy black eyelashes ringing Jacy's eyes. "Yes, he is. A very nice young girl." She put a slight emphasis on the word *young*. All the makeup Jacy was wearing couldn't disguise the fact that she was out of her twenties and well into her thirties.

"That's never stopped me before." She giggled.

Monica tamped down on her dislike and plastered a smile on her face that she doubted would fool anyone.

"Now you haven't told me," Jacy drummed her long manicured nails on the counter, "what I can help you with." She squinted at Monica. "I have an amber necklace—an antique—that would suit your coloring perfectly."

Before Monica could protest, Jacy had whipped out a black velvet pad and placed a strand of smooth round amber beads on it. It was choker length, and Monica found her hand going to her throat. She'd never been all that interested in jewelry but for some reason, she immediately wanted this necklace.

She touched one of the beads with her finger. "How much is it?" She asked even though she knew she couldn't afford it.

Jacy undid the clasp and handed the beads to Monica. "Why don't you try it on first?"

Monica put the beads around her neck. They felt cool against her skin. Jacy pushed a mirror toward her, and Monica looked into it. Jacy was right—the beads were the perfect color for her. She sighed, took the necklace off and handed it back to Jacy.

"Don't you like it?"

"I'm afraid I can't afford it."

"But I haven't even told you the price yet."

Jacy mentioned a number that was out of reach but not so far out that Monica immediately ruled out the purchase. If she scrimped a bit here, and cut a few corners there . . .

"I'm not in a position to buy the necklace now, but is there any chance you could hold it for me for a month or two?"

Jacy pursed her pink lips. "I don't know . . . how about if I let you know if someone else shows an interest and give you first dibs on it?"

"That sounds good." Monica fished around in her purse and pulled out her clipping. It was already starting to get worn in the creases.

She spread the newspaper story on the counter and pointed to the picture of Roger Tripp.

"I'm trying to find someone who might have seen this man," Monica pointed to the picture again, "in the vicinity of the village green at the time of Preston Crowley's murder."

Jacy stared at the picture intently and finally picked up the clipping and held it under the light. She tapped the paper with her index finger, which had a large Band-Aid wrapped around it.

"This fellow does look familiar. I've seen him coming and going from the Pepper Pot while they've been working on it."

"Can you remember if you saw him the opening night of the Winter Walk?"

Monica realized she was holding her breath and let it out in a rush.

"Yes, I'm quite certain I did. It was right before that sleigh came barreling down the street and scared everyone half to death." She tapped the picture again. "He was moving quickly—almost running—with his coat flying wide open, even though it was mighty cold that day."

Chapter 16

Monica left Bijou feeling so exhilarated she didn't even notice that the temperature had dropped yet again and the wind off the lake had picked up even more.

She finally had a lead—a solid lead. Jacy was quite certain she'd seen Roger Tripp—running furiously—at the time of the murder. It looked as if he had been in the right place at the right time. That, combined with a strong motive for hating Crowley, made him the perfect suspect.

Monica ducked into the diner and slipped into a vacant booth. They were getting ready to close—the waitress was collecting salt and pepper shakers on a tray and giving the tables a final swipe with a cloth.

She stomped over to where Monica was sitting.

"Yeah?" She pulled her pad out of her pocket. "You want something to eat because the kitchen is about to close."

"No, no, just a cup of coffee."

The woman grunted and walked back behind the counter where the dregs of the day's coffee sat warming on a hot pad.

Monica wasn't interested in the coffee—she just wanted a warm, quiet place to make a phone call. She dug around in her purse and pulled out her cell phone and a dog-eared business card.

Monica was punching in the numbers when the waitress appeared with her coffee, banging it down on the table so that it sloshed over the rim of the cup and into the saucer. While Monica waited for the phone to be answered, she picked up the cup and slid a napkin underneath to soak up the drips.

Finally her call went through.

"Detective Stevens, please."

Another interminable wait while the waitress continued to glare at Monica, and Gus, behind the grill, banged implements around as if to emphasize the point that they were waiting for her to drink her coffee so they could close.

Monica did her best to ignore them as she waited. Finally, she was rewarded when Detective Stevens's voice came over the line.

Monica identified herself and proceeded to tell Stevens what she'd discovered about Roger Tripp and how Jacy Belair claimed to have seen him running from something the afternoon of the Winter Walk.

Stevens sounded half doubtful and half amused but promised Monica she would follow up on the lead. Monica clicked off the call feeling that if Stevens had been in the room and not on the other end of the telephone line, she would have patted Monica on the head and said, *My, what a bright girl you are.*

She took a gulp of her coffee, which, as she had suspected, was bitter and burnt tasting. She pulled a couple of bills out of her wallet, tossed them on the table and got up to leave. Monica hadn't taken more than a step down the sidewalk when she heard the click of the front door of the diner being locked behind her.

She shivered as the cold wind slipped down the neck of her coat and up the sleeves. She began to walk faster, anxious to get inside her car and turn on the heat. She was almost there when she had a thought. Maybe the young man who had been tasked with keeping track of the horse that was meant to pull the sleigh had seen Tripp in the vicinity. Surely it was worth asking him.

The only problem, of course, was that Monica had no idea who he was. But she had a pretty good idea who would know—Hennie and Gerda VanVelsen. She turned on her heel, pulled her collar up around her ears and headed toward Gumdrops—she ought to be able to catch up with the sisters before they closed for the day.

Hennie was about to lock the front door to the shop when Monica pushed it open. The older woman was holding a large ring dripping with keys that made her look like the chatelaine of an old castle.

"Hello, dear," Hennie greeted Monica warmly. "We were about to close, but if there's something you need . . ."

The curtain to the back room rattled, was pushed aside and Gerda entered the shop. "I heard voices, Hennie. Is there someone—" She stopped short when she saw Monica. "Oh, hello, dear."

The shop smelled of sugar and spice. Monica took a deep breath. Entering Gumdrops was a bit like entering a magical kingdom made of candy. The VanVelsen twins contributed to the illusion, looking as if they had just stepped out of a Disney movie.

"Is it some of the Wilhelmina peppermints you're after?" Hennie's hand hovered over a tin of the mints.

"Yes," Monica blurted out. "I'll definitely take some peppermints." It didn't seem right not to buy something when she was holding the sisters up. No doubt they had a pot of erwtensoep—Dutch pea soup—waiting on the stove for their dinner.

"Have you learned anything new about Crowley's murder?" Hennie asked as she slid Monica's purchase into a white paper bag with *Gumdrops* on the front in candy-colored letters.

Monica handed her a bill and took the package in exchange.

"I do have a lead. I've been showing a picture of Roger Tripp, the owner of the Pepper Pot, around town. He had good reason to dislike Crowley, and Jacy Belair, who owns Bijou, claims to have seen him running furiously right before the sleigh with Crowley's body came flying down the street."

"Well!" Hennie exclaimed, and Gerda nodded her head in agreement.

Hennie leaned across the counter. "It sounds like you're making progress. What do the police think—have you heard?"

Monica scowled. "I passed the information on to Detective Stevens, but I don't think she was terribly impressed with my detective skills."

"But surely she'll check it out?"

"I hope so."

Hennie shook her head. "That Belair woman seems a

bit flighty to me. I understand she's from down South somewhere. I don't know how good of a witness she'd make."

Gerda frowned at her sister. "Don't forget that our dear
mother's second cousin once removed on her father's side
was from Charleston."

Hennie snorted. "I don't know that that exactly makes
us Southerners. The connection is terribly remote."

"That's true." Gerda fiddled with the strand of pearls
around her neck.

"Still, the police might take the information more seriously if it can be corroborated by someone else," Monica
said. "That's why I thought I would talk to the boy who was
responsible for looking after the horse and sleigh. Perhaps
he also saw Tripp in the area that afternoon."

Gerda and Hennie looked at each other.

"That's Penny Kuiper's oldest boy—Ryan," Hennie
said. "He gets his red hair from his great-grandmother."

Gerda nodded. "Penny's grandmother—Ryan's great-
grandmother—was in our class at Cranberry Cove High.
Viola was good at languages, as I recall." Gerda laughed.
"I'm afraid I have a tin ear myself."

"Me, too. Although we did learn Dutch from our parents," Hennie said. "Viola's daughter was a bit of a disap-
pointment. Married twice, then ran off a third time with a
Fuller Brush salesman." Hennie shook her head. "Penny
grew up with her father—he was the second husband, mind
you. She didn't have any children with the first husband.
If I recall, that marriage lasted less than a year."

Monica wondered how she could bring the subject
back to the present generation and Ryan Kuiper.

Hennie clapped her hands together. "But I don't suppose

you're interested in all that. When you get to be our age, memories are all you have." She smiled at Monica.

"Do you happen to know where I can find Ryan Kuiper?"

"He used to work at the drugstore here in town—after school and on weekends. Rode his bike into town every day—the Kuipers live way out near Old Bridge Road. I suppose he still works there?" Hennie looked at Gerda, and she nodded.

"He was there just the other day when I went in to pick up my prescription. Dr. Vredevoodg gave me something for my acid stomach."

Monica glanced at her watch. "What time does the drugstore close?"

"Not until nine o'clock, dear. You've plenty of time."

Once outside Gumdrops, Monica hesitated. It was getting late, and she had no idea what time her mother had planned dinner for. Of course, the drugstore was on her way to the car—surely she ought to see if she could speak to Ryan now? It wouldn't take that long to show him the newspaper clipping and see if he recognized Roger Tripp.

The Cranberry Cove Drugstore was ready for St. Valentine's Day with red, white and pink hearts liberally sprinkled throughout. The row of Christmas cards that had been going for half price had been replaced with a selection of Valentine's Day cards and a smattering of St. Patrick's Day cards. The owners of the Cranberry Cove Drugstore believed in looking ahead.

The store was quiet, with one customer waiting at the

prescription desk and a father and his two children at the soda counter digging into hot chocolate topped with a swirling mound of whipped cream. Monica went up and down the empty aisles until she came to a young man with a shock of red hair stocking the shelves in the grocery aisle. Along with the usual drugstore fare, the store stocked canned goods like soup and tuna, cleaning products and frozen dinners, ice cream and pizza.

Monica approached him quietly, pretending to study the array of room deodorizers on the shelf in front of her. She glanced at Ryan out of the corner of her eye. He was tall and gangly, with a mop of hair that fell over his forehead and a crop of angry-looking acne on his chin.

He was putting out the last packages of toilet paper from the carton on the dolly next to him when Monica turned to him.

"Are you Ryan Kuiper by any chance?"

He looked startled, and for a minute, Monica thought he would deny it. His Adam's apple bobbed up and down a few times before he answered.

"Yeah." It was more of a grunt than an actual word.

"Do you mind if I ask you a question? I'm Monica Albertson, by the way."

He looked around as if he was scoping out an avenue of escape.

Monica held out her hand, and he stared at it for a moment before switching the roll of toilet paper he was holding to the other hand and shaking hers.

His hand was clammy. Monica got the impression that he was scared. But of what?

"You were in charge of the horse and sleigh the afternoon of the opening of the Winter Walk, is that right?"

Monica made it sound more like a statement than a question.

"Yes. Jingle Bells."

"Pardon?"

"The horse. Her name is Jingle Bells. She lives on the farm down the road. I used to ride her when I was a kid. That was why Mr. Crowley asked me."

"To watch out for her?"

"Yeah." He stuck his finger in the roll of toilet paper and spun it around and around.

"Where did you stay with the horse while you waited for Miss Winter Walk?"

"Near the village green. They brought the sled over on a truck on account of there wasn't any snow yet. Jingle Bells came in her trailer, like she normally would."

"Were you with Jingle Bells the whole time?"

Ryan picked at the bit of acne on his chin. "The police already asked me that," he said, his eyes sliding away from Monica's.

"So you never left Jingle Bells and went off somewhere to . . . to meet someone or do something?"

"Why should I?" Ryan replied in a voice that would have sounded challenging if it hadn't cracked halfway through the sentence.

"I don't know," Monica said. She stuck a hand in her purse and pulled out the now rather worn clipping from the newspaper. She unfolded it and held it in front of Ryan. "Do you recognize this man?"

He brushed the hair away from his eyes and stared at the picture. "I don't know his name."

"That's okay. I'm wondering if he looks familiar and if you might have seen him around the horse or sleigh."

"Maybe." Ryan picked at his chin again. "I might have." He shook his head and his bangs flopped up and down. "Yeah, I'm pretty sure I did."

He looked at Monica, but again his eyes didn't meet hers. It wasn't exactly the corroboration she was looking for.

"One more thing." Monica smiled at Ryan reassuringly.

"Okay."

"You never left the horse or the sleigh, right?"

He nodded and twirled the roll of toilet paper around his finger again.

"But if you didn't leave the horse at any time for any reason, how did Mayor Crowley's body get in the sleigh? You would have to have seen something."

A panicky look crossed Ryan's face, and he turned and glanced over his shoulder. "Boss wants me," he said before taking off at a trot.

Funny, Monica thought, she hadn't heard anyone calling him.

Monica headed toward home, hoping that she wasn't going to be late for dinner. Even so, it had been worth it. Like Jacy, Ryan thought he'd seen Tripp around the murder scene. And even though he swore to the contrary, Ryan was obviously lying about never having left the horse and sleigh alone.

Monica was surprised to see Gina's car when she pulled into the driveway. Had the traffic accident caused Nancy and Gina to bury the hatchet for real this time?

Monica parked her car, got out and opened her back door. Delicious aromas immediately swept over her—the mingled scents of butter, herbs and wine. Her stomach growled in response.

The table was set in the kitchen—Nancy had dug out Monica's white tablecloth and the set of linen napkins she'd gotten from a friend who didn't want them. Gina was busy arranging a bouquet of carnations in a vase while Nancy peered at something in the oven. Monica took a deep breath—the atmosphere was calm and not sparking with hostility.

Mittens was the first to greet Monica, weaving in and out between her legs and rubbing against her pants. She bent down and picked the kitten up. Mittens allowed Monica to hold her for all of thirty seconds before demanding to be put down. She gave Monica a look that clearly said *I've got some exploring to do* as she scampered into the living room.

"Everything smells so good," Monica said.

Nancy turned from the stove. "Chicken cordon bleu, rice pilaf and roasted asparagus. And Gina's made a lovely trifle for dessert."

Monica was surprised—she didn't realize her stepmother's culinary skills extended beyond making dinner reservations.

Gina must have noticed her reaction. "I've been watching those cooking shows on television. You can learn a lot from them."

"You look like you're bursting to tell us something," Nancy said as she lifted the lid and gave a stir to the pot on the stove. Steam rose up to bathe her face and curl the ends of her hair. "Why don't you pour us a glass of the nice pinot grigio I picked up at the market." She jerked her head in the direction of the refrigerator.

Monica retrieved the wine and three glasses. The cork came out of the bottle with a quiet but satisfying pop, and Monica poured a measure into each of the glasses before handing them around.

Nancy brushed her hair back from her forehead, took the glass Monica handed her and sipped from it. "Now tell us what you've learned before you burst." She leaned against the countertop next to the stove while Monica and Gina took seats at the table.

Monica stared into her glass of wine and took a deep breath. "I've found two people who can place Roger Tripp, the owner of the Pepper Pot, at the scene of the murder."

"Who?" Nancy and Gina chorused.

They looked at each other, exchanged glances and laughed.

Monica decided to draw out the suspense and savor her brief moment in the spotlight. She took a leisurely sip of her wine and smiled to herself when she could feel Nancy's and Gina's impatience.

She put down her glass. "Okay, first it was Jacy Belair."

"Who?" Nancy and Gina chorused again.

"She owns Bijou, the new jewelry store in town."

"She has some lovely things in her window," Gina said.

"You always did like your jewelry," Nancy said.

There was silence for a moment and Monica wondered if the détente between the two women had come to an abrupt end. Gina shrugged but didn't say anything and Monica breathed a sigh of relief.

Nancy turned to the stove and lowered the gas under the pot. "You said two people saw him. Who's the other person?"

"Ryan Kuiper."

"Who?" Nancy and Gina said in unison again.

"He's the boy who was in charge of dealing with the horse and sleigh."

Gina ran her finger around and around the rim of her wineglass. "You know what I wonder? How did Preston's body get in the sled? If that boy was watching the horse and sleigh the entire time . . ."

"He must have wandered off," Nancy said as she pulled the pot off the stove. She turned to Monica. "Where are your serving dishes, dear?"

Monica got up and opened a cupboard. "He swears he didn't." She pulled out several large bowls.

Nancy looked at them. "These were your grandmother's, weren't they?"

Monica nodded.

"I didn't know you'd kept them." Nancy looked pleased. "How did Preston get the sleigh to the village green?" Nancy spooned the rice pilaf into one of the dishes. "The horse couldn't have pulled it all the way."

Gina jumped up, took the dish from Nancy and put it on the table. "I imagine some kind of truck? A flatbed?"

"Do you think Preston's body might have already been in the sleigh? That boy—Ryan?—might have focused all his attention on the horse and didn't notice." Nancy began to arrange the chicken cordon bleu on a platter.

"Not notice a dead body?" Gina laughed. "How could that be?"

"You know teenaged boys. Perhaps some girl caught his eye?" Nancy put the platter on the table.

"You could be right," Gina said. "Some girl caught his

eye and he wandered off to talk to her, leaving the horse tied to a post. That would have given someone time to put Preston's body in the sled."

"And then it was just a matter of untying the horse and sending it off running," Monica added as she unfurled her napkin and placed it on her lap.

The meal was delicious, as Monica knew it would be. Her mother was an accomplished cook. Gina's trifle was the perfect finish.

"Not bad," Gina said as she tasted her first mouthful. "If I do say so myself. Maybe this cooking thing isn't as hard as I always thought it was."

Nancy gave a smug smile but didn't say anything.

"And now I'm stuffed," Gina said, putting down her spoon and pushing back her chair. She glanced at the dirty dishes on the counter. "Now if the kitchen would only clean itself."

Monica was loading the dishwasher when the doorbell rang. "I wonder who that is?" She dried her hands on a towel.

"Jeff?" Nancy said.

"No, he would come around to the back door, and he usually doesn't bother to ring the bell or knock. Just pops in."

Mittens followed Monica out of the kitchen, down the hall, through the living room to the front door. She seemed as curious as Monica was to know who had rung the bell. Despite her height, the small diamond paned windows set in the door were too high up for Monica to be able to see who was there. In Chicago she would never have opened her door without checking the peephole first, but this was Cranberry Cove.

Mittens mewled and wound in and out between Monica's legs as she pulled open the door. . . .

And gasped in surprise when she saw who was standing on her doorstep.

Chapter 17

"Dad! What are you doing . . . I didn't expect . . . why are you here?" Monica couldn't stop the words as they tumbled out in surprise.

"Don't I get a hug?" John Albertson held out his arms. He was zipped into a black leather jacket that was a far cry from the cashmere jackets he used to wear when he and her mother were together.

Monica gave him a quick embrace. Her mind was whirling with questions—why was her father here, what did he want and what would happen when he found Nancy and Gina in the same room?

"I hope you're not going to leave me on the doorstep."

"No, of course not. Please come in."

John dwarfed Monica's small living room with his presence. He was tall and slender and his hair, which had been the same color as Monica's, was now a very distinguished looking dark gray.

He pulled off his leather gloves as he looked around. Mittens rubbed against his leg, and he bent down and picked the kitten up.

"And who is this?"

"Mittens," Monica said, still distracted by her father's sudden presence.

"She?" He looked at Monica, who nodded. "Is adorable."

Mittens actually let John hold her for several seconds before squirming out of his grasp and jumping to the floor.

"I hope I'm not interrupting something. It smells wonderful in here—were you having dinner?"

"Just finished actually," Monica said, wondering when he was going to reveal the reason behind his unexpected visit.

He cleared his throat. He actually looked nervous—something Monica had never seen before.

"I'm looking for Gina. I heard she'd moved here, but no one seems to know where she's living—I've been sending her checks to a post office box." He looked down at his feet.

Monica had barely opened her mouth when both Nancy and Gina walked into the living room.

"I heard a male voice—" Nancy began but stopped abruptly when she saw her ex-husband.

Gina was right behind her, and she, too, stopped in her tracks at the sight of John Albertson standing in Monica's living room.

"Gina," John said, after nodding in Nancy's direction, "I need to speak to you."

"Well, go ahead then." Gina lifted her chin.

"Not here. Can we go somewhere and I'll buy you a drink?"

Gina laughed. "Cranberry Cove is all tucked in tight for the night, John. They roll up the sidewalks early around here. And I have to get to bed myself. I've got a shop to run now."

John ran his hands through his wavy gray hair. "Just for a minute then."

"You can say whatever you have to say right here."

"Please," John said, and for a moment Monica felt sorry for him. "Can we go somewhere private?" He looked around the room as if something would suggest itself. He cast a pleading glance at Monica and Nancy, but they both ignored it.

"Can we go out to my car then?"

Gina looked at Nancy and Monica as if she hoped they would tell her what to do.

"Please?" John said again. "It's . . . it's important." He looked down at his shoes.

"Fine," Gina said finally. "But only for a moment. Like I told you, I go to bed early now."

Gina retrieved her coat from the back of the chair where she'd tossed it earlier, shrugged it on and followed John out the front door. Monica and Nancy turned and looked at each other. Nancy raised her eyebrows but didn't say anything. Monica silently followed her mother out to the kitchen.

"Coffee?" Monica asked, opening the pantry door and getting out a canister of coffee.

"Why not?" Nancy dropped into a chair at the table and rested her head in her hands.

Monica measured coffee and water into the machine

and turned it on. Within minutes hot coffee was gurgling and splashing into the pot.

"What on earth is he doing here?" Nancy finally said when Monica handed her a steaming cup.

"I can't imagine." Monica sat opposite her mother and blew on her coffee before taking a sip.

It was probably only ten minutes but it seemed longer before they heard the front door slam, and Gina walked back into the kitchen. Her face was flushed, although whether from the cold or strong emotions wasn't obvious. She looked utterly flustered.

Nancy fidgeted with her coffee cup, nearly knocking it over before blurting out, "Well, what did John want?"

Gina paced back and forth. Nancy and Monica tried to follow her movements but only succeeded in looking as if they were at a tennis match.

Gina finally stopped pacing and stood in front of them. "Get this. That bimbo who stole John away from me has dumped him—moved out and run off with a tattooed guitar player. She left John high and dry—ran up his credit cards and then scampered."

Nancy looked confused. "But what does this have to do with you?"

Gina laughed. "He wants me back. He wants me to go home to Chicago with him."

"What did you say?" Monica felt as if she was watching some made-for-television movie.

"I couldn't believe it! The nerve!" Gina slammed her fist into the open palm of her other hand. "He dumps me and now he expects me to forget all the . . . the hurt and anguish and take him back? Because he doesn't want to be *alone*?"

Gina took off her coat and threw it across a chair. She turned to face Nancy and Monica. "I've discovered I like being alone. This is the first time in my life I've been independent and on my own. My shop is starting to do well, I have my own home where I can do what I want. Why should I give all that up?"

"I'm glad you said that," Nancy said, pushing back her chair and standing up. She went over to Gina and put an arm around her. "Because if you agreed to take that scoundrel back after what he's done, I'd never speak to you again."

Monica spent the early morning hours in the kitchen baking and cooking—cranberry scones, cranberry coffee cake and a fresh batch of cranberry salsa. By the time she'd filled two baskets with the delicious goodies, the kitchen was redolent with the scents of vanilla and sugar.

Nancy was still asleep when Monica slipped on her jacket. Mittens meowed loudly at her, rubbed against her legs, then stalked off to stretch out in a sunbeam by the kitchen window, where she proceeded to groom herself thoroughly.

Monica headed out the door and down the path to the farm store. The sun was out, the wind had died down and it was quite mild for January, the temperature having risen to almost forty degrees. Monica stopped briefly to loosen her scarf and stuff her knitted hat into her pocket.

Monica heard a shout coming from behind her. She turned and waved to Jeff, who was driving the sander across the ice-covered bog, laying down a layer of sand. The trees ringing the bog, which had been flaming with color in the autumn, were bare now, stretching their naked branches toward the deep blue sky. Monica took a moment to savor the scene before continuing on toward the white-shingled building that housed the store.

Nora was already there, her cranberry-printed apron tied around her plump waist. She was busy cleaning the pastry case when Monica walked in.

"Howdy." Nora flapped her sponge in Monica's direction. "You've been baking—I can smell it already."

"Lots of things," Monica said as she began to empty her baskets. "Scones, cake and some more salsa."

She stacked the salsa containers on top of each other, opened the cooler with her elbow and began to arrange them on the shelves.

"You're early today," she said over her shoulder to Nora.

"Rick drove the kids to school this morning, which saved me a good half hour."

Monica had barely finished arranging the scones on a decorative platter when their first customer walked in. Monica recognized her as the wife of the farmer down the road. They'd met at one of the church potlucks, but Monica hadn't seen her for a while.

"Morning," the woman said as she approached the counter. Her jacket hung open and she was wearing a sweatshirt with hearts and flowers appliqued on it underneath.

Monica returned the greeting. "What can I get you?"

"I'll take a couple of your scones, please. I've got a friend coming over this afternoon. It'll be some company since Dieter is off at one of his farmers' conferences."

"Will he be gone long?" Monica selected two scones and placed them in a white bakery bag.

"Couple of days is all. Organic farming is what he's gone to learn about."

The woman leaned against the counter, obviously in no hurry to leave. "I heard you had a booth at the Winter Walk. How did it go? I was going to get up something to sell my homemade preserves, but I wasn't sure it would be worth the trouble."

"We did very well. Sold everything I took. I'd say the whole event was pretty successful, and I imagine the town council will vote to continue the Walk."

"I'm sorry I missed all the excitement. I heard about it afterward, and I said to Dieter I should have gone—we'll never have something like that happen here in town again."

"Let's hope not."

"The whole thing must have scared poor Candy to death. She was Miss Winter Walk—her mother goes to our church." She shook her head. "Flighty girl—dating that Ryan Kuiper."

"Ryan Kuiper?"

"Yes. But Della, that's Candy's mother, said they broke up a couple of weeks ago and good thing, too, with Ryan being four years younger than Candy. It's time she found a man her own age and settled down."

Monica barely heard the rest of the woman's conversation as she rang up the purchase. So Candy—aka Miss Winter Walk—had dated Ryan Kuiper. Was that significant in any way? She was sure it was, but she couldn't quite grasp why.

They had a decent stream of customers all morning, which made Monica happy. The farm was still on somewhat shaky financial ground, although the money from the fall crop had certainly helped. But Jeff was always worrying about money, and Monica hated to see him like that.

She had to make a trip into town for some things at the drugstore and maybe treat herself to lunch at the diner if there was time. She'd love a bowl of their famous chili, which wasn't even on the menu—Greg had clued her in to its existence. Ordering it proved you were a local and in the know. Although Gus, the short-order cook and diner owner, could tell if you weren't from Cranberry Cove the minute you walked in the door.

Monica had been considered an outsider when she first arrived in town, but lately Gus had taken to nodding at her, which meant she was moving up the food chain as far as he was concerned.

Monica found a space in front of Bijou, and cast a longing glance at the store's façade. Jacy was rearranging the window display and waved when she saw Monica. She raised her eyebrows, but Monica shook her head. She'd really liked that amber necklace but couldn't quite justify the cost.

She moved on to the drugstore where Rieka, the secretary from the town hall, was waiting by the prescription counter. She didn't seem to recognize Monica, which was fine with her. The fewer people who remembered her going around asking questions, the better. Back in September, asking questions had nearly ended her life, and if it wasn't for Tempest, her mother and Gina being suspects in Preston's murder, she wouldn't dream of doing it again.

Monica spent a few minutes in front of the shampoo display. They had a shampoo for every type of hair imaginable—fine hair, thick hair, hair that needed more volume, hair that was too dry, hair that was color-treated. The array was dizzying, and in the end Monica picked up a bottle of the same shampoo she always bought.

She grabbed a tube of toothpaste from a display that was almost as vast as the shampoo selection—offering you a choice as to whether you wanted your teeth whitened, wanted to prevent the buildup of plaque or wanted to avoid gingivitis. Next, Monica made her way down the cosmetics aisle and picked up a bottle of lotion—the lack of humidity in the winter air was making her skin dry.

Finally, having collected all her purchases, Monica made her way to the checkout counter. She pulled her wallet out of her purse, and along with it came a grocery receipt from her last big shopping trip. It dropped to the floor, where it coiled like a snake. Monica sighed and swore to herself that this time she really was going to clean out her purse—it became the repository for all sorts of things she didn't know what to do with but was afraid to toss out.

She bent to pick up the fallen receipt and noticed there was another piece of paper kicked under the base of the cashier's desk. She thought she would be a good citizen and pick it up as well. She could dispose of it when she got home.

Monica shoved the receipt back into her purse and was about to do the same with the other piece of paper when she noticed it was a page torn from a calendar with something scribbled on it. Curiosity got the better of her and as she waited she unfolded the crumpled scrap. It looked as if it had been ripped off of one of those daily desk calendars—on one side the date was the day of the Winter Walk. A time had been circled with the notation *Village green/sleigh.*

Monica turned the page over to the Thursday before the Winter Walk began. A note in slanted handwriting was written horizontally across the page.

Monica stuffed the paper in her pocket, paid her bill and went out the door. As soon as she was outside, she retrieved the calendar page and read the note scrawled across it.

> *Ryan, meet me at the gazebo on the village green at 3:30 pm Saturday. It's important. P. S. Don't tell anyone.*

It was signed *Candy*.

Monica knew the gazebo was a popular place for courting couples to meet—but in the summer, not when the temperatures were below freezing. Candy must have had something very important to tell Ryan.

Or else . . . at 3:30 pm on the day of the Winter Walk, Ryan was supposed to be tending to the horse that was going to pull the sleigh bearing Candy and Preston Crowley. Did Candy know Ryan was going to be in charge of the sleigh? And did she lure him away on purpose?

Chapter 18

What now? Monica wondered. Where did this information fit in with everything else she already knew?

Monica stood on the sidewalk, lost in thought, until someone brushed against her.

"Sorry," the young man called over his shoulder.

Monica smiled at him. "My fault," she yelled as she headed down the street.

She decided she would talk to Candy, although she wouldn't be at all surprised if Candy denied knowing anything about the note. Candy worked part-time at Bijou—perhaps she'd be lucky and catch her there.

Monica was about to step off the curb when a pickup truck blared its horn at her as it rumbled down Beach Hollow Road. She jumped back. She'd better pay more attention to what she was doing or she would end up as dead as poor Preston Crowley.

Monica finally made it safely across the street and

headed toward Bijou. She was disappointed when she pushed open the door to the shop to discover that Jacy was alone behind the counter, showing an older woman a selection of gold crosses.

The woman finally decided on her purchase and left the store. Jacy looked up and gave a smug smile when she saw Monica. "I knew you'd come back," she said as she began to reach into the glass display case. "This necklace was made for you." She placed the strand of amber beads on the counter.

Monica was flattered and embarrassed at the same time. She looked longingly at the necklace.

"I'd love to purchase the piece this minute, but I'm afraid I'm going to have to wait a bit longer."

Jacy looked confused. She drummed her pink nails on the counter. "Is there something else I can show you? Do you need a gift? We have an array of options—Christening presents, wedding presents, birthdays, Valentine's Day. . . ." She stopped when she saw Monica's face.

"Actually I'm looking for someone."

"Looking for a gift for someone?"

"No, looking for a person."

Jacy looked around the shop as if to verify that it was empty. "Who? I'm afraid I'm the only one here."

"I wanted to speak to Candy—your assistant."

Jacy looked momentarily startled and then snorted. "Calling her an assistant is a bit of a stretch. She's always late and still hasn't figured out the cash register." She studied her nails and picked at the cuticle of her index finger. Jacy sighed. "I guess it's better than nothing. Otherwise I'd be here all day, six days a week, with no break. At least I can visit the little girl's room or go out and pick up something to eat."

Monica wasn't sure what to say, so she said nothing.

Jacy looked at Monica and the expression in her eyes was sharp. "What do you want with Candy?"

Monica felt the blood drain from her face. She hadn't thought that far ahead—she'd just barged into the shop without a suitable excuse. She stuttered briefly, desperately trying to think.

"I wondered if she'd like to pick up some more hours—we need some help at the farm store—"

"That girl? She doesn't exactly have what you call a work ethic. She's on the lookout for easy money—some guy with a wallet full of cash who'll fall for her dyed blond hair, big blue eyes and complete lack of an IQ."

"Do you know where Candy lives? I'd like to speak to her anyway."

Jacy gave Monica an appraising stare. "I'm not sure," she said.

That was strange, Monica thought. Most employers took down the address, social security number and contact info of their employees. Then she remembered Mauricio, who had worked for Jeff. Difficulty finding workers sometimes led to a lackadaisical attitude toward the appropriate papers.

"Do you have a telephone number for her?"

"Probably. But I don't have time to look for it right now." Jacy turned her back on Monica and began to rearrange a display of jeweled clocks on the shelf behind her.

Monica sighed. Detecting was certainly never easy. No wonder Detective Stevens had those deep lines bracketing her mouth even though she was only in her forties.

The VanVelsen sisters knew Candy and her mother—

perhaps they would know how Monica could get in touch with her.

Monica left Gumdrops with Candy's address on a scrap of paper tucked firmly into her pocket.

She backed the Focus out of the parking space and headed north down Beach Hollow Road, following the directions from the VanVelsen sisters. At the end of Beach Hollow, where the road forked, she took a right as instructed. She passed an empty field dotted with scrubby grass and gnarled bushes on her right and a stand of tall, sand-dusted pines on her left. She continued to climb until she reached the street the VanVelsens had indicated. Monica retrieved the slip of paper from her pocket and checked it to be sure.

Candy had a room in one of the tangle of houses crammed together on the hill overlooking the lake. Most of the homes were gold mines for their owners—rented out weekly or monthly to tourists who wanted to spend the summer, or at least part of it, within walking distance of the lake and downtown Cranberry Cove. The owners usually didn't rent rooms to people year-round—certainly not someone like Candy who couldn't possibly afford to pay very much.

When Monica saw the house, she understood how Candy had been able to handle the cost. The house looked as if it hadn't been renovated in decades, and the entire structure appeared to be listing to the right. The owner might have been able to get some college students to take it on for their summer break, but it wasn't the sort of place people would bring their families.

Some sort of reconstruction was under way. A truck

was parked out front with several two by fours sticking out the open back door, and Monica heard the whine of a saw coming from somewhere inside the house.

Before she could even knock, a woman opened the front door. She was obviously intent on something because she seemed startled to see Monica on her doorstep. She was wearing peach scrubs and had a mass of frizzy light brown hair. The hospital ID pinned to her top read *Carrie Zeilstra, Nurse Aide*. She was older than Candy—probably close to Monica's age.

"Can I help you?"

Monica cleared her throat. "Is Candy here?"

"She lives here if that's what you're asking, but she's not home at the moment."

"Do you know when she'll be back?"

"Probably soon. She wanted to get away from the noise." The woman jerked her head in the direction of the house. The whining of the saw had stopped, only to be replaced by the sound of hammering. "I inherited this place from my grandparents. They hadn't done a lick of work on the house in years. I swear the appliances in the kitchen were the original ones installed when they moved in." She brushed some hair out of her eyes. "Over the years the damp from the lake warped the floors so that if you dropped something it would roll to the other side of the room." She wrapped her arms around herself. "I couldn't rent it out the way it was."

"But Candy—"

The woman shook her head. "She'll have to leave come summer when the house is finished. Meanwhile she has a place to stay, and I make a few bucks to put toward that." She cocked her shoulder in the direction of the truck.

"Candy claims she's going to get a nice place of her own

now that she's going to have some money. I can't imagine where it came from—maybe someone died, I don't know. But she's been talking about it for a couple of days now," the woman said.

"Do you remember when she first mentioned it?"

The woman frowned. "I think it was right before the Winter Walk started, but I'm not sure. When you're picking up shifts for everyone who's sick, and even pulling double shifts, the days start to run together. This is my first day off in ten days."

"Was Candy planning on moving out right away?"

"No, and I'm glad—this old place gets a bit creepy at night." She laughed. "Maybe I've read too many Stephen King novels." Her expression turned serious. "Although Candy has been acting a little jittery the last day or two. It's not like her. Maybe I infected her with my own fears."

"So that was unusual for her?"

"Yeah, she's normally a pretty laid-back type, if you know what I mean."

Monica thanked the woman, declined to leave a message and walked back to her car. Candy had come into some money and at the same time she'd begun acting jittery. Were the two related? Did they have anything to do with Preston's death? Monica had no idea. Maybe if she let the facts stew in the back of her mind, something would come to light.

Monica backed out of the driveway. The truck was behind her—it looked as if the workmen were calling it a day. She gave the house one last glance. She didn't know much about construction, but in her opinion, it would be a miracle if the place was ready for the summer trade.

She was headed down the hill when the truck pulled out in front and passed her. Monica shrugged. She wasn't in any hurry. She was enjoying the view of the lake, the rays of the lowering sun glinting off the ice floes.

She passed the field again, on her left this time, and the cluster of pine trees on her right. She caught a glimpse of something out of the corner of her eye. She had no idea what it was, but it looked out of place enough for her to pull over to the side of the road and stop.

Something red lay at the base of one of the tall trees. Monica squinted at it—it looked like a purse. She stared at it for a few moments longer, then turned the car off, unbuckled her seat belt and got out. The wind immediately grabbed hold of her scarf and tossed it into the air. Monica grabbed it and tucked the ends into her coat.

Now that she was closer, she could see that the object was definitely a purse. Had it been there on her way up the hill? She wasn't sure—she might have been looking at the field on the other side of the road.

How strange that someone had lost their purse in such an isolated spot. Monica couldn't be sure from such a distance, but the purse looked like red corduroy with a long strap—the kind that can cross over the body.

She wasn't sure what to do. Would someone come back for it? Should she take it to the police? She walked closer and closer to the handbag until she was near enough to see that something was wrapped around the strap.

It was a hand—a hand attached to a body that looked an awful lot like Candy's.

Chapter 19

Candy was sprawled on her back, her right knee bent, her left arm outstretched and her blond hair splayed across the snow-covered ground. She was wearing a lavender parka with white fake fur around the collar, a scarf, mittens and boots.

Monica called Candy's name but the rational part of her brain knew she was already dead. She sidled closer to get a better look. There was a smear of blood across Candy's forehead and an ominous-looking dent in her temple.

Monica stifled the scream that rose unbidden to her throat and scuttled back to her car. Her teeth were chattering uncontrollably, and she turned the dial on the heater to high as she dug her cell phone out of her purse.

She waited several long, frustrating minutes while the operator at the police station attempted to locate Detective Stevens, but finally Monica was put through. Their conversation was short and Stevens promised to be on the scene as quickly as humanly possible. Stevens ended the call with a warning to Monica to not touch anything.

Monica wondered if she ought to get out of the car and stand by Candy. Not that she could do anything, but she hated to think of the poor girl lying there all alone on that frozen windblown field. But Monica was still shivering from the cold and shock and decided she would stay in the car a little longer.

It looked to her as if Candy had been headed into town. Her landlord had said she wanted to get away from the noise of the construction at the house. Had the killing been random—some drifter looking for cash? Monica could picture the scene in her mind with great clarity, as if it were etched there permanently—Candy's purse on the ground and her fingers still curled around the strap. The purse itself was closed and latched so it was unlikely someone had been after her credit cards and her money.

Monica had almost stopped shivering by the time the first patrol car arrived, spewing loose bits of macadam as it came to an abrupt stop on the shoulder of the road. Monica recognized the first officer who got out as having been at the scene when Crowley's body was discovered—the other, thinner one looked familiar but she couldn't place him. Most likely she'd seen him directing traffic somewhere.

They both hastened to the body and stood looking down at it for several minutes. They were gesturing to each other, but Monica couldn't make out what was going on. Finally the heavier one headed toward Monica's car.

She rolled down her window and waited, her breath making clouds in the cold air.

"Are you the person who called us?" he asked, pushing back his hat and leaning over so he was level with Monica's window.

She nodded. Her teeth had begun to chatter again as the cold air from the open window rushed into the car. Shock was making her react more strongly than usual to the frigid temperature.

"Detective Stevens should be here shortly. I'm afraid I'm going to have to ask you to wait."

"That's fine."

The officer walked off to help his partner with the bright yellow-and-black tape that would rope off the scene and warn people to stay away. The brisk wind was whipping it around and it took both officers to secure it.

Monica averted her head from the sight of Candy's lifeless body. Who would do such a thing? Random crime was unheard of in Cranberry Cove, which made it likely that someone had targeted Candy for a specific reason. Had Candy been a danger to someone? To the same person who had murdered Crowley?

Monica was thinking about it when Detective Stevens pulled up. She tightened the belt of her coat as she made her way over to Monica's car. The wind blew a strand of her short blond hair across her face, and she swiped at it impatiently. There were lines of fatigue around her eyes.

"You look tired," Monica said when she rolled down her window.

"The baby's teething." Stevens smiled briefly. "And I've got a murder case on my hands." She glanced over her shoulder. "Two cases now, from the looks of things. What can you tell me about this?" She waved a hand toward the roped-off area of the field.

"I was driving past when the bright red of Candy's

purse caught my eye. At first I thought someone had lost their handbag." Monica's voice began to shake. "Then I saw . . . then I saw Candy."

"The woman's name is Candy? Do you know her last name?"

Monica shook her head. "No. But she worked at Bijou, the jewelry store in town, and she's renting a room in a house up the hill."

Monica scrambled in her purse and pulled out the scrap of paper with Candy's address on it. She handed it to Stevens. "Here's the address. It's not far." She pointed up the hill behind her.

"Hey." A shout came from one of the officers and Stevens whirled around.

"Be right there." She tapped Monica's car door. "Mind waiting a few more minutes?"

"No."

As soon as Stevens walked away, Monica put her window back up. She sat thinking. Candy had obviously been a danger to someone. Why? Did she know something? Perhaps she had seen someone or something the day of the Winter Walk and the killer had found out? According to the note Monica had found, Candy was meeting Ryan in the gazebo on the village green. Could she have seen something then? If so, was Ryan in danger as well?

Monica jumped when Stevens tapped on her window. She shivered as she zapped the window down again.

"We found something," Stevens said, holding out a plastic evidence bag. "It's a napkin from that new restaurant in town—the Pepper Pot." She rubbed her eyes with her other hand. "Since the baby, we haven't gotten out much, but I thought the place hadn't opened yet. I'm pretty sure it was closed the opening day of the Winter Walk."

"It's still closed," Monica said glancing at the crumpled napkin visible through the clear plastic.

"I wonder how she got hold of this then?" Stevens said, almost to herself.

She looked at Monica, but Monica didn't have an answer either.

Monica was on her way back to Sassamanash Farm when she stopped at a light. Hers was the only car at the intersection. She looked behind her, down the hill in the other direction and to both sides. There wasn't another vehicle in sight. Monica glared at the red light ahead of her and wondered who had decided that a traffic light was needed at this particular spot. She was still waiting when she heard her phone ding from the depths of her purse, indicating she had a message.

As she pulled out her cell, the light turned green. She looked around but she was still the only one waiting at the intersection. She took a second to read the text before dropping the phone back into her purse and transferring her foot from the brake to the gas pedal.

The text was from Jeff, and he had something he wanted to show her. He didn't say what, and Monica was curious.

She headed down the hill to where the farm could be seen in the distance. A few minutes later, she was pulling into her driveway. Her mother's car was there, so Nancy obviously hadn't gone out.

As soon as Monica opened the back door, Mittens skittered over to say hello. She picked the kitten up and held her close, relishing the softness of Mittens's fur against her skin. Mittens soon twisted from Monica's grasp and leapt to the floor, where she amused herself by chasing a piece of fluff that was being blown about by the air from the heating vent. The kitten's antics made Monica smile and briefly forget the horror of finding Candy's body.

Monica was hanging her jacket on the coatrack when her mother walked into the kitchen.

"Hello, dear," Nancy said, her finger holding her place in a book. She brandished it at Monica. "I've been enjoying my book—it's an intriguing mystery set in World War Two London. I think you'd enjoy it. It's so peaceful and quiet out here on the farm that in spite of everything I've found myself relaxing."

She looked at Monica, who had begun to shiver.

"What's wrong? Are you cold? Let me make you a cup of tea." Nancy put her book facedown on the table and reached for the kettle on Monica's stove. "Has something happened?" She twisted around to look at Monica as she placed the kettle under the tap.

Monica nodded and told her about finding Candy's body.

"How dreadful," Nancy said as she turned on the burner.

"I'm sorry." Monica sniffed. "I didn't mean to ruin your peaceful afternoon."

"Nonsense. I'm sorry you had to go through that."

"Has Jeff been around? He messaged me that he had something to show me."

Nancy shook her head as she poured steaming tea into a mug, added some sugar and handed it to Monica. She wrapped her hands around it gratefully, suddenly realizing they were as cold as the ice that now covered the cranberry bogs.

Monica finished her tea and put the mug in the dishwasher. "I'd better go find Jeff. He rarely ever texts me, so it must be something he considers important." She turned to Nancy. "And you can get back to your book in peace."

"Are you sure you want to go out again? You were shaking like a leaf."

"I'm fine. The tea has warmed me up. Besides, I'm curious about what Jeff found."

Monica bundled up in her down parka, scarf, heavy gloves and knitted hat. She was still freezing—it must be from the shock. She'd never gotten her lunch either but fortunately she was no longer hungry. She began to walk briskly, hoping the exercise would warm her up.

The sun was lower in the sky, lengthening her shadow on the path in front of her. Monica assumed Jeff was still out on the bogs doing the sanding. She could hear the faint drone of the sander in the distance. She left the path and headed in the direction of the sound.

The sound got louder as Monica approached the distant bog, where she could make out two sanders going back and forth methodically across the ice. They were laying down a half-inch layer of sand as neatly as if they were rolling paint on a wall.

Monica waved as she approached. One of the crew was standing at the edge of the bog. He had a knit cap pulled down over a wreath of blond curls. Monica thought she recognized him as a regular member of Jeff's team.

He smiled as Monica got closer. He was drinking from

a stainless steel thermos and swiped a hand across his mouth. "Hey," he said. "Looking for Jeff?"

"Yes." Monica looked toward where the sanders were swishing back and forth across the bog. Neither driver looked like Jeff. "Do you know where he is?"

The fellow pointed to a spot in the distance. "See those piles over there? That's sand." He jerked a thumb toward the sanders behind him. "Jeff's been loading the sand onto the trucks to bring out to the bogs. He ought to be over there now. Dennis has just gone for another load."

"Thanks," Monica said and headed off in the direction the worker had indicated.

The spot he'd pointed to didn't look that far away, but by the time Monica got there she was quite warm and actually loosened her scarf a bit. Jeff was standing at the base of a large pile of sand, talking to another crew member. A truck filled with more sand idled nearby.

"Sis," Jeff called when he saw Monica walking across the field.

The other fellow—Monica assumed he was Dennis—slapped Jeff on the back, hopped into the cab of the truck and began to pull away.

Despite the cold, Jeff had shed his jacket and was working in a dark green sweatshirt. His brows were drawn together in a frown and his expression was serious when Monica reached him.

"I'm glad you're here."

His expression made him look vulnerable and younger than his twenty-five years. Monica felt her heart constrict at the sight of him. She'd felt protective of her baby brother from the moment she first saw him, and that hadn't changed over the years.

"I got your text. You found something?"

Jeff nodded and ran a hand across the back of his neck. "Yeah, but I don't know what to make of it. That's why I was hoping you could. . . ." He trailed off.

"Why don't you show me what it is."

Jeff led her over to a blue plastic tarp he'd spread out on the ground. On top of it was a woman's coat. It was cream-colored wool with a shawl collar and two ornate cut crystal buttons, rimmed in red stones and shaped like flowers. There were two other buttonholes but the buttons themselves were missing.

Jeff poked at the garment with the toe of his boot. "I was loading sand into the truck when I found this buried in the pile." He jerked his head in the direction of the sand. "I don't know what to make of it." He looked slightly embarrassed. "Obviously someone was trying to hide it, but why?" He looked at Monica.

She knelt down beside the coat, careful not to touch it. There was a rust-colored stain down the front—blood? Something about the garment looked familiar, but Monica couldn't quite place it. Maybe it would come to her later.

"What should we do?" Jeff shifted impatiently from one foot to the other. "Do you think it's okay if I toss it in the trash?"

"No." The word burst out of Monica with the force of an explosion. She was convinced the coat had something to do with Crowley's murder. Why hide it otherwise? It looked to be expensive, with those fancy buttons. . . . Buttons! Monica bent over the coat for a closer look. She'd seen buttons like these before. Monica rubbed her forehead trying to remember why they looked so familiar when it suddenly came to her.

"Tempest found a button like the ones on this coat on the floor of her shop. I can't imagine there are two people in Cranberry Cove with a garment like this. Whoever hid the coat here had been in Twilight at some point."

"So what?" Jeff pushed back his hat and scratched his forehead. "I mean, lots of people must go into that shop."

"The weapon used to kill Crowley was stolen from Twilight."

Jeff continued to look puzzled.

"And the murderer must have been wearing this coat at the time. And they didn't notice that one of the buttons had fallen off." She bent closer and examined the fabric. "That could be blood." She pointed at the stains.

Monica stumbled to her feet and backed away from the tarp. "I think we'd better call Detective Stevens." She pointed to the coat. "This might be important evidence."

Jeff didn't look convinced. "If you say so." He sighed. "You don't think they'll try to stop us from working, do you?"

Monica looked around. The ground was lightly covered with snow but any footprints had been obliterated by crisscrossing tire tracks. She doubted the ground would yield much in the way of evidence. Most likely the coat was what the police would be interested in.

The rumble of a truck as it rattled over the frozen ruts in the ground broke the silence. Jeff jerked his thumb toward the vehicle. "Looks like Dennis is back for some more sand. I'd better see to it."

Monica nodded. "Sure."

Monica was glad she'd stashed her cell phone in her jacket pocket. She pulled it out, ripped off her gloves and once again dialed 911.

The dispatcher sounded bored when Monica reached her but promised to send someone around. Monica wondered how long that would take. She stuffed her hands in her pockets and waited, her eyes scanning the road leading to the bog for any sign of a vehicle.

About ten minutes later Monica heard a car in the distance. At first it was a speck on the horizon, but it slowly came into focus as it bounced along the crude dirt road. Monica recognized it as Stevens's car.

Stevens got out of her dusty gray Taurus and leaned against the door for a moment, her eyes evaluating the scene.

"What have you got this time?" she said when she walked over to where Monica was waiting.

Monica pointed to the coat spread out on the tarp. "Jeff—he's my brother—"

"Yeah, I remember him."

Monica felt a frisson of fear. Last time, Jeff had been the suspect in a murder investigation, but surely there was nothing to tie him to this one.

"Anyway," she continued, "Jeff was filling one of the trucks with sand from that pile over there," Monica pointed to it, "when he found the coat."

Stevens pinched the bridge of her nose. "What's the sand for?"

"During the winter, the bogs are flooded. When the ice is thick enough, growers spread sand on top. As the ice melts in the spring, the sand sifts onto the vines and provides protection from insects and helps to choke out weeds."

"Interesting." Stevens stared up at the pile of sand. "Is this area closed off in any way at night?"

"Closed off?"

"I mean can anyone get to this area? There aren't any guard dogs roaming around or anything like that?"

"Oh, no. But I don't think all that many people know about it—well, maybe the people who have been on tours of the farm."

"Who are those people?"

"Tourists mostly. The occasional class trip."

"I see."

Stevens approached the tarp and knelt carefully on the edge. She stared at the coat, without touching it, for several long minutes.

"That could be blood." She pointed to the stain on the front. "Then again, whoever owned the coat might have simply dripped ketchup from a burger they ate in the car." She sighed and got to her feet. "The lab will be able to tell us for sure. Let's hope there's not too much of a backlog at the moment."

"Do you see those buttons?" Monica asked, pointing at the coat.

Stevens scrubbed a hand across her face. She swayed slightly and Monica looked at her in alarm.

"Sorry, too many late nights with the baby." She gave a sudden grin that lit her face. "But so worth it. Assuming I don't lose my job." She massaged her forehead for a second before looking at Monica and smiling reassuringly. "So what about the buttons?"

"Tempest Storm found a button matching these in her shop." Monica pointed to the coat. "As you can see, two of them are missing."

"Maybe the coat belongs to Ms. Storm."

Monica looked at the coat, trying to quell her alarm. Would this evidence incriminate Tempest even further?

"It looks too small for Tempest. She's a tall woman, and broad-shouldered."

"The lab results should reveal some clues." Stevens pulled a small camera from the pocket of her coat. "Mind if I snap a few pictures?"

"No, not at all. Go right ahead." Monica stepped back and out of the way.

The cold was beginning to get to her—she hoped Stevens wouldn't be too long.

A few minutes later, Stevens stuffed the camera back in her pocket. "I've got some evidence bags in my car." She started toward the dirt road where she'd left her Taurus. "You don't have to wait if you don't want to," she called over her shoulder to Monica.

Monica was more than happy to head back to her cottage. On the way she kept picturing the coat Jeff had retrieved from the sand pile. Was it really too small to be Tempest's?

One thing was for certain—if the coat belonged to the murderer, then Roger Tripp was out of the running as a suspect.

Chapter 20

Monica was surprised to see Gina's car in the driveway
when she got back to her cottage. She was even more
surprised to smell pizza when she opened the back door.

"Just in time," Gina said as she set plates out on the
table.

Mittens sat off to the side, twitching her tail back and
forth. She scampered over to Monica and began to rub
against her legs.

Gina was wearing a zebra-print tunic over black leggings. It was quite a contrast to Nancy's carefully pressed
and creased blue jeans, baby blue cashmere pullover and
suede driving shoes.

Monica was surprised that her mother would deign to
eat pizza. She was usually so health conscious.

Gina was about to turn away when she spun around
and looked Monica over carefully.

"Something's happened. You look terrible."

"Gina's right. What's happened?" Nancy looked up from the paper napkin she was carefully folding into a triangle.

Monica told them about finding the bloodstained coat in the sand pile.

"How gruesome." Nancy shivered as she transferred the pizza from the cardboard box to a platter.

Gina watched her, one eyebrow raised. "We could have eaten that out of the box, you know."

"Yes, and we could also eat it off paper towels instead of plates, but one must have at least a few standards," Nancy said pleasantly.

Monica tensed, but Gina just laughed.

"I've been thinking," Gina said.

Nancy feigned surprise and Monica shot her a warning look.

"The murders have to be connected," Gina continued as she helped herself to a slice of the pie. "But what danger could a silly ninny like Candy pose to anybody?"

"She knew something that's a danger to the murderer?" Nancy suggested.

"She knew that Ryan wasn't at his post with the horse but was meeting her in the gazebo instead," Monica said.

"But unless she saw something while she was there—" Gina began.

"Wait." Monica held up her hand. She had to think it through. Things were starting to come together.

"Her landlord said she'd recently come into some money."

Nancy raised her eyebrows.

"But that she was also acting uncharacteristically frightened but wouldn't say what was bothering her."

Monica absentmindedly picked a mushroom off her piece of pizza and ate it. "What if the killer paid her to lure Ryan away from the scene? That would account for Candy coming into money . . . and being frightened. Maybe she was bright enough to put two and two together and realize she was a danger to the murderer."

"I'll bet it was the fellow who owns that new restaurant. What was his name?" Gina turned to Monica.

"Roger Tripp. Although I doubt he's our murderer. Jeff just found a woman's coat buried in the pile of sand by the bogs. It looks as if there are bloodstains on the front and there are buttons missing—buttons that look just like the one Tempest found in her shop."

"So that person is probably the one who stole that thing . . . what was it called?"

"An athame."

"Stole the athame that killed Crowley," Nancy finished.

"Now we just have to find out who the coat belonged to," Gina said, biting into her pizza with relish, oblivious to the tomato sauce dripping down her chin.

"I wonder," Nancy said, casting a disapproving eye in Gina's direction, "if that's going to be—"

Nancy was interrupted by the sound of the front doorbell. The three women looked at each other, and Monica pushed back her chair.

"I'll see who it is."

Mittens followed on Monica's heels out to the foyer, then got bored and scampered off to bat at the living room curtains as Monica opened the front door.

A number of things went through Monica's mind—the caller wasn't likely to be Jeff, nothing could be as startling as having her father arrive on her doorstep, and finally the certainty that it was Detective Stevens and she had found something.

"Sorry to bother you," Detective Stevens said when Monica opened the door.

"No problem." Monica took in the reddened tip of Stevens's nose and her hands stuffed into the pockets of her jacket. "Come in and get warm."

"I could certainly do with that." Stevens stepped across the threshold and slipped out of her shoes. "Don't want to track dirt all over your place." She looked around. "It's so clean. I'm afraid our house smells like dirty diapers and spit-up and is awash with baby toys." She smiled. "Not that I would have it any other way."

A thought flashed across Monica's mind—would she ever have children? It wasn't too late. She hadn't ever given it much thought—she'd been focused on getting her café off the ground and then when she lost Ted . . .

"I wanted to ask Mrs. Albertson something." Stevens interrupted Monica's thoughts.

"My mother?" Monica asked in surprise.

"If it isn't too much trouble. Assuming she's here . . ."

Where else would she be, Monica thought. There weren't many places to go in Cranberry Cove once the sun went down. Except maybe for Flynn's—a seedy bar down by the harbor. The thought of her mother perched on a bar stool knocking back a shot of whiskey made Monica smile. Stevens gave her a strange look but didn't say anything before following Monica down the hall and out to the kitchen.

Nancy and Gina were seated at the kitchen table finishing their pizza. Both turned to stare when Stevens walked into the room.

Stevens gave an apologetic smile.

"Would you like a cup of tea?" Nancy jumped up, ever the hostess. "You look cold."

"Yes, please. I am rather cold still. "

"Let me take your coat." Monica held out her hand for Stevens's jacket, which she hung on the coat tree.

Stevens brushed at her shoulder, and Monica noticed her face turn slightly red.

"It looks as if the baby missed the spit-up cloth." She gave a chagrined smile. She sniffed. "I don't think I smell."

Nancy and Gina laughed.

"I remember wanting to buy a hazmat suit when Jeff was a baby," Gina said. "First it's the spit-up, then it's fingers sticky with peanut butter or jelly."

"And don't forget finger paint." Nancy put a mug in front of Stevens. "Once when Monica was in preschool, I arrived early to pick her up—while they were doing finger painting. She was so excited she came running to me, throwing her arms around me and completely ruining my beige slacks. They had red and yellow fingerprints all over them."

They laughed, and Monica wondered how she could steer the conversation away from anecdotes about her obviously less than stellar past. Before she could think of anything, Stevens cut the conversation short.

"As much as I enjoy chatting with you all, I've actually come to ask you some questions."

"Me?" Gina and Nancy said in unison as they pointed to themselves.

"Both of you, yes. I'm glad I've caught you together." Stevens ran a hand over her face. "It will save me some time. That seems to be a precious commodity these days."

The room was quiet as she pulled a plastic evidence bag from her pocket. Monica could see there was a piece of paper inside, along with something else—something shiny.

Stevens pulled her chair closer to the table and upended the bag. A diamond solitaire ring tumbled out but she had to fish around to retrieve the piece of paper that was also inside. She smoothed out the paper and placed the ring on top.

Gina looked at the diamond and whistled. "I wonder what lucky woman is getting that?"

"That's what I'm wondering," Stevens said. She turned the ring so that the stone caught the light, and looked back and forth between Nancy and Gina.

"I don't see why you think we can help—"

"The ring—and the receipt—were found in Preston Crowley's pocket the day he was murdered."

Gina shot a triumphant look at Nancy. "He was going to propose!" She put her hands against her chest, her eyes shut.

"But he was seeing both of you. . . ."

Gina's eyes flew open. "Yes, but we've been going out longer—"

"How do you know?" Nancy shot back.

Stevens held up the receipt. "At least Crowley shopped locally. It looks like the ring came from Bijou here in town."

Gina pointed at the paper. "Does it say anything on there—a name or some kind of . . . hint?"

"I'm afraid not. Maybe you should both try it on—like Cinderella's glass slipper. Of course, it might have been meant for someone else entirely."

"Not a chance," Gina said as she reached for the ring and

slipped it onto her finger. She had to struggle a bit to get it past her knuckle but when she did, she held her hand up and admired the winking diamond. "See? It fits perfectly."

"It looks a little snug to me," Nancy said, holding her hand out for her turn.

Gina turned slightly red as she attempted to tug off the ring, but eventually it came free.

Nancy slipped it onto her own well-manicured finger. It slid on easily enough but when she held up her hand, the diamond flipped around her finger.

"Looks a little big to me," Gina pointed out.

Stevens laughed. "Maybe it's not a Cinderella tale after all but Goldilocks. Too big, too small—I wonder who would fit it just right?"

Monica was up early the next morning to do some baking. But first, of course, Mittens needed to be fed. The kitten waited patiently by her bowl as Monica got her food from the cupboard. She occasionally emitted a soft meow as if to say *Hurry up, please, I'm hungry.* Monica filled the dish and stepped back. Mittens approached her replenished food slowly, gave it a sniff and pranced off with her tail in the air. Monica sighed but knew Mittens would be back later to eat.

Monica was working on perfecting a new concoction for the farm store—a cranberry, raisin and pecan bread. When she'd owned her own café, she'd loved experimenting with new recipes, and she hoped to continue. Her dough, which was in a blue-and-white-striped bowl and covered with a white cloth, was sitting on the counter. Monica lifted the dish towel and peered inside. The mound of dough was plump and airy looking, and a delicious yeasty aroma rose from the bowl.

Monica gently punched down the dough, letting her fist sink into its soft interior. She watched as it slowly deflated. Punching down the dough was not as harsh as it sounded—it helped release some of the gas bubbles formed by the yeast during rising and produced a finer grain.

Monica upended the bowl onto the countertop dusted with flour. She enjoyed kneading—the feeling of the dough becoming more and more elastic under her hands. Finally she shaped it into loaf form, put it in a pan and slid it into the hot oven.

Monica was wiping down the counter when the back door opened, letting in a gust of cold air.

"Hey, sis," Jeff said, unceremoniously taking a seat at the kitchen table. "What smells so good?"

"Cranberry, raisin and pecan bread. It's a new experiment." Monica hesitated with her hand on the handle of the coffeepot. "Coffee?"

"Sure." Jeff yawned widely as if to punctuate his need for a good dose of caffeine.

Monica poured herself a cup and joined her brother at the table.

"Are you done sanding the bogs?"

"Yes. Got the last of it done yesterday. Now it's on to all the other winter chores."

Monica looked at him curiously.

"There's never a dull moment on a cranberry farm." Jeff smiled. "Winter is the perfect time for repairing equipment, performing routine maintenance, stuff we don't have time for the rest of the year."

"It's a lot of work."

Jeff scratched his head. "Sure is. But I wouldn't have it any other way." His expression became serious. "If I have any chance at all with Lauren, I've got to make the farm a success. I can't afford to have two strikes against me." He gestured with his chin toward his injured arm.

Jeff had finally agreed to get counseling to come to grips with his injury and the things he'd seen while stationed in Afghanistan, but Monica realized it was going to take quite a bit more time before he was completely ready to move past it and let go.

"I don't think Lauren's after your money," Monica said, trying to lighten the mood.

Jeff laughed. "That's one thing that's for sure. Even if I do make a success of Sassamanash Farm, it's not exactly going to be a life of luxury." He ran his finger around the rim of his coffee cup, making it squeak. It was something Monica had shown him how to do when he was a little boy. He looked up at Monica. "Did I tell you about Lauren's interview?"

"No." Monica felt a sinking feeling in the pit of her stomach.

"In Chicago." Jeff grimaced. "She says she's not interested in the job but the company recruited her at some campus job fair."

"And she's going?"

"I told her she'd better. I don't want her settling for life here in Cranberry Cove always wondering *what if.*"

"What if she gets the job and decides to move to Chicago?"

Jeff grimaced and looked down at his feet. "I'll have to accept it. Better that than always worrying that she felt she'd settled when she could have had something . . . something bigger in life."

The oven timer pinged and Monica jumped up to check on her loaf of bread. She pulled it from the oven—it was golden brown on the outside and dotted with cranberries and raisins. The smell was ambrosial.

"Hey, sis," Jeff said, giving her a cheeky grin. "Do you need someone to sample that for you?"

"Let it cool for a few minutes," Monica said, turning the loaf out onto a wire rack.

"Maybe you can bring me a piece later." He looked at his watch. "I've got to get going." He gave Monica a sheepish grin. "But I do have a huge favor to ask if you don't mind."

"Of course. What is it?"

Jeff dug a hand into his pocket and pulled out a piece of metal that Monica assumed was some sort of bolt.

"One of the water reels broke down—fortunately we were almost done with the harvest when it happened. Keith is helping me repair it, and he says we need five more of these." He twirled the bolt in front of Monica. "They ought to have them at the hardware store. I'd go myself but," he glanced down at his work clothes, "I'm not fit for human consumption at the moment. I don't think even Gus would let me into the diner like this and that place is hardly white tie and tails."

Monica glanced at Jeff's worn and grimy overalls and the grease and dirt that created a line under his fingernails.

"I think I have to agree with you. I'd be glad to run into town and pick them up for you. If I show the clerk that . . . thing," she pointed at the piece of metal in the palm of Jeff's hand, "will he be able to tell me where to find them?"

"Sure." Jeff tossed the bolt to Monica. "I really appreciate it, sis."

• • •

Monica finished cleaning up the kitchen, played with Mittens until the kitten became bored with laser tag and went off in search of a sunbeam, then left a note for her mother that she was going out.

The Focus didn't want to start at first, and Monica could feel sweat breaking out around her collar. She didn't have the money for a new car at the moment—she didn't even have enough money for a garage bill more expensive than an oil change. Fortunately the car started on the fourth try, and Monica was soon headed toward downtown Cranberry Cove.

She found a space right in front of Bart's Butcher shop, which was sandwiched between the hardware store and Book 'Em. Monica headed toward the hardware store, jingling the bolt Jeff had given her in her pocket as if it was a worry stone, the tip of her index finger tracing the round hole in the center. Bart waved to her as she went past his window, where a tempting crown roast of pork held pride of place.

An older man waited on Monica in the hardware store. He wore a heavy-duty apron with pockets along the front that held a ruler and a tape measure. With brusque efficiency he herded her down the store's middle aisle, finally stopping in front of a large plastic box that housed at least a dozen drawers. Peering over the tops of his glasses, his bushy gray eyebrows drawn together, he selected the five bolts Jeff had sent Monica into town to get.

He slipped them into a small brown paper bag and, with a stubby yellow pencil desperately in need of sharpening, wrote out a sales check and handed both to

Monica. Monica thanked him and headed toward the front of the store.

"Hey, Ralph," the woman behind the checkout counter yelled, and the salesman who had waited on Monica spun around, an expectant look on his face. "Can you bring this lady a pack of finishing nails?" She indicated a woman who had a number of purchases spread out on the counter by the register.

The clerk loped off and Monica got in line. Fortunately the woman at the register wasn't the same one who'd been there the day Monica had gone in asking about Roger Tripp. She was older and carried an air of authority about her that suggested to Monica she might be one of the owners.

The two women chatted while they waited for Ralph to come back with the packet of finishing nails the woman wanted.

Monica found herself thinking about Jeff and Lauren—would Jeff be able to handle it if Lauren decided to take that job in Chicago? She'd made such a difference in Jeff in such a short time—when Jeff had returned from Afghanistan his eyes were perpetually shadowed, his shoulders slumped and his attitude bitter. Lauren had brought the humor out in him again and had given him a more positive outlook on life. Monica hoped that wouldn't all drain away if she left.

A few words of the women's conversation drifted toward Monica and caught her attention—specifically a name: Preston Crowley. That made Monica stand up and take notice. She leaned in and began to listen more carefully.

"I heard he took up with several women at once," the customer said in a tone that left no doubt as to her disapproval. She was wearing baggy, high-waisted jeans and had her graying hair cut short—the kind of cut that women always talked about as being a *wash and go* style.

"I know I've seen him with that gal who runs that smelly place next door—the one with all those oils."

"Making Scents?" the cashier asked.

"That's the one." The customer nodded, her chin nearly disappearing into the folds of her neck. "And I heard talk of there being someone from out of town as well."

"And just between you and me," the woman behind the register lowered her voice and Monica quickly pretended to be interested in the screen of her cell phone, "I've seen him going in and out of that new jewelry shop—whatever the heck it's called."

"Bijou," the customer said. "Maybe he was buying something?"

The clerk raised her eyebrows suggestively. "I don't think so. Bob took me to the Cranberry Cove Inn last month—it was our fiftieth, and believe you me, I never thought we'd make it that long what with some of the things he's done—and there was Preston Crowley, entertaining that woman who owns the jewelry store. She sure looked fancy—made me wish I'd bought a new dress for the occasion. But what on earth would I do with it after?"

"Really? I heard she comes from down south somewhere—Mississippi or Alabama or one of them places. She sure sounds like it."

"Yeah. Reminds me of Dolly Parton. I always did like her records."

By now Ralph had returned with the packet of finishing nails he'd been sent for, and the customer paid for her purchases and left.

Monica rather absentmindedly plunked down a couple

of bills for the bolts and left with the bag tucked securely into her jacket pocket. If what the clerk had said was true, Crowley was even more of a ladies' man than they'd originally imagined.

Monica was headed toward her car when the door to Book 'Em opened and Greg walked out. He was coatless and his shoulders were hunched against the cold. He stopped when he saw Monica.

"I'm going for a late breakfast at the diner. Do you have time to join me?"

"I've already eaten, but I wouldn't mind a cup of coffee."

Monica followed as Greg hurried toward the diner, shivering, and pulled open the door.

Monica was shocked to see that Gus was not at his usual post behind the grill, orchestrating the cooking of half a dozen items at once. In his place was a young man in a short-sleeved black T-shirt with tattoos on both prominent biceps.

"I wonder where Gus is," Greg said as they slipped into an unoccupied booth. "He's here tending to the grill every time I've come in, no matter what or when. I hope nothing's happened to him."

The waitress slapped a couple of plastic menus down on their table and was about to turn away when Greg stopped her.

"Where's Gus? Is he okay?"

The woman shrugged. "So far as I know. Billy's filling in for him this morning. Someone said Gus is getting married, but I don't believe it."

Before Greg or Monica could ask any more questions she was off, another half dozen menus tucked under her arm and a steaming coffeepot in her hand.

"Married! Well if that doesn't beat all," Greg said as he pushed his menu to the side. "I guess I've never known much of anything about Gus. He was just . . . Gus. Always here, always frying potatoes and flipping burgers. I never thought about whether he was married or had a family."

In a way, Monica had been as anonymous as that in Chicago—the lady behind the counter serving her customers daily with coffee and fresh baked goods, not knowing anything about them and them not knowing anything about her. Everybody in Cranberry Cove might be aware of your business—if not right away then soon enough—and she was discovering she rather liked it. The customers that came into the farm shop spent time talking to whoever was behind the counter, sharing news, giving their opinions and spreading a little gossip.

Monica fiddled with the edge of her napkin. "I found out something interesting about Preston Crowley today." She paused for a moment. "Although maybe you already know."

Greg raised an eyebrow. "What's that?"

"It seems that he and Jacy Belair, the woman who owns Bijou, were something of an item."

Greg nodded and smiled at the waitress as she held the pot of coffee over his cup.

"Jacy and Preston?"

Monica nodded and signaled to the waitress to pour her some coffee as well. She waited until the woman turned away and headed toward the booth behind them, then leaned across the table.

"The police found a diamond solitaire ring in Preston's pocket and a receipt from Bijou." She laughed. "Both my mother and Gina are convinced it was for them." Monica reached for a packet of sugar and stirred it into her coffee. "But maybe it was actually for Jacy?"

Greg frowned as he stirred his coffee. "But it would hardly be a surprise then, would it?" He was quiet for a moment. "But maybe it wasn't meant to be."

"What do you mean?"

"Maybe the ring wasn't for Jacy. Or maybe Crowley changed his mind." Greg put an index finger on his menu and spun it around and around. "I remember seeing Crowley the day before the Winter Walk opening. I was putting some salt down on the sidewalk outside Book 'Em. He was standing at the counter inside Bijou with Jacy on the other side. Obviously I couldn't hear anything they were saying, but I could see them well enough and Crowley was making heated gestures—at one point I even saw him pounding the counter."

By now the waitress had reappeared at their table with her order pad in hand.

Greg handed back their menus, and the waitress stuck them under her arm. "I'll have the farmer's breakfast," he said. "Eggs over easy, and can I have whole wheat toast with that?"

The waitress grunted, made a note on her pad and headed toward the grill.

Greg waited until she was several feet away before continuing. "I couldn't see Jacy's reaction, but all of a sudden, Crowley stormed out of the shop, slamming the door so hard I could hear it bang all the way across the street.

"He was obviously furious about something." Greg tore

open a packet of sugar and added it to his coffee. "He crossed the street—not even looking, but fortunately no cars were coming. I was standing near the curb spreading the salt, and he slammed right into me. Then he glared at me like it was my fault."

"Lover's quarrel?" Monica blew on her coffee. Steam was still rising from the thick, white mug.

"If they were an item like you said, that seems likely, doesn't it?"

"Either they had an argument and she told him to keep the ring or she found out about the other women—"

"With the same result. The ring ended up back in his pocket."

Chapter 21

It was snowing lightly when Monica and Greg left the diner. They hesitated on the sidewalk outside for a moment before Greg leaned forward and gave Monica a brief kiss.

She felt a warm glow as she walked toward her car. It wasn't as if she'd never been kissed before, she reminded herself. But this felt *right* somehow. She whistled as she started up the Focus—which obligingly turned over on the first try—and backed out of her space.

It occurred to her that her mother had cooked her some very nice meals and perhaps she ought to reciprocate. She put on her blinker and headed to the gourmet store that was in the strip mall on the highway to buy some provisions.

Women choked the aisles of Fresh Gourmet when Monica got there. She eyed their carts with awe and a bit of envy. They all obviously knew more about cooking than she did. She knew her way around an oven and could whip up a baked good as easily as some people opened a can, but she'd not done much cooking beyond throwing a steak under the broiler and fixing a salad.

When she'd lived in Chicago, she and Ted had usually grabbed takeout—sushi, Thai food or something equally exotic. After baking for her café, the last thing Monica had wanted to do was to spend more time standing in the kitchen.

The fish counter had some lovely ruby-red, wild-caught salmon fillets. Monica asked for half a pound, and tossed the paper-wrapped bundle into her cart. She would make a dill sauce to go with it.

She found fresh dill in the produce section and added that to her cart. There were some lovely fingerling potatoes that ought to go well with the fish, and she selected an appropriate amount of those along with two handfuls of fresh green beans. All they would need would be a pat or two of butter.

As Monica cruised down the dairy aisle, a cloth-bedecked table caught her eye. She wheeled her cart closer. Small containers held an assortment of jams and jellies and there was a basket filled with crackers as well. Monica put a dab of lime curd on a cracker and popped it into her mouth. Suddenly, she stopped mid-chew.

Why not do the same thing at the farm store? There was an unused round table in the processing room that she could cover with one of the cranberry-printed cloths. She could set out samples of her cranberry salsa, along with her homemade jams and jellies.

She spun around and headed toward the cracker aisle, where she flung several boxes of water biscuits into her cart. She'd eventually have to find a cheaper option—

some way to buy in bulk—but for the moment these would do.

Feeling as if she'd accomplished something extraordinary, Monica loaded her purchases into her car and headed back toward Cranberry Cove. She could see Lake Michigan in the distance—a thin strip of blue capped with frothy splashes of white. From this distance it looked as if the hovering dark clouds were mere inches from the water. The roads were dusted with a sprinkling of snow, but Monica had no trouble negotiating the route back home. Nonetheless, she was glad when she pulled into her own driveway.

Mittens was waiting at the door and stalked Monica as she emptied her grocery bags and stashed her purchases. Nancy was in the living room reading, and said she was fine when Monica offered a cup of tea, insisting she could make her own.

Monica headed back out the door, swinging the plastic bag with the crackers she'd bought. She was excited to put her new idea into play.

A man and woman were leaving the store when Monica got there. They were dressed in expensive down parkas, and the woman had a silk scarf tied at her throat.

"Hey," Nora said when Monica walked in.

"Looks like we've had some customers." Monica tilted her head toward the door and the couple who had just left.

"Yes," Nora said, pushing her round glasses up the bridge of her nose with her index finger. "They're from out of town. They were quite disappointed to discover that the Winter Walk was over. I told them to watch for it next year. Howard—he's in my husband's golf league and is on the city council—said the town is very interested in repeating the event."

Nora wiped a smudge off the counter with the edge of her apron.

"We've had our share of customers so far today." Nora gestured toward the bakery case. "Your cranberry coffee cake is all gone, and there's only one scone left."

"And I've just had the greatest idea."

Nora looked on quizzically as Monica unloaded the boxes of crackers from her shopping bag.

"What are those for?" Nora leaned her elbows on the counter.

"I thought we'd set up a table with samples of our salsa and jams and jellies. Maybe even bites of our coffee cake and other baked goods."

"That's a great idea! Once people get a taste, they'll be hooked."

Monica dragged a round table that had been pushed against the wall into a more prominent position and removed the smattering of objects that had accumulated on top.

"Hand me one of those tablecloths, would you?" She pointed to the shelf behind the counter.

Nora handed her a white cloth printed with cranberries. Monica shook it out and spread it over the table.

"We need something to put the crackers in." Monica looked around the shop. She spied a basket hanging from a hook in the ceiling.

"Here." Nora pulled a chair out from behind the counter. "Stand on this."

Monica perched on the chair while Nora held it steady. She could just reach the basket with her fingertips, but with some teasing, she managed to get it off the hook. She let it drop to the floor.

While Nora put the chair away, Monica unfurled two napkins and layered them inside the basket. Then she ripped the plastic wrap off the boxes of crackers and emptied them into the basket.

She stood back to study the effect. Perfect. Now for the samples. She grabbed a container of salsa from the cooler, along with several jars of jam—cranberry orange, cranberry pepper, and cran-apple. She started to open the jars then realized she hadn't put on her apron. With her luck, she'd end up with red speckles all over her white turtleneck.

Monica grabbed her apron from the hook by the counter and slipped it on. She opened the jars and set them out around the basket.

"What do you think?" She turned to Nora.

"It's just what the shop needed." Nora's eyes glowed. She was almost as dedicated to the Sassamanash Farm store as Monica was.

"Now for some spoons . . ." Monica put a finger to her lips while she thought. "We have a box of plastic ones somewhere." She rummaged around behind the counter and finally found the box she was looking for.

The top of the box was a bit dusty, so Monica dashed at it with a paper towel. The dust got up her nose and made her sneeze. She reached into the pocket of her apron, where she almost always had a tissue or two.

Something poked her, and she withdrew her hand abruptly. She'd pricked her index finger on something—a small droplet of blood was forming on top as she watched.

What on earth had she stuffed in her pocket? She

certainly wouldn't have put anything sharp in it. She reached back in—more carefully this time, and managed to extract the object without poking herself again.

She held it in the palm of her hand and examined it. It was a tiny doll—rather crude—made of cloth with tiny beads representing its eyes, nose and mouth. A handful of red feathers sprouted from the top of its head. And right where its heart would be, a long straight pin was stuck deep into its chest.

"What is that?" Nora pushed up her glasses and peered at the object in Monica's hand.

"I don't know." Monica's voice quavered. "It looks like—"

"A voodoo doll."

Monica stifled a scream and dropped the doll on the floor.

Chapter 22

Monica and Nora stood stock-still, staring at the bit of cloth and feathers that Monica had dropped on the floor.

"Someone must have slipped that into my apron pocket when no one was looking."

"But why?" Nora poked at the doll with the toe of her shoe. "Who would do something like that?" She turned to Monica with a worried look on her face. "It's meant to be bad luck, isn't it?" Her eyes were huge behind her round glasses. "I've heard that people can . . . can die from the spell it casts."

At first Monica couldn't imagine who would have done such a thing, but realization dawned on her with the force of a punch to the stomach. It had to have been the murderer. She must have touched a nerve, and he or she was trying to scare her off.

She started to shiver. "I think you have to believe in it for it to be effective." She knew she'd read that somewhere, and she devoutly hoped it was true. Because she didn't believe in voodoo—not one single bit.

Nora looked at her in alarm. "Are you okay?"

"Yes. It's the shock. I'll be fine." She plopped down on the wooden bench by the door to the shop—a spot where bored husbands usually sat while their wives looked around. She looked at Nora. "Can you remember who stopped by today? Anyone familiar?"

Nora wrinkled her nose. "There was Brenda Hyder—her son is in my son's class." Nora rolled her eyes. "He's something of the class troublemaker from what I've heard." Nora took off her glasses and polished them with her apron. "One woman reeked of perfume—it made me sneeze—and she wore all these bracelets that tinkled together when she moved her arm. Then there was this terribly thin woman—she smelled of cigarettes and that was almost worse. I didn't think anyone still smoked these days."

None of the descriptions rang a bell with Monica.

"And that couple from out of town, of course." Nora wrinkled her forehead. "Others as well . . . but no one stands out particularly. Sorry."

Monica waved a hand. "That's fine."

The doll was still on the floor. Nora poked it with her toe again.

"What should we do with it?" She shuddered. "I don't even want to touch it."

"I'm going to show it to Detective Stevens." Monica gingerly picked the doll up by its foot.

"You think it has something to do with Preston Crowley's murder?"

"I don't know. It could be someone pulling a prank—

some kid who thought it would be funny. But I don't think that seems very likely, do you?"

Nora shook her head. "No, I'm afraid not." She pointed at the doll. "Do you want something to wrap that in? I have a clean handkerchief in my purse."

"I don't think the police will be able to get any fingerprints off of it," Monica said.

"True, but I don't want you to prick yourself with that pin again." Nora retrieved her purse from behind the counter, opened it and handed Monica a plain white handkerchief.

Monica wrapped the voodoo doll in it carefully and placed it on the counter. She pulled her cell phone from the pocket of her jeans and dialed the police station. The dispatcher promised to send someone around as soon as possible.

Monica heard the sound of a car's engine and glanced out the window. The car pulled into a space, and a young couple got out.

They wandered around the shop, and Monica was pleased when, after sampling some of her jellies and salsa, they purchased several jars to take home.

They were leaving when Monica heard the sound of another car. The door opened and Detective Stevens walked in. "Long time, no see," she said as she pulled off her gloves and blew on her chapped and reddened hands.

"I'll be glad when this winter is over," she said unwinding her scarf and loosening her coat. "Getting the baby ready to go out in this weather takes an eternity. I can't wait until I can walk outside with him in his onesie with bare feet." She smiled. "He definitely doesn't like socks—kicks them off every time I put them on him."

Nora smiled back. "Try getting him a pair of soft booties with laces. Even though it will take a few minutes to
get them on, he won't be able to take them off and you'll
save time in the long run."

"Thanks, I'll try that." Stevens pulled a notepad and
pen from the pocket of her coat. "Do you want to show
me what you found?"

Monica led her over to the counter, where the voodoo
doll lay wrapped in Nora's handkerchief. She slowly peeled
back the fabric and stood back so Stevens could examine
the doll.

Stevens rolled the doll over with the tip of her pen. "Not
much of a chance of fingerprints, but it's best to be cautious." She pulled her camera from her other pocket and
took several photographs of the doll—front and back.

She put her camera away and turned to Monica. "You
found this where?"

Monica stuck her hand in her apron's pocket. "In here.
I was looking for a tissue and pricked my finger on that."
She pointed to the pin protruding from the doll's chest.

"Where do you normally keep your apron?"

Monica led her over to the hook in the wall next to the
counter.

Stevens looked around. "So if someone wanted to access
your apron, they wouldn't have to go behind the counter."
She looked from Nora to Monica. "If someone went behind
the counter, I'm sure you would have noticed."

Nora turned slightly red. "I did leave the counter for a
moment." She glanced at Monica apologetically. "To use
the *ladies' room*." She whispered the last two words.

Stevens looked surprised. "You were alone in the shop?"

"We don't worry too much about shoplifting," Monica explained. "It's never been a real problem."

Stevens nodded. "Fortunately for all of us, Cranberry Cove is hardly a hotbed of crime." She made a face. "Except for these murders, of course. And the one last fall. Let's hope that doesn't become a pattern. Was anyone in the shop when you came back out of the ladies' room?"

Nora squeezed her eyes shut. "I think so. A couple of people maybe."

"Can you remember what they looked like?"

"I think there was a couple wearing fancy parkas . . . no, wait, that was later." She shrugged. "People come and go all day. I'm afraid I don't pay much attention—except to provide customer service, of course."

Stevens gave one last look at the doll, touching the pin with the tip of her ballpoint. "Do you have any idea why someone would put this in your apron pocket?"

Monica hesitated. "I don't know. My first thought was that it was a prank of some sort."

"And your second thought?" Stevens asked with a wry smile.

"That someone is trying to scare me."

Stevens tilted her head. "Do you have any idea why someone would do that—try to scare you?"

"I don't know," Monica said. "Maybe they think I know something . . . something I don't even realize I know."

Stevens tapped her pen against the counter. "I don't like this." She shook her head. "If someone is trying to scare you, who's to say they'll stop at this?" She nudged the doll.

Suddenly the import of what had happened hit Monica full force. What would the killer do next?

Stevens scratched her head. "Where would you get a voodoo doll anyway?" She snapped her fingers. "Maybe that shop—Twilight. The one Tempest Storm owns. That knife was from her shop, too."

"I don't think Tempest would carry something like a voodoo doll. That's not the sort of thing she's into at all. Besides, there are other people who had a reason to hate Preston. Roger Tripp, for instance. Preston held up the permit on his restaurant so it couldn't open in time for the Winter Walk. Preston didn't want any competition for his restaurant at the Cranberry Cove Inn. Or . . . or Jacy Belair. Greg Harper saw her and Preston arguing quite heatedly."

Stevens looked doubtful. "Still I'll send someone around to check."

She folded the handkerchief back around the doll and carefully slipped it into a plastic evidence bag she pulled from her purse. She turned to Monica, her expression serious. "If anything suspicious happens—anything at all—call nine-one-one immediately. If it turns out to be nothing—great. But if it doesn't, I want someone on the spot as quickly as possible."

Stevens placed the evidence bag with the doll in her purse and began to do up her coat again and rewind her scarf.

She had her hand on the door when she turned around suddenly. "Please be careful. Don't be a hero, okay?"

Stevens left, and after checking that Nora could handle things, Monica went home. She spent several long minutes sitting on the couch in her living room, staring at the wall. She had to admit she was scared—the voodoo doll had frightened her, but Stevens's words had scared her even more. The killer must have gotten wind of her snooping and obviously suspected she knew something—but what?

"You must be starving." Nancy's voice startled her, and she spun around. Monica hadn't heard her come down the stairs. "Or did you get lunch in town?"

Monica shook her head. She was starving, she realized suddenly. She followed her mother out to the kitchen, where she opened the refrigerator and stared at the contents. Nothing appealed to her. She closed the door, turned around and noticed the cranberry raisin and pecan bread she'd made that morning but hadn't yet sampled. She'd toast a piece of that and have it along with a dab of cranberry orange preserves and a boiled egg.

"Would you like to try a piece of bread? It's a new recipe I've concocted."

"Thank you, dear, that would be lovely."

Monica put a pan of water on the stove to boil and retrieved an egg from the refrigerator. She'd been looking into keeping a few chickens and thought she might start when summer came. They could sell the fresh eggs at the farm store.

While Monica waited for the bread to toast and her egg to cook, she thought of telling her mother about the voodoo doll but decided against it. Nancy would worry and what good would that do?

Monica put a slice of bread on each of two plates and set them on the table, then got the butter dish and a jar of cranberry orange preserves from the fridge.

She took a bite of the bread before buttering it and rolled it around in her mouth, testing the flavor and texture. It was quite good. The sweetness of the raisins counteracted the tartness of the cranberries and the pecans added a nice crunch.

"What do you think?" Monica asked Nancy as she added butter and preserves to the rest of her slice.

Nancy nibbled on the end, closing her eyes as she analyzed the taste.

"Delicious," she said finally, opening her eyes. "Really excellent. You've turned into a spectacular baker!" She tapped her plate with her index finger. "People are going to come to Cranberry Cove just to get a taste of your wonderful treats."

Monica tried to hide the glow of satisfaction she felt. She was proud of her baking skills. Now if only her sleuthing skills were as good.

Chapter 23

As Monica cleared away the dishes after they'd finished their bread, she thought about Crowley's murder. She wished there was someone she could bounce ideas off of—sort of like a modern day Sherlock Holmes and Watson. Although she suspected she was more Watson than Sherlock.

She was wiping down the counter when the thought came to her—she'd talk to Greg. He was smart, observant, analytical, and he knew his way around a mystery.

Monica finished cleaning up the kitchen, called to her mother that she was going out and quickly headed back into town. The roads were slipperier than they had been earlier, and Monica mentally crossed her fingers as the Focus churned its way up the hill between Sassamanash Farm and Cranberry Cove.

The downside of the hill was a bit like an amusement ride, with her little car skidding and slipping and sliding.

But ultimately she made it to the bottom of the hill and back onto flat ground.

Beach Hollow Road was nearly deserted when Monica got there. There were two cars parked in front of the diner—one in front of the drugstore, one in front of the hardware store—and the rest of the spaces were empty. She pulled into a spot right in front of Book 'Em, grateful that she didn't have to brave the snow and wind, both of which had picked up in the last hour, for more than a few feet.

Book 'Em was empty when Monica pushed open the door, but Greg soon came out from the back room, drying his hands on a paper towel.

"What a pleasant surprise. I was considering closing since all my customers seem to have been frightened away by the snow." He squeezed Monica's arm and gave her a light kiss. "What brings you out in such foul weather? Of course I always suspected you were the intrepid sort."

"It's Crowley's murder."

"Have there been some new developments?" Greg tossed his paper towel into a nearby trashcan.

"Yes, and I'd like your thoughts on what I've learned so far."

"You're playing at being Miss Marple, aren't you?" Greg teased. "Although you're far too young and pretty for that part . . . Nora Charles, maybe?" He grinned. "I hope that means I get to play Nick."

Monica did her best to stem the blush she could feel rising from her neck to her face. Sadly, her attempt was an abysmal failure, and she knew she was as red as one of the cherry lollipops the VanVelsens sold in Gumdrops.

"Come on. Let's make ourselves a cup of tea." Greg stopped. "Or, would you prefer coffee?"

"Tea would be wonderful."

Monica followed him into the back room. While he fiddled with the tea things, she tried to organize her thoughts so she could present everything in as logical a fashion as possible.

Greg heated water in two mugs in the microwave and dug tea bags out of a very cluttered cupboard. When the microwave dinged, he retrieved the cups and plopped in the tea bags. He handed one of the mugs to Monica and stirred some sugar into the other one for himself.

"Let's go sit down."

He led Monica to the corner of the bookshop and a worn brown corduroy sofa that was sagging in the middle. Monica sat down and suddenly felt as if she were falling down a hole—the ancient cushions having been reduced to little more than bare springs.

"One minute," Greg said, jumping up and heading toward the cashier's desk, where he retrieved a yellow legal pad and a pen. "We can make a list of everything that's relevant," he said as he plunked down on the opposite side of the sofa, sending a tidal wave of undulating cushions over to where Monica was sitting.

He put his mug on the floor, then held his pen poised above the pad. "Okay, what do we already know?"

Monica thought for a moment. "Ryan was lured away from the horse and sleigh with a note from his former girlfriend, Candy. She wanted him to meet her in the gazebo."

"And why is that significant?" Greg raised his rather shaggy eyebrows.

"Her landlady said that Candy suddenly came into money but at the same time she began acting as if she was frightened of something . . . or someone."

Greg scribbled some notes on his pad. "Could someone have paid Candy to lure Ryan from the scene?"

"Yes, I think that's possible—probable even, given that she came into some money. And she was scared. I gather Candy wasn't all that smart but she must have had enough native intelligence—or survival instinct—to realize that she was in danger from the killer, given what she knew."

"What else?" Greg retrieved his mug from the floor and took a sip.

"The killer is female. Unless they hatched some incredibly complicated plan to throw everyone off the track."

"And what makes you think that?" Greg held his pen poised above his pad.

"Tempest found a very unique button on the floor of her shop. It obviously came from a woman's garment." Monica ticked the items off on her fingers. "And a coat—again, a woman's—was found buried in the sand pile at Sassamanash Farms. The police have sent it to be analyzed, but it looked as if there was blood on the front of it."

"I didn't know that," Greg said as he scribbled more notes.

"And the buttons on the coat matched the one found in Tempest's shop. I think the killer lost it when she stole the athame from Twilight."

Greg tapped his pen against the pad. "Quite likely," he murmured.

The cushions on the worn and rickety old sofa canted toward the center, and Monica eventually found herself thigh-to-thigh with Greg. The warmth was very pleasing, and she found herself relaxing for the first time in a long time.

"Anything else?"

Monica hesitated. She hadn't told her mother about the voodoo doll. Should she tell Greg? But Greg wasn't her mother—he was grounded, down-to-earth and not likely to panic.

"Today at the farm store I found a voodoo doll had been put in the pocket of my apron."

"What?" Greg bolted upright, sending shock waves through the worn sofa cushions. "I don't like that. I don't like that one bit." He turned to Monica and took her hands in his. "Promise me you'll be careful? We're dealing with a murderer who has killed twice already. She won't hesitate to kill again if she feels threatened."

Monica felt a chill wash over her despite the warmth of Greg's hands. He was right. What Monica was doing could be dangerous—very dangerous indeed.

She would just have to be more careful from now on.

Monica was headed toward her car when she noticed Jacy summoning her from the window of Bijou. Monica crossed the street and entered the shop.

"Hi, there," Jacy said. "I was wondering about those amber beads. I can't get over how good they looked on you." She smiled, reached into the counter and pulled out the necklace.

Monica looked at it longingly. "I do love them," she admitted. "And maybe soon . . ."

"Sure." Jacy replaced the beads. She glanced out the window. "Cold out there?"

"Yes, although the snow has stopped. I don't know about you, but I'm ready for spring."

"Heavens, yes," Jacy said. "And me without a winter

coat—just this old corduroy jacket that's nowhere near warm enough. I suppose I'm going to have to find the time to make a trip to that mall over near Grand Rapids. The good news is all the winter things will be on sale." She frowned. "I'd love to get my hands on the thief who took off with my coat."

"Your coat was stolen?"

"Yes. Can you believe it? I was dying to get out of the shop so I went down to the diner for a bite to eat. You know those hooks by the front door where everyone hangs their coats and things?"

Monica nodded.

"I hung my coat on one of those. The only seat available was a stool at the counter so I could hardly keep my coat with me. When I went to get it, it was . . . gone." Jacy snapped her fingers. "I thought maybe somebody put their coat over mine, but no, it was missing—someone had taken it." She let out an explosive sigh. "I gave the staff a piece of my mind, believe me."

"Maybe someone mistook it for their coat. . . ."

Jacy shook her head. "Not likely. I've never seen anyone in town with one like it. It was cream colored with these really pretty buttons."

Monica felt her heart speed up. "Buttons?"

"Yes. They were really unique—crystal, in the shape of a flower with dark red stones all around."

Monica felt her jaw drop and quickly shut her mouth. The coat Jacy was describing was the one found in the sand pile out at the farm—the one with blood on it that Crowley's killer apparently wore.

If Jacy was telling the truth and her coat had been stolen, that meant the killer could have been anybody . . . including a man. Including Roger Tripp.

• • •

Monica nearly collided with a fellow in work boots and a heavy parka as she left Bijou.

"Sorry."

He grunted in return.

Monica was thinking furiously. Was Jacy telling the truth? Or was she trying to cover up for the fact that she was the killer? As far as Monica knew, Jacy had no reason to hate Crowley. Greg had seen them arguing, but that didn't mean it was anything serious. People argued all the time without resorting to killing each other.

Monica was headed toward her car when she turned on her heel and began walking toward the diner. If someone could corroborate Jacy's story, that would put her in the clear. And if, as Jacy had said, she'd given the staff a piece of her mind, everyone at the diner was bound to remember it.

Chapter 24

The diner was nearly empty when Monica got there. A lone customer was sitting at the counter nursing a cup of coffee. The waitress stood in front of him on the other side, her elbows resting on the counter, chatting. Gus was scraping down the grill and looked up, his eyebrows drawn together, when Monica walked in. It would be like Gus to get married in the morning and then show up for work in the afternoon.

In the nearly six months Monica had been living in Cranberry Cove, she'd never exchanged a word with Gus—not good morning or good afternoon or even hello—although Gus did now favor her with a nod when she entered.

Monica approached the grill where Gus was working with an absurd feeling of trepidation—as if she was about to have an audience with the Pope or the Queen of England. Which was absurd. For all anyone knew, Gus was actually shy and needed prompting to talk.

"Good afternoon." Monica thought a simple greeting would be a good start.

Gus grunted.

"Can I ask you a question?"

Another grunt. Monica couldn't tell if it meant yes or no, so she decided to plunge on.

"Jacy Belair who owns Bijou," Monica pointed vaguely in the direction of the jewelry store, "said someone stole her coat from one of the hooks," this time Monica pointed in their direction, "while she was here having lunch."

Gus continued scraping the grill without looking up. And this time he didn't even bother to grunt.

The waitress left her customer and sidled over. Monica remembered when she was new—she'd replaced Cora, who had been an old hand—and how harried she'd been at first. Now she'd become a seasoned pro.

"Are you asking about the time that woman lost her coat?"

"Yes—Jacy, from Bijou. She said someone stole it from here."

The waitress fiddled with the pad in her pocket. "She made a huge stink, that's for sure. All the customers stopped eating and watched like it was some kind of television show—one of those reality shows, you know?"

It seemed to be a rhetorical question so Monica just nodded.

"She really pitched a fit. Claimed she'd gotten the coat from some fancy department store. I don't remember which—it's not like I shop in places like that." She gave a laugh that ended in a rumbling cough. "I'm more the Walmart type myself." She turned to glance at Gus, who was giving her a dirty look. She shrugged. "There was something special about the buttons—I don't remember what exactly—but apparently the plastic ones like I've got on my coat weren't good enough for her."

So Jacy had been telling the truth. Monica thanked the waitress, said good-bye to Gus, who was still bent over the grill, and headed toward her car.

A young man stopped her just as she was about to open her car door. He handed her a photocopied flyer, then continued down the street. It was probably for a free car wash or announcing that a new pizza place had opened up outside of town, Monica thought. The headline caught her eye and she stopped to read it.

The Pepper Pot was having a grand opening the next afternoon and everyone was invited. Drinks and hors d'oeuvres were on the house.

Monica folded the piece of paper, stuck it in her purse and started up her car. Maybe Nancy would want to go— and Gina, too. Perhaps she could even convince Jeff to stop work long enough to join them. And maybe she would ask Greg to go, too, Monica thought, glancing at Book 'Em.

Monica had almost forgotten that she'd promised to make dinner that night. Fortunately salmon didn't take that long to cook, nor did green beans and potatoes.

As soon as Monica got the paper-wrapped piece of salmon out of the refrigerator, Mittens, who had previously been exploring the nether regions of the cottage, shot into the kitchen, simultaneously screeching to a halt at Monica's feet and emitting a loud, warbling and demanding *meow*.

"Don't worry—I'll save you a piece," Monica promised the kitten as she unwrapped the fish.

She was thinking as she scrubbed the fingerling potatoes under running water. It seemed as if Jacy's coat had, indeed, been stolen from the diner. Had Roger Tripp taken it? The coat would not only shield his own clothes from any blood but would also incriminate Jacy. She knew Roger had good reason to hate Crowley, but what did he have against Jacy? Had he stolen her coat on purpose or was it just happenstance that hers was the one he grabbed from the hook in the diner?

Monica cut up the potatoes, drizzled them with olive oil and some chopped garlic, and put them in the oven to roast.

"What smells so good?" Nancy asked several minutes later when she walked into the kitchen.

"Potatoes with olive oil and garlic."

"It smells heavenly." She peered into the pot on the stove. "And green beans, I see."

"To go with the salmon and dill sauce I'm making."

Nancy retrieved placemats, napkins and cutlery from the cupboards and drawers and began to set the table. Ever since her arrival, they'd been using linen napkins and setting the table properly. It was a far cry from eating standing at the counter, Monica thought. She rather enjoyed it.

"I wonder when the police will let me go home," Nancy asked.

She fiddled with her knife while Monica put the salmon under the broiler.

Monica closed the oven door and turned around with her hands on her hips. "I don't know how far along they are in the investigation. I haven't heard anything from Detective Stevens. Maybe that coat they found will provide some clues."

"I hope so. I'm enjoying being with you—we so rarely have time together anymore—but I am getting a little bit . . . bored."

Monica stuck a hand into her purse, which was sitting out on the counter, and pulled out the flyer the fellow had handed her that afternoon. "The Pepper Pot, that new restaurant on Beach Hollow Road, is opening tomorrow, and they're having a launch party. Free drinks and food—the entire town will be there." She handed Nancy the flyer.

"That does sound fun. Are you going?"

"Yes. And I hope you'll join me?"

"I think I will."

Monica was relieved to see Nora behind the counter at the farm store the next morning. She was afraid that the voodoo doll might have scared her off. But fortunately Nora was the no-nonsense sort, and was at work bright and early as usual.

"Are you going to the opening at that new restaurant this afternoon?" she asked as she arranged the baked goods Monica had brought with her.

"Yes, are you?"

Nora laughed. "I don't think so. There's no one to watch the kids, and I can't imagine the havoc they would wreak if let loose in a place like that. Hopefully Rick and I can sneak away for dinner once it's open. Rick's parents—they live just outside of Cleveland—visit a couple of times a year and are happy to watch the kids while we grab some couple time."

Monica was putting the salsa in the cooler when she heard a noise coming from the processing room behind the store. Was Jeff there? She opened the door between the two spaces and stuck her head around the corner.

"Good morning."

Jeff looked up from the machine he was working on— the Bailey separator, a machine that separated the good cranberries from the rotten ones. He was wearing a pair of ripped and stained overalls, his hands were covered with grease and there was a smear of black on his right cheek.

"I thought I heard someone back here."

Jeff smiled. "I'm giving the machinery a bit of a tune-up so we're ready for next year's harvest. The sanding is finished so now I can turn my attention to other things." He grinned. "It's kind of nice to be inside for a change, although I know I'll be coming down with cabin fever by the end of February."

"Have you heard about the big opening splash at the Pepper Pot?"

Jeff wrinkled his brow. "The Pepper Pot?"

"It's that new restaurant in town."

"I'd forgotten about that place." Jeff pushed a lock of hair off his forehead, leaving another smear of grease on his face. "What's up?"

"They're throwing a grand opening with free drinks and hors d'oeuvres this afternoon. Why don't you come? You could bring Lauren—I'm sure she'd enjoy it."

A shadow crossed Jeff's face. "She's in Chicago for that interview."

"Oh." Monica had forgotten about that. She looked at her brother. "You're worried, aren't you?"

He shrugged. "What is that song? *Que sera sera . . .* whatever will be will be. . . .'"

"I don't think you have anything to worry about," Monica said as she let the door close.

Monica spent the morning at the farm store helping Nora serve customers, then headed back to her cottage in plenty of time to freshen up for the afternoon's event.

She dove into the back of her closet where she kept what she thought of as her Chicago clothes—dresses and other outfits she'd worn when going out with Ted. She unearthed a dark green sweaterdress and a pair of suede boots. She was surprised that when she slipped into the dress it was a little loose. She hadn't been aware of losing weight, although she knew she had been working hard.

"Gina's picking us up," Monica said when she found Nancy sitting in the living room, reading.

Nancy was wearing black slacks, a green and blue geometric print silk blouse and pearl studs in her ears. Monica marveled at the fact that her mother's style hadn't changed a bit over the years—the pants may have gotten wider or narrower at the hem according to the style of the day, but other than that, she always looked the perfect lady—stylish but without appearing to be a slave to fashion.

Suddenly a horn blared outside.

"That must be Gina," Nancy said with a little quirk to her lips. "Are you coming with us or is Greg picking you up?"

"We're meeting there. No need for him to come all the way out here to the farm when I can hitch a ride with you."

Monica and Nancy slipped into Gina's Mercedes.

"I thought Jeff was coming," Monica said.

"He's still getting ready. He'll join us there."

Gina backed out of the driveway at full speed, and Monica could see her mother gripping the front passenger seat door handle.

"I have to say, I'm a little worried about Jeffie," Gina said as she ran through a four-way stop without even slowing down. "Lauren is off on some job interview in Chicago, and he's moping around like someone who just lost their last dime in the slot machine in some second-rate Vegas casino."

"I'm sure he's worried for nothing," Monica said, hoping that was true.

"Maybe tonight will cheer him up a bit," Gina said as they idled down Beach Hollow Road.

Parking in downtown Cranberry Cove was at a premium—an unusual event in the middle of the winter. They were passing Book 'Em when Greg came out of the shop and waved them down. He was wearing a corduroy sport coat and knitted tie, and it looked as if he'd slicked his hair down with some sort of product, because for once it wasn't flopping over his forehead.

Gina zapped down her window, and Greg bent over and leaned his elbows on the sill.

"Why don't you get out here, and I'll park your car for you."

"You are a true gentleman," Gina said as Greg held her door open. "Isn't he, ladies?"

Greg opened Monica's door, and when she slid out, he gave her a quick kiss, pressed her hand and whispered, "You look lovely."

She saw her mother raise an eyebrow and give a small smile. A look passed between her and Gina that made Monica suspect they'd been talking about her.

Greg drove away in Gina's Mercedes, and the three women pulled their collars closer and, leaning into the wind that was blowing across the lake, made their way to the Pepper Pot.

The noise of the crowd inside the restaurant was a faint rumble in the distance but grew louder and louder the closer they got. Someone opened the door to the restaurant and the babble of voices intensified as if someone had turned up the volume.

By the time they reached the front door, Monica was shivering. It was partly the cold, but also a strange feeling that something critical was going to happen this afternoon.

Chapter 25

"If this crowd is anything to go by, the restaurant is sure to be a success," Gina said as they slipped out of their coats.

"Free food and drink always attract a crowd," Nancy said as she passed her coat to the girl manning the coat check. "Let's see how many show up when they have to pay for their meal."

Monica looked around. There were a lot of people she'd never seen before but some she recognized as well—several were regulars at the farm store, stopping by on their way to work for their daily fix of cranberry scones or coffee cake. She noticed the VanVelsen sisters, pressed close together by the crowd, which increased the effect of seeing double. They were wearing long velvet skirts, white stock-tie blouses and plaid boiled wool jackets, and Monica was quite sure that the whole ensemble had been taken out of mothballs for the event. They made quite a contrast to Gina's short, skintight dress in a cream knit shot through with gold threads and her over-the-knee black suede boots.

The long wood bar glittered with glasses, bottles of wine and hammered metal tubs filled with ice and cold drinks. Perpendicular to the bar was a cloth-covered table set with hors d'oeuvres. With tantalizing smells emanating from the kitchen, a fire glowing in the stone fireplace and the dark wood and ceiling beams, the Pepper Pot was as cozy as a private home.

Monica made her way through the crowd, conversing briefly with a gentleman who said he was an English teacher at the local high school before moving on when she spied Greg by the front door.

"Did I already tell you that you're looking lovely today?" he asked, giving her a peck on the cheek. "Would you like something to drink?"

Without waiting for an answer, he took Monica's hand and led her over to the bar.

"Quite the selection," he said turning several bottles around so he could read the labels. He tapped one of them. "This is a very nice chardonnay if you'd like white."

"Perfect."

Greg chose two glasses and poured them each a measure of wine. He handed one to Monica and held his up in a toast. *"May you live all of the days of your life."* He smiled. "Jonathan Swift," he said apologetically. He touched Monica's arm lightly. "I don't know about you, but I'm starved. Would you like to get something to eat?"

He led Monica over to the buffet table.

"Everything looks delicious," Monica said, hesitating with her plate in her hand. There were stuffed mushrooms, cold shrimp, mini-quiches, cocktail meatballs and assorted dips. She selected a few things and added them to her plate.

She and Greg were chatting when Nancy came up to them.

"I don't believe we've met." She held out her hand. "I'm Nancy Albertson, Monica's mother."

Greg put his plate down on the table next to them and shook Nancy's hand.

"Greg Harper. I own Book 'Em here in town. We sell both new and used books."

"Monica always did like to read," Nancy said, taking a sip of her wine. "She was constantly walking around with her nose in a book. When the other kids were outside playing, she was devouring Nancy Drew mysteries."

"We have something in common then." Greg smiled at Monica.

Monica hoped Nancy wouldn't reveal anything too embarrassing about her childhood, and was relieved when a rather distinguished-looking gray-haired gentleman came up to Nancy and the two wandered off.

Monica had just finished the nibbles on her plate when a waiter appeared to take the dirty dish away.

"Good service," Greg said. "That bodes well for the restaurant."

Monica set her wineglass down on a table. "If you'll excuse me for a moment . . . ?"

"Certainly. Look for me by the food." Greg jerked a thumb behind him. "I didn't have any lunch today, and I'm still hungry."

Monica laughed and began to wend her way through the crowd toward the restrooms at the back of the restaurant.

The dark wood motif was carried through into the

ladies' room, where the walls were paneled and a white china bowl propped on top of a wooden cabinet substituted for an ordinary sink. A stack of fluffy white hand towels were stacked in a woven straw basket and the bar of hand soap smelled of lavender. The room itself was perfumed, although Monica couldn't tell whether that was a special touch on the part of the restaurant or a cloud of perfume left behind by a previous occupant.

Monica locked the door behind her and approached the stall, which was enclosed in wood panels and had an actual door. The lighting was rather dim but even so, Monica could see there was something sparkling at the bottom of the toilet bowl.

She fumbled in her purse for her cell phone and, using the flashlight feature, shone the beam on the water in the bowl. It looked as if someone had lost an earring. She leaned closer and gasped, nearly dropping her phone in the toilet.

It was the second button missing from Jacy's stolen coat.

Monica shuddered and reached a hand into the water, trying not to squirm in disgust. The water was cold and every time she tried to grab the button, it floated away. She finally got ahold of it and fished it out of the toilet.

She immediately ran hot water in the sink and, using what seemed like half a bar of soap, washed both the button and her hands thoroughly. She slipped the button into the pocket of her dress and returned to the stall briefly. She washed her hands again, checked her lipstick—not that she would be able to touch it up since she'd forgotten the tube in the bathroom at home—and ran a hand through her hair.

The fragrance that had scented the air upon her arrival had dissipated—it must have been someone's perfume lingering in the small space.

Monica left the restroom and was about to go look for Greg when she heard voices coming from an open door down the hall. She tiptoed closer.

"What are you doing here?" Monica heard a masculine voice demand. It sounded like Roger Tripp. The room looked like an office from what she could see through the cracked door.

"I think it would look odd if I was the only person in Cranberry Cove to not show up, don't you think?" a woman drawled.

It was Jacy. Monica was sure of it. She sidled a little closer.

Roger grunted. "Do you have my money? This place isn't going to pay for itself anytime soon."

There was a rustling sound followed by footsteps. Monica moved away quickly, barely daring to breathe until she'd turned the corner and joined the crowd in the restaurant.

Greg was right where he'd said he'd be—by the food. He was holding a plate heaped with hors d'oeuvres. He held it out toward Monica when she joined him.

"Care for something?" He looked at Monica and frowned. "Is everything okay?"

"Yes." Monica glanced around. "Can we go somewhere a little more private? I have to show you something."

They moved into the dining room proper, where half a dozen people—mostly older—sat at the empty tables. Greg steered Monica toward one of them.

"What's up?" he asked as soon as they sat down.

Monica stuck her hand in her pocket and pulled out the crystal and rhinestone button. She placed it on the table.

"This is the second button that was missing from the coat the killer used to cover up with when killing Preston Crowley. I found it dropped in the toilet in the ladies' room." Monica looked around but no one was near them. "It must have fallen off the coat at some point while the killer had it in their possession."

"And maybe they didn't notice it at first. . . ." Greg raised his eyebrows. "They must have found it afterward and realized they needed to get rid of it." Greg laughed. "Just their bad luck to steal a coat with such distinctive buttons."

"If Roger Tripp is the murderer, how easy would it be for him to dispose of the button here at the restaurant? Maybe he thought it had been flushed away." Monica put the button back in her pocket.

"You're a regular Hercule Poirot." Greg smiled. "No, you're better than Hercule Poirot."

"Who is this Hercule . . . what did you say his name was?"

Monica and Greg both jumped at the sound of the voice and spun around to find Jacy standing behind them. She was wearing cream-colored slacks, a cream lace blouse and plenty of jewelry.

Greg gave an abrupt laugh. "He's a detective in Agatha Christie's mystery novels."

"I've never been too keen on reading," Jacy said, fiddling with one of her bracelets. "Maybe I'll try one of those books someday."

"Stop by the store anytime," Greg said. "I'd be glad to help you choose something."

"Great turnout today," Monica said, anxious to change the subject.

How much of their conversation had Jacy overheard? she wondered. The last thing she wanted was for Roger Tripp to get wind of her discovery.

"That was amusing," Nancy said, kicking off her shoes after Gina dropped her and Monica off at Monica's cottage.

Monica stooped down to say hello to Mittens who was acting as if Monica had been gone for days instead of mere hours.

"I met a rather interesting gentleman," Nancy said. "He said he owns a food service distributorship." She laughed. "I thought I'd check him out on the Internet. After Preston, I don't want any more surprises." Nancy sat down in the armchair by the fireplace and rubbed her right foot. "I think I'm getting too old for high heels."

"Do you want to use my computer?"

"Now? Oh, why not. Let's go out to the kitchen. I could do with a cup of tea."

While Monica put the kettle on to boil, Nancy pecked at the computer keys.

"What do you know," she said finally. "It looks like he is legit." She turned the computer around so Monica could see the screen.

"Are you going to see him again?" Monica asked as she put the mugs of tea down on the table.

"Possibly. He said he travels to Chicago on occasion and suggested we have dinner sometime. We'll see what happens."

Nancy was about to close down the computer when Monica had a thought.

"Just leave it for now. There's something I want to look up."

Nancy picked up her mug. "I'm going to take this up with me and lie down for a bit if you don't mind. All those people and the noise have given me a bit of a headache."

"Hope you feel better," Monica said as she sat down in front of her computer, her mug of tea at her elbow.

She brought up her favorite search engine and typed in Jacy Belair's name. Her mother had given her the idea—no one seemed to know much about her, not even the VanVelsen sisters who were the town historians.

Her search brought up a number of entries. It looked as if Jacy was on Facebook, like everyone else these days. There was the announcement in the local paper about the opening of Bijou and another entry from a site that promised to put you in touch with your classmates.

Monica kept scrolling. She had hoped to find something more. She had the feeling that Jacy was somehow at the center of this whole case, although she couldn't exactly say why or in what capacity. Quite possibly she was a victim, because it seemed as if Tripp had stolen Jacy's coat on purpose in order to incriminate her. Did he hate her for some reason?

Monica continued to scroll through the entries her search engine had found until one of them brought her up short. It was an article from the *Times-Picayune* about the death of Parker "Beau" Belair, owner of Café Mondial, a company that imported coffee from all over the world.

Monica's tea grew cold as she read through the article. It seemed that Beau, as the article referred to him, had been married several times, had had a daughter with his second wife, and had ultimately married Jacy Devereaux, a woman nearly forty years his junior. He'd died under somewhat mysterious circumstances, having been in perfect health previously and having just played eighteen holes of golf with his friends before collapsing several hours after arriving back home. The autopsy had been inconclusive, but fingers were pointed at his new wife, who inherited all the money upon his death, which included a stately home in Louisiana and a summer home on the shores of Lake Michigan in Cranberry Cove.

Beau's daughter had died in an unfortunate accident several years earlier, and until he married Jacy, his sole heir had been his grandson.

His grandson just happened to be Roger Tripp.

Chapter 26

Monica involuntarily pushed back from the computer. The information wasn't what she had expected. She picked up her mug, but her tea had grown cold. She got up, stretched and made herself another cup. The wind had intensified and was hammering against the window and creeping around the edges of the old loose panes.

She grabbed a fleece she kept hanging from the coatrack and slipped into it, pulling it close around her. There were more entries listed—most of them from the *Times-Picayune*. She began reading the articles. Some were recaps of Beau Belair's life and career while others focused on the manner of his death. Nothing was said outright, nor was anything ever proven as far as she could tell, but the consensus seemed to be that Beau's young wife Jacy had somehow had a hand in his death.

Monica clicked to the next article, written several months after Beau's death. It seemed that Roger Tripp,

Beau's grandson, was not only contesting the will, but hiring a private investigator to look into his grandfather's death.

It was obvious there was no love lost between Roger and Jacy. But would he go so far as to incriminate her in a murder? Monica leaned back, her warm cup of tea cradled in her hands. Maybe in Roger's mind, he wanted Jacy to pay for what he imagined she had done to his grandfather . . . and for cheating him out of an inheritance he had most likely been counting on.

Monica was turning off her computer when her cell phone rang. As usual, it was at the bottom of her purse, and she was convinced she had missed the call, so she was surprised when someone answered her greeting.

"Monica? This is Detective Stevens. I hope I'm not disturbing you."

"Not at all."

"I thought you would find this funny." Stevens chuckled.

Monica couldn't imagine anything about this murder being even remotely amusing.

"What is that?"

"Do you remember the ring we found in Crowley's pocket on the day he died?"

"Yes. With the receipt from Bijou."

"We'll be looking into Bijou as soon as this case is put to bed. Our dispatcher's father is a jeweler, and she's been around gems her whole life. The diamond looked fishy to her so she had her father take a look. It didn't take him long to figure it out."

"Figure what out?"

"I don't know if it will make your mother and stepmother feel better or worse, but the diamond was fake."

"Fake!" Monica exclaimed, turning around to see that Nancy had walked into the kitchen.

"What's fake?" Nancy asked when Monica clicked off the call. She opened one of the cupboards. "Do you have any ibuprofen?"

Monica got out a small bottle of tablets she kept in one of the kitchen drawers and handed it to her mother.

"The diamond ring found in Preston Crowley's pocket was fake."

"Fake? I can't believe it," Nancy said, her hands on her hips. "Did Preston really think he could fool me like that?" She frowned. "Maybe it was meant for Gina after all," she added dismissively.

Monica was starting to get hungry despite all the hors d'oeuvres she'd eaten at the Pepper Pot. She really hadn't done much more than pick, she assured herself—plus everything had been bite-sized. She opened the refrigerator and looked inside: some beer for Jeff, a small wedge of cheese, a bag of apples, the usual condiments and not much else.

She was contemplating a run to the store when the telephone rang.

It was Greg—he was throwing together some dinner and wondered if she'd like to join him. He didn't have to ask twice.

Monica checked with her mother, and Nancy said she'd be fine—she wasn't hungry anyway, so she'd just have a cup of tea and another slice of the cranberry raisin pecan bread later.

Monica hummed as the Focus crested the hill into

town. Even though she'd seen Greg that afternoon, she was looking forward to seeing him again.

He lived in an apartment over the bookstore, so Monica parked in front of Danielle's, which had just closed for the winter, and headed down the block to Book 'Em.

Much like the building where Edith lived, the door to Greg's building was unmarked and next to the shop. Monica had probably passed it dozens of times without noticing it. She rang the brass doorbell that was off to the side.

She heard someone coming down the stairs and then Greg flung the door open. He was wearing a white chef's apron, and his hair looked as if he'd been running his hands through it.

"Come in." He smiled when he saw Monica.

He led her up some carpeted stairs and through a doorway at the top.

"It's not much, but it's home." He gestured around the small but cozy apartment. "After my wife died, I couldn't see rattling around in that house all by myself. I owned this building so I had this space fixed up and moved in."

Monica looked around. There were books everywhere, of course—lying facedown on the coffee table, stacked next to the sofa and crammed into the bookshelves that ran along three of the walls in the dining area, where a small gateleg table had been pulled into the center of the room and set for dinner for two. The furniture was the type you could sink into with a good book and be comfortable for hours.

Monica followed Greg to the kitchen, which was little more than a galley. An open bottle of red wine sat out on the counter.

"I imagine this has breathed enough," he said with a laugh. "Would you care for a glass?"

"Yes, thanks."

He retrieved two balloon wineglasses from a cupboard, gave them a swift polish with a dish towel and filled them both. He handed one to Monica.

He motioned to a steak that sat out, its butcher paper wrapping suggesting it had come from Bart and not a supermarket.

"I'm not much of a cook, but I can grill a steak and make mashed potatoes. I hope that will do."

"Perfectly."

They took their wine out to the living room, where they sank into the overstuffed sofa.

"I've been thinking about Crowley's murder some more," Monica said as she took a sip of her wine before placing the glass on the coffee table. "I did some investigating online."

Greg grinned. "What would Miss Marple have made of Google, do you suppose?" He cradled his wineglass in his hands. "What did you discover?"

Monica told him about the articles in the *Times-Picayune* about Beau Belair.

"So Jacy really had been a rich summer tourist at one point."

"There's more. Roger Tripp is the grandson of Jacy's late husband, and it seems he was quite disappointed when the family inheritance went to Jacy instead of to him."

Greg whistled. "That puts things in a whole new light, don't you think?"

"Yes. And although nothing was ever proven, Roger

was convinced that Jacy had had a hand in his grandfather's sudden death."

"Sour grapes at losing the inheritance?"

"I don't know." Monica reached for her wineglass. "According to the articles, the police did look into Tripp's claim, but Beau had been cremated, and there wasn't enough evidence to warrant going any further."

"So Roger obviously holds quite a grudge against Jacy. That supports our theory that he's trying to frame her for Crowley's murder. He certainly had enough reasons to hate Crowley as well." Greg put his hands on his knees and started to get up. "How about I start our steak? I don't know about you, but I'm starved all of a sudden."

They went out to the kitchen, where Greg lit the broiler and rubbed the steak with garlic and some seasoned salt. Monica leaned against the doorjamb watching him. She was suddenly overcome with a rush of affection that surprised her.

Monica told Greg about the conversation she'd overheard between Roger and Jacy—where Roger had been demanding money for something.

Greg stopped with his hand on the refrigerator door. He spun around toward Monica. "Do you think he's blackmailing her?"

"That's what it sounded like to me."

"All the more reason to try to pin the murder on her then." Greg brought a salad out of the refrigerator and carried it over to the table in the dining area.

Something was niggling at the back of Monica's mind, but she couldn't get hold of the thought. She felt as if she was missing something—something important. A clue?

Or the meaning behind a clue? The harder she thought, the more elusive the information became. Perhaps it would come to her later.

Greg grilled the steak and heated the mashed potatoes while Monica whisked dressing for the salad.

"Would you like a refill?" Greg pointed to her nearly empty glass.

Monica held it out. "Yes, please."

They carried their glasses and the food to the table. Greg held out a chair for Monica and then sat down opposite.

They chatted companionably through dinner—mostly about books, but also about themselves. That elusive thought still haunted Monica, but whenever she felt she was about to grab it, it floated away again.

They were clearing away the dishes when Monica finally realized what was wrong with the conclusions they'd drawn about the murder.

She was so startled, she exclaimed, "Oh!"

"What is it?" Greg turned in alarm. "Are you okay?"

"I thought of something. It's been nagging at me all night." Monica ran through everything in her mind. It made sense. "We've got hold of the wrong end of the stick, as they say."

"How so?" Greg closed the dishwasher and leaned against the counter.

"I don't think Roger Tripp is trying to frame Jacy. I think it's the other way around—Jacy's trying to frame Roger."

"Whoa! What makes you think that?" Greg asked as he refilled their wineglasses. He gestured toward the doorway. "Shall we go sit down?"

They sat on the sofa and Monica began to explain her

theory—piecing it together in her own mind as she went along.

"First there's this button from Jacy's coat—the coat she claims was stolen."

"The button you found in Roger Tripp's restaurant."

"Yes. So obviously we—I—thought Roger was the one who stole Jacy's coat with the intention of covering up his part in the murder and, coincidentally, incriminating her."

"So what's wrong with that theory?"

"Another button from that coat was found in Tempest's shop—Twilight. Crowley was killed with an athame Tempest claims must have been stolen from her shop because she didn't sell it to anyone."

"So Roger stole the athame—"

Monica was already shaking her head. "If Roger was the one who took it, why would he bring Jacy's coat with him to the shop? He wouldn't want to be seen with it, don't you think? He'd have stashed it in his car or gone back to the restaurant with it first."

"So you think that—"

"Yes. Jacy stole the athame. And the button fell off her coat while she was in the shop."

"But you found the other matching button in Roger's restaurant."

"Yes. In the ladies' room. Jacy was being too clever for her own good. Why would Roger have brought the coat into the ladies' room? Why would he even go into the ladies' room?"

"To clean it?"

"Possibly. But not while wearing Jacy's coat."

"True."

"Jacy wanted me to find that button and draw the

conclusions I did—the wrong ones. She must have noticed I was headed toward the restrooms so she dashed in ahead of me and dropped that button into the toilet." Monica snapped her fingers. "Another thing. I noticed a perfumed scent in the ladies' room. I thought it was some sort of room spray but it was Jacy's perfume. She was wearing a lot and the scent lingered even after she'd left."

Greg frowned. "If all that is true, then Jacy had to have killed Preston Crowley, and what motive would she have had for that?"

"Crowley had a diamond ring in his pocket when he died along with a receipt for the ring from Bijou. The police had it examined, and the diamond was fake."

"Hmmm," Greg murmured. "And the day before he was murdered I saw Crowley coming out of Bijou looking like a volcano about to erupt."

Monica fiddled with the stem of her wineglass. "My guess is he had had the ring appraised independently, discovered it was nearly worthless and went back to complain. Since he left in such a fury, I'm guessing he didn't get any satisfaction from Jacy. Plus the ring was still in his pocket." Monica turned toward Greg. "Crowley probably threatened to go to the police, and Jacy couldn't let him do that. I imagine there's more than one fake gem in her shop."

"A scheme she must have cooked up to make the money she needed to pay Roger the cash he was demanding."

"And remember the day of the book club? I think it was Phyllis Bouma who said Jacy had lost most of the money left to her by her husband. She probably thought this crooked scenario was the only way she could stay afloat."

Greg ran his hands through his hair. "Jacy had to know Crowley was supposed to ride in the sleigh with Miss

Winter Walk at the start of the festivities. She knew exactly where to find him—and also that practically everyone else in town would be lining Beach Hollow Road."

"She must have paid Candy to lure Ryan away from the horse and sleigh long enough for her to murder Crowley. And she murdered Candy to keep her from talking, poor thing. I doubt she would have put two and two together anyway. Who knows what Jacy told Candy? She must have had quite a surprise when she and Ryan discovered the horse and sleigh gone."

"I suppose we should go to the police?" Greg suggested. "Or do you think they're on the same path?"

Monica cupped her chin with her hands. "I don't know." She twisted around to look at Greg. "The problem is we don't have any proof. This is all conjecture."

"You'd think someone would have seen Jacy on the village green. Surely not every single inhabitant of Cranberry Cove was on Beach Hollow Road."

Greg's words caused something to click in Monica's brain. "Tempest!" she blurted out. "She was going to perform her Imbolc ceremony on the green. She said she'd set everything up for it—candles, bells, noisemakers and who knows what all."

"Does Jacy know that?"

"I don't know, why?"

"Because if she does, Tempest could be in danger."

Chapter 27

Monica left Greg's apartment with conflicting feelings—contentedness from having spent such an enjoyable evening combined with a niggling worry about Tempest and her safety. Would Jacy remember that Tempest had been on the village green attempting to hold her springtime ritual? Or was Monica worrying for no reason?

As Monica walked toward her car, she passed Twilight and noticed that the lights were on above the shop. Tempest was obviously still up. Should Monica try to warn her to beware of Jacy? Would Tempest believe her or think she was overreacting?

Monica hesitated for several minutes, standing on the sidewalk and staring at the lit window above Twilight. Through the crack in the curtains, she saw a shadow thrown up against the far wall. Two shadows. Did Tempest have company? Monica had an uneasy feeling in the pit of her stomach. She didn't want to disturb Tempest, but on the other hand, she didn't want to spend the rest of her life wishing she had done something.

The cold was beginning to penetrate her jacket, and her fingers were numb inside their gloves. She might be risking making a fool of herself, but it wouldn't be the first time. She pressed the bell alongside the door that led to Tempest's apartment.

Monica stamped her feet and clapped her freezing hands together as she waited. And waited. Maybe Tempest hadn't heard the bell? Monica had heard it peal inside the building so she knew it was working. She pressed it again and stood back so she could see the lit window up above.

One of the shadows on the far wall froze at the sound of the doorbell. Monica waited, expecting Tempest to throw the door open at any minute, but the door remained firmly closed.

Monica didn't like this one bit. Something was going on. She was fairly certain Tempest wasn't seeing anyone, so it wasn't as if she and a man were holed up in the apartment together, oblivious to distractions.

Monica paced up and down in front of the building for several minutes before retrieving her cell phone from her purse. She pulled off her right glove and quickly pressed the buttons for Tempest's telephone number. She stood for several minutes with the phone crammed against her ear until Tempest's voicemail came on. Monica hesitated but then clicked off the call. What point was there in leaving a message? If Tempest was in trouble, it would do no good. And if she wasn't, the message would sound terribly foolish in the morning.

Monica was about to stow her cell back in her bag

when it rang, startling her to the point where she almost dropped it.

"Hello?" she said breathlessly, recognizing Tempest's number on the screen. "Is everything okay? I rang your bell but—"

Monica's words were greeted by a deep, throaty laugh that didn't sound at all like Tempest's.

"Well, well, well. I knew you were clever the minute I met you. But Mama always said there was such a thing as being too clever for your own good."

The voice that oozed over the telephone line was southern in origin and dripping with sweetness like honey dribbling from a spoon.

"Jacy!" Monica exclaimed. "What are you doing? Where's Tempest? I want to speak to her immediately."

Jacy laughed again—the same throaty laugh with which she'd greeted Monica.

"Then why don't you come up?"

"I can't. Not . . . not right now," Monica stuttered.

Jacy's voice hardened, the sweetness and the laughter completely gone. "I'm going to come down and let you in. I expect you to cooperate or something very bad will happen to your friend."

Monica's hands suddenly got even colder. She turned to look over her shoulder toward Book 'Em, where she could see the warm glow of the light in Greg's apartment above. She tried willing him to look out the window but his curtains remained firmly closed.

Monica briefly contemplated bolting to her car, locking herself in and calling for help, but just then the door to the building was flung open and she was facing the business end of a small gun pointed steadily toward her chest.

Too late now. Monica looked longingly toward her Focus, which was parked only a few feet away.

"Upstairs." Jacy jerked the gun toward the stairwell.

Monica started up the steps acutely conscious of the gun pointed at her back. Her legs were shaking and she was almost to the top when she lost her footing and stumbled briefly. The thought crossed her mind that she could fall backward, taking both her and Jacy down the long, dark staircase, but then she was mounting the top step and it was too late.

The apartment was similar to Greg's—a galley kitchen and a living/dining area. The ceiling was draped with fabric, with a chandelier dripping with crystals in the center. A coat tree that looked like real tree branches stood next to the sofa. Hanging from it was the long black cloak Tempest often wore around town, which scandalized the local population who favored simple outerwear like parkas or car coats. Tempest herself was in a royal blue caftan and was sitting on the plump purple velvet couch. The light in the room was shadowy, but even so, Monica could see the frightened expression on her face. Jacy motioned for Monica to join Tempest on the sofa.

Monica's knees almost gave out as she took her seat. Tempest shot her a sidelong glance before turning her attention back to Jacy . . . and Jacy's gun, which was leveled at them with a remarkably steady hand.

"Jacy, if you let us go, nothing will happen. We won't say anything," Monica said, in as soothing a tone as she could muster with her voice quivering so badly. "We can all forget this ever happened."

Jacy threw her head back and laughed, her chandelier earrings catching the light as they swung to and fro.

"You must think I'm dumber than a box of rocks." She pointed a finger at Monica. "I looked up that character you and that bookseller were talking about at the Pepper Pot."

"What character—"

"Hercule Poirot. The librarian over at the Cranberry Cove Library was more than happy to tell me about him. I already suspected you'd been snooping around—especially when you asked about Candy—but that clinched it."

"Did you put—"

"The voodoo doll in your apron?" Jacy laughed again—the sound had a hysterical edge to it. "We believe in voodoo down South. I had to send clear to New Orleans for that doll." She jabbed a finger in Monica's direction again. "Those spells can be mighty powerful." She smiled and waved her gun at Monica and Tempest. "This is awful powerful, too."

Monica shrank back against the sofa cushions. She strained to hear any noises coming from outside, praying that Greg had sensed something was wrong and had called the police, but so far the night was quiet and still—no sirens in the distance or shouting voices, just darkness and silence.

"You won't get away with this," Monica said, feeling as if she were reading from a bad television script.

"I've already gotten away with more than you can imagine."

"Beau? Your late husband . . ."

"He was starting to eye other women—younger women. All of a sudden I wasn't young enough for him anymore. And of course there was the pre-nup. I wasn't about to give up everything I'd worked so hard for."

"And Crowley?"

"It was his fault for having that diamond appraised. I

told him I'd give him his money back, but that wasn't good enough. He insisted he was going to the police. He didn't want the reputation of his precious Cranberry Cove ruined by someone selling fake gems, he said."

Monica shifted in her seat, and Jacy waved the gun at her. "Don't get any ideas. This is loaded and I know how to use it."

"What are you going to gain by shooting me and Tempest?"

"What do I have to lose?"

Monica tried to ignore the gun pointed at her. "Was Tripp blackmailing you?"

"Yes."

"So that's why you tried to frame him for Crowley's murder."

Jacy shrugged. "That was a nice touch, don't you think?"

"And you stole the murder weapon from my shop." Tempest sounded indignant.

Jacy started pacing in front of the sofa. "Everyone in town thinks you're nuts, so I figured they'd be more than happy to have a murder pinned on you."

"There are some things I won't stand for," Tempest said, two bright spots of color appearing on her otherwise pale face. "And being called a *nut* is one of them."

Tempest started to push herself up from the sofa. Monica looked at Jacy and was horrified to see that she was leveling her gun at Tempest, her finger already on the trigger.

Monica looked around frantically. The coat tree next to the sofa was within arm's reach. She yanked Tempest's black cloak off the hook and tossed it at Jacy, where it settled over her head obscuring her vision. Jacy batted at the material frantically, only succeeding in tightening the cape around her further.

Seizing the moment of opportunity, Tempest lunged at Jacy, managing to knock her to the ground. Monica hoped the fall had knocked the gun from Jacy's hand.

Monica threw herself on top of Jacy, banging her shin against the coffee table as she went down. The sharp pain brought tears to her eyes and momentarily blurred her vision. Jacy was fighting ferociously against the fabric swirled around her.

The gun went off so suddenly and the noise was so deafening that it took Monica several seconds to react.

Chapter 28

The bullet missed and shredded the back of Tempest's velvet sofa, burying itself somewhere in the wall behind it. Monica, Tempest and Jacy all screamed, although Jacy's scream was muffled by the fabric still swathed around her. Jacy continued to struggle, and Monica tried to strengthen her grip on the figure writhing in her grasp.

"Can you hold her while I telephone the police?" Tempest asked.

"I don't know," Monica said. She was already drenched in sweat, although whether it was from the exertion or fear, she didn't know.

Just then they heard the sound of a siren in the distance, growing louder with every passing second.

"Looks like someone's already called the police," Monica said. "They must have heard the gunshot."

Jacy renewed her struggle and managed to throw Tempest off of her. Monica was losing her grip as well.

Suddenly, the door to Tempest's apartment flew open and ricocheted against the wall.

"Greg!" Monica said in mingled tones of surprise and relief.

Greg immediately assessed the situation and joined them on the floor, where he easily pinned Jacy to the ground. Within a few moments, he'd also managed to secure the gun.

"I was already on my way over here," he said panting slightly. "I had a bad feeling about things. When I heard the shot, I rang nine-one-one immediately. The police should be here any minute."

At that moment, the sirens reached a crescendo and trailed off into silence. Colored lights from the flashers swirled across the wall of Tempest's apartment. They heard shouts and the thud of footsteps on the stairs and then two burly policemen burst into the room.

"Who fired the shot?" one of them demanded, pushing his hat back on his head. A deep red crease ran across his forehead where the brim had been.

Tempest and Monica motioned toward Jacy, who had managed to free her arms from the confines of Tempest's cloak and pull it off her head. One of the policemen kept his eye on Tempest and Monica while the other one grabbed Jacy.

"Are you the fellow who called us?" the one holding Jacy, who continued to struggle, asked Greg.

"Yes. I heard the gunshot and became alarmed. As a matter of fact, here's the gun." He handed it over with a look of relief on his face.

The policeman was handcuffing Jacy when Stevens arrived.

"I'm afraid you'll have to stick around. I'm going to need to ask you some questions," she said to Monica.

"Let's go into the kitchen," Tempest said, walking unsteadily ahead of them in her long, regal caftan.

Greg put his arms around Monica and she leaned her head against his shoulder. His strong arms felt incredibly good, especially since it was the one and only time in her life she thought she might actually faint.

Monica was never so glad to get back to her cottage. The lights were on, glowing warmly in the dark, welcoming her home. The long driveway was nearly full—Nancy's car was there and so was Gina's Mercedes. Monica pulled in behind them, Greg following her lead. He'd insisted on seeing her home, and she was glad of the offer.

"What happened?" Nancy said as soon as Monica walked in the door. "You look terrible—as if you've been in a fight."

Monica ran a hand over her hair and looked down at herself. She hadn't realized that her clothes were still askew from her struggle with Jacy. Mittens trotted over and gave her a peremptory greeting, accompanied by several loud *meows*.

"You look like you could do with a drink," Gina said, opening the cupboard and getting out some glasses. "Luckily I brought a bottle of wine with me."

She was pouring the wine when the back door opened and Jeff walked in, stopping to wipe his muddy work boots on the mat by the door.

"What happened?" he said as soon as he saw Monica.

"Monica is about to tell us." Gina handed Monica a glass. She jerked her head toward Jeff. "There's some beer in the refrigerator if you'd like."

"I think I will." Jeff opened the door and pulled out a bottle.

He turned around and held a hand out to Greg. "It's Greg, right? From Book 'Em."

"Yes." Greg returned the handshake.

"I'm Jeff—Monica's brother."

Monica noticed her mother's lips tighten slightly. Her mother had wanted another child, but it hadn't happened, and then suddenly John Albertson was gone and about to have a son.

Jeff leaned against the wall while the women took a seat. Greg stood behind Monica with his hands on her shoulders protectively.

Monica explained about the fight with Jacy and her subsequent arrest.

"In other words," Nancy said, twirling her wineglass by the stem, "Jacy had that girl Candy lure that young man away from the horse and sleigh so she could murder Crowley."

"Yes," Monica said. "Crowley was going to expose her for selling fake gems, and at the same time, Tripp was blackmailing her. She had to do something and quickly. At first she thought she could pin the crime on Tempest, who is, shall we say, slightly different . . . which makes the townspeople suspicious of her in the first place. When that didn't work, she had the idea of trying to throw blame on Tripp."

Gina snapped her fingers. "Now I remember something. The afternoon of the first day of the Winter Walk— it was shortly before the sleigh appeared with Crowley's body—someone came into my shop for some essential lavender oil, and they mentioned that they'd just been in Bijou and no one was there to wait on them."

Jeff swiped at the foam of beer along his upper lip. "That day Jacy came out to watch us sand the cranberry bogs. I always thought that was kind of peculiar—"

"What do you mean?" Monica teased. "It was your charm that attracted her."

Jeff snorted. "I think it was the opportunity to bury the offending coat in one of our sand piles. She probably didn't realize that we would be digging in them so soon."

"She didn't strike me as being particularly bright." Gina reached for the bottle of wine and topped off her glass. "Why not dump the coat in another town? Or burn it or something."

"I'd have tossed it in the lake," Greg said. He frowned. "Although I suppose it would wash up eventually."

They amused themselves for several minutes discussing how Jacy should have gotten rid of the incriminating coat.

"How did Lauren's interview go?" Monica looked at Jeff. "Any news?"

Jeff grimaced and looked down at his hands. "The company offered her a summer internship after she graduates. It could lead to a full-time job," he said, so quietly Monica almost didn't hear him.

"She's not taking it, is she?" Monica asked.

Jeff squared his shoulders. "Yes. I told her she had to do it. She has to get a taste of life outside Cranberry Cove otherwise how will she—how will *I*—know she's content here?"

Monica bit her lip. "What if she decides to stay in the big city?"

Jeff grimaced. "It's a chance I'll have to take. I want her to be sure."

Nancy pushed her chair back. "It's time I started packing. I'm going home in the morning."

"Have a safe trip," Gina said, and Monica thought she sounded as if she meant it.

"I should be going, too. Come on, Jeffie." Gina put her arm around his shoulders. "Let's you and me go out to dinner."

Monica saw everyone out the door and then it was just she and Greg standing in the kitchen.

Greg picked up the bottle that was still sitting on the kitchen table along with their glasses. "Why don't we take our wine into the living room, build a nice warm fire in that fireplace of yours and get cozy on the couch?"

Monica smiled. She couldn't think of anything else she'd rather do.

Also from
Peg Cochran

Berried Secrets
A Cranberry Cove Mystery

When Monica Albertson comes to Cranberry
Cove—a charming town on the eastern shore
of Lake Michigan—to help her half brother, Jeff, on
his cranberry farm, the last thing she expects
to harvest is a dead body.

It seems that Sam Culbert, who ran the farm while
Jeff was deployed overseas, had some juicy
secrets that soon would prove fatal, and Jeff is ripe
for the picking as a prime suspect. Forming an uneasy
alliance with her high-maintenance stepmother,
Monica has her hands full trying to save the farm while
searching for a killer. Culbert made plenty of enemies
in the quaint small town…but which one was desperate
enough to kill?

"Cozy fans and foodies rejoice—there's a place just
for you and it's called Cranberry Cove."
—Ellery Adams, *New York Times* bestselling author

pegcochran.com
facebook.com/PegCochran
penguin.com

Penguin
Random
House